CW01113185

SEPT JOURS

BY
GN HETHERINGTON

First Published in 2021 by GNH Publishing.

The right of Gary Hetherington to be identified as the author of this work has been asserted by him in accordance with the Copyright, Designs and Patents Act 1988.

Copyright © Gary Hetherington

All rights reserved. No part of this book may be reproduced, stored in a retrieval system or transmitted in any form or by any means, electronic, mechanical, photocopying, recording or otherwise, without the prior permission of the publisher.

www.gnhbooks.co.uk

The story, the places and characters are a work of fiction.

grâce à :

the wonderful people who care and love the stories I manage to create, especially my angels Jackie Waite, June Russell, Sandra Scott, Pam Pletts, Suse Telford, Joy Edwards and Jennifer Trieb and my beaux parents, Bill & Chris Bailey. Big mwah to Julien Doré & Sheena Easton for their daily inspiration.

There are other books, check out: www.gnhbooks.co.uk for more info.

Special thanks to the incredibly talented Maria Almeida. We've been working together for five years now, and for such a young artist, she is exceptional and has breathed life into all of my crazy ideas and turned them into amazing works of art. Thank you Maria, you're the best. Extra special thanks to my French teacher, Bastien Greve for all his hard work and for being such a great help. Thanks also to Mai Cadiz for her help with the manuscript.

For my trio of daily love, snuggles, cuddles and survival, Hugo & Noah and *especially* my husband, Dan. My days are all about you.

As always, all I can do is send my love to those I have lost and who manage to both break and make my days, ye bastards - Charlie, Seth and Dawn. Jusqu'à ce que nous nous revoyions.

Notes:

The story, the places and characters are a work of fiction.

For further information, exclusive content and to join the mailing list, head over to:

www.gnhbooks.co.uk

We are also on Facebook, Twitter and Instagram. Join us there!

The artwork on the cover, the website and social media accounts were created in conjunction with two incredible talents Maria Almeida and Deborah Dalcin and I'm indebted to them for bringing my characters to life.

For Charlie, Seth and Dawn. *Tu me manques.*

Also available:

Hugo Duchamp Investigates:

Un Homme Qui Attend (2015)
Les Fantômes du Chateau (2016)
Les Noms Sur Les Tombes (2016)
L'ombre de l'île (2017)
L'assassiner de Sebastian Dubois (2017)
L'impondérable (2018)
Le Cri du Cœur (2019)
La Famille Lacroix (2019)
Les Mauvais Garçons (2020)
Prisonnier Dix (2021)
Le Bateau au fond de l'océan (2022)
Chemin de Compostelle (2022)

The Coco Brunhild Mysteries:

Sept Jours (2021)
Métro Boulot Dodo (2022)
Cercueils en spirale (2022)
Quatre Semaines (2023)

Also available:

Hugo & Josef (2021)
Hugo & Madeline (2023)
Josef (2023)

LUNDI

(MONDAY)

09H00

Charlotte "Coco" Brunhild turned to the side, pushing a large, over-sized antique Chanel bag between her legs. She sucked in her stomach, the material of her frayed blue and green woollen overcoat offering a protest. She tutted loudly, the angry click filling the small ancient lift. She did not know why she had suddenly gained four kilos. She dismissed the notion it may have something to do with the late-night pizzas, pitchers of mojitos, or the myriad of chocolate wrappers crumpled in her pockets. No, it was *far* more likely to be something else - a hormonal imbalance she concluded, was far more probable. She closed her eyes, allowing herself a brief moment of self-pity before pushing it away as quickly. She had been around long enough to know there was no amount of self-pity which would benefit her or make sense of her crazy life.

The lift lurched, metal straining against ancient stones. A loud, shrill ring informing her the call button had been pressed on another floor. She tutted again, blue eyes flicking around the cramped space. There was barely room for her let alone anyone else, and knowing her luck, the dank-haired greasy, spotty man from the eighth floor would try to squeeze next to her again, spraying her with garlic-infused breath and enveloping her in the stench of slimy armpits snaking out from a hole-ridden vest, an odour she had never before smelled, nor wished to again.

The doors slid open, and she prepared herself, hoping to flash him with a look that said, *I'm a cop, so quit messing with me and walk down the stairs. You could do with the exercise after all, greaseball,* look. Instead, she was faced with a small, but perfectly formed face. Perhaps one of the most beautiful she had seen. It was delicate and smooth and it could almost be a young woman, with olive skin and the darkest eyes Coco had ever seen. He was, she supposed, a young man barely out of his teens whose eyes, despite their beauty, hid a depth of emotion she could not fathom. He was staring directly at her, but for some reason, it felt as if he was not. The intensity of his gaze seemed to go straight through her. She thought perhaps she recognised him - an occupational hazard in her profession. A quick search through the recesses of her mind could not locate him in her memory banks. Not conclusive, she realised, but she suspected it meant he was not a con. If not, then where did she recognise him from? Not the apartment block, she was sure.

She had only lived in Rue de Penfeld, an old tenement building on the wrong side of Paris, for a month, and had done her very best to keep as far away as possible from the miscreants who shared the air of the building she was now forced to call home. She had realised flashing her police ID to the landlord was going to get her nowhere. He had taken one look at her and she had known exactly what he was thinking - *that's supposed to impress me? If you were anyone special, you wouldn't be in this shit-hole. Even the cockroaches don't wanna live here.*

There was something about the young man which seemed off. It was not just down to the intensity of his stare. It was almost as if he was in the wrong place, at the wrong time. Her eyes flicked slyly over him. He was dressed in a blazer, red stripes running around the lapels, and a pair of neatly ironed black trousers. She stole a glance at her own trousers, realising once again she had yet to even bother unpacking an iron, if she even had one to begin with. When she looked up, she caught his eye. He was staring at her in a way she did not understand. It was not combative, rather… rather it was challenging. As if he was asking her a question.

'Whatcha looking at, dude?' she asked in as even a tone as she could manage, hoping to convey firmness and confidence.

He turned his head to the side, a pink tongue flicking across his rosebud lips. 'Was I looking at you?' he replied.

Coco exhaled. His voice matched his face - soft and angelic.

She scratched her head, unsure if he was being sarcastic or flippant. She was used to it with her two oldest children. They wore their sarcasm and contempt for her as a badge of honour. She felt no such malice from her new friend.

'You're a cop, aren't you?' he asked.

Coco's eyes widened. She had decided long ago, being a flic was hardly something to be proud of, especially with her chequered past, and more so in the neighbourhood she had been forced to call home, once the child support cheques had ground to a halt. She had barely nodded felicitations to anyone for fear of attracting attention.

'Who said that?' she snapped back.

'Your kid,' he said with a lazy smile, before adding his name, '*Julien.*'

Coco bit her lip, silently cursing her oldest son and his big mouth. Her eyes flicked over young Monsieur-rosebud-lips again and she knew immediately why her *of-course-I'm-not-gay-how-dare-you-ask* twenty-year-old son had spilled his guts despite Coco's explicit instructions to all her kids to keep their mouths shut.

'Well, he's got a big mouth, that kid of mine,' she said, turning her head. She stopped. There was something about his demeanour which bothered her, because it had suddenly changed.

His shoulders had hunched forward, and he was rummaging desperately through his pockets. The hairs on the back of Coco's neck stood on edge and every instinct in her told her something was off, something was very off. Seconds passed before he found what he was looking for, and it took Coco as long to realise what he was now holding in his left hand. It was thin and long, gleaming silver, and she realised it was a blade, most likely a scalpel. Something which could cause serious damage. She pressed her body against the side of the elevator, steadying herself as it rocked. She knew from memory it would be less than ten seconds until it hit the ground floor, and a further ten seconds for the ancient doors to slowly creak open. *Twenty seconds.* Twenty seconds was not so long in the grand scheme of things, she reasoned. But she was a police officer, and she had seen more times than she cared to recall what could happen to a person in twenty seconds.

She exhaled, trying desperately to remember whatever training course she had been on which might have covered the events which were unfolding in front of her. All she could remember was responding to the instructor's question. What would you do if an attacker came at you? With the response, *I'd knee him in the nuts so hard he'd feel them in the back of his throat.* It had gotten her a laugh, and a slap on the ass from the cute Belgian instructor, but little else. Coco contemplated the young rosebud boy and wondered whether he had even grown any yet. She reasoned that if in doubt, do what she did best. *Talk.*

'Hey kid,' she drawled, trying her best to sound nonchalant. 'Whatever you're thinking. *Don't.* Cos, I'm packing.'

It worked. His eyes widened in confusion. 'Packing?'

She smiled. He had loosened his grip on the scalpel. If she was swift, she realised she could probably wrestle him for it. The trouble was, Charlotte 'Coco' Brunhild had been described as many things, never as swift.

'If you know I'm a cop, then you have to know I have a gun.'

The youth smiled. 'And you oughta know we're in a tiny, rickety elevator. If you shoot me and miss, the chances are the bullet is going to ricochet around so much it'll make Swiss cheese out of both of us.' He paused. 'Is that what you want? You have four kids, don't you? And their fathers? Two are AWOL and the last one, isn't he in prison for the next twenty to thirty? I'm sure you don't want to risk them ending up in a children's home, do you?'

Coco felt her hackles rising. She balled her fingers into fists because she knew at least she could dislocate the little punk's jaw if she landed him one. Charlotte Brunhild was many things, but she was a bear when it came to her cubs. No matter how much of an annoyance they were, they were HER annoyance.

He smiled again and lifted the scalpel to his chin, scraping it across the smooth, stubble-free skin. 'Don't worry, Captain,' he said, 'I'm not here to hurt you. I'm here to ask you to do something for me.'

Her eyes widened, pulling her wool coat close to her chest. 'And what is that, exactly?'

He moved the scalpel to his neck. 'Find out who made me do this,' he whispered.

Coco gasped. She was not sure what scenario she imagined, but instinctively she knew what came next would haunt her.

He closed his eyes as he slid the scalpel across his throat, splattering her face with his blood.

10H00

'Am I hearing this right? On your first day back after your "suspension," you not only did not make it into the Commissariat on time, you actually called us out to the scene of a crime. A crime scene where you were the only witness or,' the pause was lengthy, 'as I'm sure the press will call it considering your history, the potential perpetrator. S'il vous plaît, I'd be delighted if you could correct me, if I have made a mistake in my assessment of the situation.'

Coco pulled her head back sharply, regarding the tall, slender woman with a mixture of irritation and interest. She had never met her before, but Coco had heard all about Commander Imane Demissy, the new chief in charge of the Commissariat de Police du 7e arrondissement. Coco stretched her shoulders, ready to do what she did best. Fly by the seat of her pants. She closed her eyes. That had only worked with… that had only worked *before*. She stared at the Commander, pulling her wide lips into a smile. 'Well, it saved on my mileage expenses, I suppose,' she offered.

Commander Demissy took her own time, pulling her own head back, eyes widening with interest. 'I had hoped we would have a chance to talk, in private, before anything happened, but I should have known, working in the seventh arrondissement was going to be unorthodox, to say the least, especially considering everything that happened. But I should tell you, just so there is no confusion, I'm not a woman you can trifle with, Captain Brunhild, and nor am I a pushover. And more importantly, the inappropriate humour I'm told is part of your modus operandi, won't wash with me.'

Coco nudged the Commander. 'Hey, we're both chicks in a man's world, aren't we? We know the score.'

The Commander pushed her away. Her eyes were dark, but

they shined with a burning light. 'Don't play the woman card with me, Captain Brunhild, because it won't get you anywhere. I am a Black Muslim and a second-generation refugee. I'm only where I am today because I speak well, my skin isn't "too" offensive, but more importantly, I'm married to a *white, rich* Frenchman, who is known in all the right circles. I am under no illusions, those are the only reasons I have been allowed into the,' she made air quote gestures with her fingers, ' "club." '

Coco nodded. 'Ah, that's right. You're hitched to the fiddle player.'

Commander Demissy glared at her. 'My husband is a classical violinist,' she snapped. 'But my point, if you would allow me to make it, is that my sex, *your* sex is irrelevant to me. It took me long enough to make my own way here, I'll be damned if you take me down with you. Do your job and we won't have a problem. Expect me to accommodate your eccentricities and we will. Do you understand what I am saying?'

Coco shrugged. 'Well, I speak French too, so, sure,' she muttered, flicking blue hair over her shoulders.

Demissy raised an eyebrow, the slightest beginning of a smile on her lips. 'There's only one reason they assigned me to your command. They want me to fail, and they think you'll be the one to make sure I do.'

Coco snorted. 'Well, they and you appear to hold me in the highest esteem.'

The Commander waved her hand. 'I'm not interested in what came before, rather what comes next. I don't care about your problems…'

'My *problems*?' Coco interjected, her nostrils flaring. 'What happened has nothing to do with me.'

Demissy shrugged, smoothing her hijab, the purple hue matched the lipstick she always wore because she had decided at an early age if she was going to defy her father by working, she might as well go the whole way on her path towards eternal damnation. 'That's not what they say.'

Coco did her own air quotes. 'Then "they" are dead wrong and ought to keep their fat mouths shut.' She narrowed her eyes. 'You don't think I know what they say behind my back? *No smoke without fire. She must have known. Hell, she was probably in on it from the beginning.* All bullshit.'

'Captain, s'il vous plait, watch your language.'

Coco turned her head to study the Commander. 'You interest me.'

Demissy pulled back her head. 'Interest you?' she asked with obvious concern.

Coco cackled. 'Don't flatter yourself, Commander. As much as I despise men right now, I'm not about to start batting for the other side.' She shuddered. 'There's nothing wrong with it, I suppose, but just the thought of another woman's…'

'Don't finish that sentence, Captain Brunhild, I beg of you.' She lowered her voice. 'Ecouté, I'm not suggesting you had anything to do with your… with your… with what the former Commander was involved in.'

Coco closed her eyes and stopped listening. She did not need to hear the words to understand what was being said, what was being insinuated because it was all she thought about and the only conclusion she had come to was that she could not disagree with the gossip. *She must have known. I must have known.* Coco had spent the preceding months going over and over what had happened when Commander Mordecai Stanic, her former boss and the father of Coco's two youngest children, had been discovered to have committed some heinous crimes. Crimes including false imprisonment and rape, leading to further convictions for manslaughter and tampering with police evidence. He had committed his crimes while leading a successful double life, and the only solace Coco had found in all of it was that he had pleaded guilty, therefore negating her own involvement any further. In the end he had done it for his children, or so Coco chose to believe, rather than the hefty sentence reduction the Procurer had offered to ease the embarrassment for the Police Nationale.

Coco had ridden many storms, survived many cracks in the road ahead of her, but she was not sure she would survive this one. But she had to. She had to at least try for her four children. They had lost everything - their home, their security, and the father and step-father who they had all loved. She had to keep taking two steps forward for them. The only time she allowed herself to scream was each night after work, under the warmth of the shower where she would release her frustrations into the cosmos, hoping against hope it would make her feel better. The jury was still out on that; she realised, and it terrified her she might never feel better. That she might never forgive herself, even if she was sure she had nothing to forgive herself for. Because in the darkness of night, when she could not sleep, her demons told her she could have done something. She *should* have done something.

The Commander opened her mouth to reply, but the door opened, a young police officer appearing. She turned, eyes flicking over Coco's coat. 'You're covered in the boy's blood. Get yourself cleaned up, get a goddamn AIDS test and change into something decent, then meet me back at the Commissariat in one hour. I will personally take your statement.'

Coco watched her leave. 'How is he? How's the kid?'

Commander Demissy did not stop. 'He's alive. For now. No thanks to you,' she hissed over her shoulder.

No thanks to me, Coco mouthed, glancing at the blood on her hands. The hands she had pressed against his spurting neck for what seemed like an eternity until the Pompiers had arrived.

11H00

Lieutenant Cedric Degarmo drained the contents of the milkshake and threw it towards the bin. It missed and hit the floor, causing the lid to flip open and the remaining liquid to spill onto the already heavily stained carpet. 'Putain,' he cursed, glancing over his shoulder to reassure himself nobody had spotted the accident. He pulled a t-shirt from his desk drawer, sniffed it, his nose crinkling in disgust. He threw it at the spillage.

Coco flopped onto the sofa in the corner of the office they shared, a gust of dust covering her thighs. She wiped it away huffily with an exasperated sigh. He shot her a look of disdain. 'Have you even showered?' he asked.

Coco licked her finger and pressed it against a red smudge on her chin and then licked it. Cedric pressed his fist against his mouth as if suppressing a retch. 'Relax,' Coco sniffed, 'it's only jam from my pastry.' She narrowed her eyes, looking down at the "Jesus is my homie" T-shirt she had changed into. 'It's laundry day, and I'm a little behind, but it's pretty clean still.'

'Every day is laundry day according to you,' Cedric said with a sigh. He pushed his hand across his buzz-cut head, fixing her with an icy-blue stare. 'Haven't you still got the German au pair? Can't she work a washing machine?'

'Helga,' Coco retorted huffily, 'isn't paid to work a washing machine. Actually, she's barely paid at all. In fact, I think the only reason she's still here is because she's in her fifties now and has spent the last ten years telling her family and friends in Düsseldorf, she's living the highlife in "gay Paris," when in reality she's sleeping on a foldout at the bottom of my bed.'

'Your life is weird,' Cedric muttered.

'Aint that the truth,' Coco laughed. 'It's not so bad, except she snores and farts like a pig.'

Cedric raised an eyebrow, telling her she could be talking about herself.

Coco had met Cedric fresh from his time in police college. His first assignment was to work with her. His first day had been spent helping her deliver her third child, something she had thanked him for by naming the child after him. A fact which had resulted in everyone assuming he was the father. She had also, much to his annoyance, taken to telling random strangers, that although Cedric had seen her vagina, he had never gone near it. Despite it all, they had worked well together for almost ten years and she was patently aware after the problems with Mordecai, he could have justifiably chosen to transfer into another department. As far as Coco was aware, he had not even applied to do so. A fact which surprised her, because under similar circumstances, she was not sure she would not have run for the hills herself.

Commander Imane Demissy cleared her throat. 'While I admire your ability to prioritise your personal lives,' she began, 'I wonder,' she shrugged, 'whether the amount of money taxpayers in the Republic pay you both for your service, is meant for your… challenging life discussions, or rather,' she said, her nostrils flaring, 'solving damn crimes.' She shook her head. 'Captain Brunhild, follow me to my office for your statement, and you, Lieutenant Degarmo, perhaps you could not spend your time drinking milkshake and instead try to discover why someone,' she smiled at Coco, *allegedly* tried to cut his own throat this morning?' She shrugged. 'I mean, a name would be something to start with, or am I wrong? Isn't that what the police are supposed to do?' She pointed at Coco. 'Captain, follow me.'

She turned around, manoeuvring around the cramped office, the sounds of her heels echoing around the room. Coco pushed herself out of the chair, following her. She smiled at Cedric as she gesticulated behind Demissy's back. The Commander did not look back. 'If you continue to do that, Captain Brunhild, I'll break every one of those fingers.'

12H00

'His name is Elliot Bain, he's seventeen years old, and he lives in apartment 4e in your building,' Cedric relayed to Coco.

Coco scratched her head. 'I was sure I'd never seen him before, but apparently Julien spoke with him,' she said, glancing at her cell phone. 'I've left him four messages, but as usual he's ignoring me.' She turned her head back to Cedric. 'What did you find about Elliot Bain? Does he have a record?'

Cedric shook his head. 'Nope, the pompiers found his ID in his wallet.'

Coco jumped to her feet. 'Well, let's go take a look and see if he left a clue in his house. He must have parents,' she added. 'My favourite part of the job, ruining people's lives.'

'How did your meeting go with the new Commander?'

Coco shrugged. 'Well, she hates me, hates the fact they have saddled her with this department and that I'm apparently going to ruin her career and my own, so...' she trailed off, 'working with her is going to be F U N.'

Coco watched with annoyance as Cedric leapt ahead of her, jumping the spiral staircase steps three at a time. She turned her head towards the elevator, crime scene tape covering the door. 'Well, at least he lived on the fourth floor,' she muttered to herself, realising that if the elevator was still out of service later, she would have to climb the stairs again to her own apartment on the tenth floor. She had chosen it because it was on the top floor and had access to the roof, offering amazing views of Paris and in particular, if she strained her neck hard enough, the Eiffel Tower. After uprooting her children from their home, she had felt as if giving them a view was the least she could do. But in hindsight and how out of breath she was already, the thought of traipsing up ten flights of stairs was triggering. She shook her head, irritated with herself. A boy, barely older than her own, was lying in a hospital fighting for his life, and there she was worrying about herself. She looked up, Cedric was peering at her from the stairwell, a mischievous grin on his face. She cursed at him and pulled herself up, dragging her body slowly up the staircase. Finally, after what seemed like an eternity, she stepped onto the fourth floor, her chest wheezing as she gasped for breath. She pointed at Cedric. 'If you say one sarcastic thing, I'll… I'll…'

Cedric laughed. 'You'll chase after me? I'd like to see you try!'

She shot him a filthy look and moved away, narrowing her eyes as she looked for the door to apartment 4e. She knocked on the door, cocking an ear, listening for signs of any activity inside. There were none. She knocked again, louder this time. 'Nobody home,' she groaned, staring at the staircase again.

The door to apartment 4c opened, an old lady appearing. She stared at Coco and Cedric, fear clear on her face. 'Are you the police?' she asked cautiously.

Coco nodded, pulling out her ID and holding it up. 'I'm Captain Brunhild, and this is Lieutenant Degarmo. And you are?'

'Madame Cross. Are you here about the fight?'

Coco took a step toward the old lady, causing her to step back. 'Fight?' Coco asked.

'Oui,' Madame Cross replied. 'I didn't mean to listen, but it was so loud and went on for so long.'

Coco pointed to apartment 4e. 'In there?'

'Oui,' she repeated. 'I like Nita, she's very kind to me, I don't get out much you see.'

'And she was fighting with someone?'

The woman nodded again, her face clouding. 'That son of hers, Elliot. There's never a peaceful moment when he's around.'

'Then he doesn't live here?' Coco asked.

'He goes to school,' Madame Cross replied, 'or he did,' she lowered her voice, 'I'm not one to gossip, but I get the sense he'd gotten himself in some trouble, because he's been around here much more lately, and,' she lowered her voice, 'it seemed to be one of the main things they argued about.'

Coco and Cedric exchanged a look. 'What made you think that?' Cedric asked. 'Did Madame Bain tell you?'

Madame Cross's eyes flashed warily. She shook her head. 'Not in so many words. Nita used to brag about Elliot and how he'd gotten a scholarship into some fancy school in the country and how he was going to be rich and successful. But then, maybe a week or two ago, she stopped talking about him, and then he turned up and they've been fighting ever since.' She pointed to the lift. 'What happened in there this morning? I heard an almighty commotion, but I didn't dare look. You never know what or who you're going to find if you do.' She pulled her cardigan tight around her chest. 'I'm eighty-six years old, I've had my life, but I want it to end peacefully, not at the hand of some gang-banger after stealing my pension.' She paused. 'So, what happened?' she asked again.

'There was an accident. Monsieur Elliot Bain, is in hospital.' Coco said.

Madame Cross gasped. 'Does Nita know?'

'That's what we're here for,' Coco said. 'Is there a Monsieur Bain?'

The old lady shook her head. 'Non, there isn't.' She took a breath. 'There may have been a man.'

'A man?' Coco asked.

She nodded. 'I never saw him,' she began slowly. 'But sometimes, I "heard" him,' she said with air quotes.

Coco smiled. 'Ah, I see.'

The old woman shook her head. 'I'm not one to gossip,' she said quickly, 'but after I'd heard him a few times, I asked her if she had a special friend.'

'And what did she say?' Cedric asked.

Madame Cross pursed her lips huffily. 'She had the cheek to sound offended. She said, "it must be your imagination." I told her, I don't know what kind of woman she thought I was, but I most certainly wasn't one with *that* sort of imagination.' She sighed, lowering her head conspiratorially. 'I think it has more to do with the fact it embarrassed her about the sort of man he was.'

Coco frowned. 'The sort of man he was? What do you mean?'

Madame Cross mouthed the words. 'He was ethnic.'

Coco hid a smile in Cedric's direction. 'And this man? Has he been around lately?'

Cross pulled her cardigan tight. 'As I said, I'm not the sort of woman who listens to the comings and goings of others.' She paused. 'Mais, if the police pressed me, I'd be inclined to say he has been around in the last day or two.'

Coco looked over her shoulder. 'We really need to speak to Madame Bain, but she doesn't seem to be in,' Coco added.

'Nonsense,' Madame Cross retorted. 'I would have heard her go out, and she never leaves without knocking and asking if I need anything, she's very good like that.' She bit her lip, looking anxiously at the closed door of apartment 4e. 'It really was an awful fight.' She stepped inside her apartment, reaching for a key on a small table. Her hand shook as she tried to reach it, knocking a pile of envelopes onto the floor. 'Oh dear, I'm so clumsy,' she cried.

Coco stepped inside the doorway, gently touching the old lady's arm. 'Non, you're not clumsy, you've just had a shock, that's all.' She bent and bundled the letters together. 'Here you are.' She smiled, pointing at the top envelope. 'Bills, bills, bills, that's all I seem to get as well, at least yours aren't final demands like mine!'

Madame Cross' cheeks flushed. 'I always make sure I pay my bills on time,' she said huffily.

Coco held out her hand for the door key, Madame Cross looked at it, her lips pinched tight.

'I really shouldn't be doing this,' she said, 'Nita only gave me it in case of an emergency.'

Coco extended her hand further. 'Madame Bain's son could die, so I would say that constitutes as an emergency.' She pointed. 'Please, go inside Madame. We'll call you if we need anything else from you.'

Madame Cross nodded and reluctantly went back into her apartment. Coco and Cedric moved across the corridor. Coco slipped the key in the lock and pushed open the door. 'Madame Bain,' she called out, 'it's the police. Are you there?'

They moved into the apartment. The first thing which struck Coco was the clear evidence something had happened. Papers were strewn across the floor, an upturned telephone table lay in front of them, the telephone yanked from the wall. 'Madame Bain,' Coco called out again, the wariness of the situation creeping into her voice. 'Madame Bain, are you…' She stopped dead in her tracks in the archway leading into the living room. A woman was on the sofa, staring straight at her, eyes wide and focused. And clearly dead.

'What is it?' Cedric called out from behind her, trying to squeeze through the narrow gap.

Coco stopped him. 'Call Sonny,' she said.

13H00

Dr. Shlomo Bernstein dropped his bag on the floor, pulling a skull cap off his mop of unruly black curls. He nodded in Cedric's direction.

Coco was sitting on a foldout chair, sucking on an unlit cigarette. 'I'm trying to quit,' she grumbled.

'Bon,' the doctor replied, 'they're terrible for your health.'

She snorted. 'So is air pollution, and cheese, and alcohol and red meat, and just about everything else. I'm quitting because they cost a fortune and I…' she pulled open her bag, 'don't have one. So, I'm rationing them.'

Shlomo cleared his throat. 'She's in there?' he asked, tipping his head towards the living room. Coco nodded, watching him as he made his way into the room. The door behind them opened and Ebba Blom, the Swedish forensic technician, walked in. She was tall and thin, with a shaved head and a pinched, seemingly always irritated face.

Cedric jumped to attention. 'Bonjour, jolie fille,' he said.

Without turning to him, Ebba strode purposefully past him. 'You're a disgusting pig and I hate you,' she hissed.

Cedric cackled. 'Ha! I think you protest too much, obviously to cover up your genuine feelings,' he said, touching her shoulder.

Ebba stopped, glancing at his hand. 'Keep thinking that Romeo, but if you don't take your hand off me, you won't be using it in your bed tonight, which will make for a very lonely night for you, won't it?' She slapped his hand away.

'I like you, you've got spunk,' Coco cackled, tipping her thumb towards Cedric. 'And anyone who can keep this Neanderthal on his toes, is pretty impressive in my book.'

Ebba stared at her. 'Well, I don't like you. You're weird, and you smell and your hair looks like you stuck your finger in an electricity outlet.'

Coco pulled a blue tipped strand of her hair and sniffed it. Her nose crinkled. 'Smells fine to me,' she muttered.

Shlomo appeared in the doorway. 'Anyway,' he said quickly, 'shall we get on with the job at hand?'

Ebba lowered her head. 'Sorry, boss,' she said passing him.

'Sorry, boss,' Coco repeated. She watched as the doctor began his examination of the body. 'So, how'd she die, Sonny?'

He turned his head. He pressed his head. 'Hang on a moment, Charlotte and I'll consult my psychic guide.' He laughed. 'Give me more than two seconds, d'accord?'

'That's pretty much all it took for me to get pregnant four times,' she mumbled under her breath.

Shlomo shook his head and moved closer to the woman on the sofa.

'Has she been posed?' Coco asked. 'Seems like an odd way for someone to sit.'

The doctor did not answer immediately, turning his head to the left and the right as if taking his time to assess the scene. He continued examining the body. 'She's still warm,' he said, 'and rigor mortis hasn't started. She's been dead only an hour or two.' He moved closer. 'I can see why you think she's been posed, but the truth is, people often die like this. A heart-attack, can look like this, par example.' He stopped. 'Ebba,' he said, pointing at a bottle of pills next to the woman on the sofa.

Without saying a word, Ebba picked up the pill bottle carefully and took it away.

'A bottle of pills,' Coco mused. 'Suicide?'

Shlomo shrugged, moving his head from side to side. 'There are no obvious signs of trauma.' He stared into her eyes. 'The eyes are clear, no sign of petechial haemorrhage.' He moved his eyes around her body. 'I also see no obvious signs of blood.' He turned back to face Coco and Cedric. 'It's odd.'

Coco snorted. 'No shit, Sherlock. All those years at university, really paid off, huh?'

The doctor stood upright. 'Once Ebba's finished here, I'll have the body removed and I can have a better look at her in the morgue. Maybe then I can give you some answers. Mais,' he shrugged, 'the bottle of pills, the lack of any obvious signs of distress or trauma, we may be looking at suicide.'

Cedric stepped forward. 'Then what are we thinking? Mother and son had a fight, mother kills herself, son feels guilty, runs away, only to slit his own throat in the elevator?'

'All rather too neat, if you ask me,' Coco mused. 'I was there with Elliot. He didn't seem traumatised, as you would expect if he'd just found his mother dead. He didn't seem sad, or guilty, or…'

'Or what?' Cedric interrupted.

She considered. 'I don't know how to describe it.' She stared at the woman on the sofa. 'If he left this room, and this was his mother, then no matter his feelings, I imagine it would have been, just different.' She sighed. 'Then again, what do I know? I've been a cop for twenty years, and the only thing I know for certain is that people are unpredictable. You can share a bed with a man and have no idea what he does when he's out of your bed.'

Shlomo touched her arm. 'Charlotte. I know you don't want to hear this. But I will say it, and I will keep saying it. Your former Commander was a terrible man. Just because you slept with him, doesn't make you any more perceptive. Morty was my friend too.'

'And mine,' Cedric added.

'And the point is,' Shlomo continued. 'Despite the evidence, and his admission, I still don't believe it of him.' He looked straight at Coco. 'That is where we are. We move on, tougher and together. For those of us who have little else, it is better because it is what we have chosen.'

Coco angrily pushed her fingers across the rims of her eyes.

'Bugger you, Sonny,' she cried. 'Anyway, enough with the schmaltz. Let's get on with our day. Elliot Bain tried to kill himself, because his argument with his mother triggered something in him. Commander Demissy will be happy with an open and shut case on my first day back at the Commissariat.'

'Except, she won't,' Ebba Blom interjected, the bottle of pills in her hand. 'Unless someone can explain why a woman kills herself with a handful of pills from a bottle without a single fingerprint on it.'

'No prints at all?' Coco asked.

The forensic tech laughed with clear sarcasm. 'Ah, maybe my French isn't so good after all. I had assumed my statement about there being no fingerprints was quite clear, perhaps I was wrong.'

Coco noticed the smirk on Cedric's face, shooting him a piercing glare. She turned to Shlomo. 'No prints on a bottle of pills? Isn't that strange?' She moved closer to the body. 'She isn't wearing gloves.'

He shrugged. 'It's strange, or it isn't, Charlotte. Everything we see is strange, non?'

Coco ignored him, moving closer to the body. 'I can't imagine a single scenario where someone decides to take their own life, and then wipes their prints from the bottle of pills they used, can you?'

'Peut être, her son did?' Cedric suggested.

She flashed him a doubtful look. 'Pourquoi? It would make no sense for him to do it. He may have wanted us to believe she had died of natural causes, but then he would have removed the bottle altogether. Leaving the bottle, a bottle with no prints on it, suggests only one thing to me.'

'He wanted us to investigate,' Cedric concluded.

'Or he didn't see them, or notice them,' Ebba said.

'Right before he…,' Coco began, 'before he did it, the last thing he said was, *find out who made me do this.*'

'What does that even mean?' Cedric questioned.

She shrugged. 'Find out who killed my mother? Find out who made me want to kill myself? Until he wakes up, we're not really going to know. And why was he in the lift? Where was he going? He can't have known I was going to be in the lift.' She sighed, staring at the body. 'Too many questions with no answers. D'accord. Let's get Madame Cross in here before we remove the body. I'd like a confirmation this woman is Elliot Bain's mother.' She turned her head. 'And also, I'd like her to take a look around the apartment. She's the only person we know who has been here before. She might spot if something is out of place or looks strange.'

13H15

Madame Cross stared at the body. She ambled across the room, pressing her hand against the wall. She stopped by the window, lifting her head slowly and deliberately as she turned it.

'Something terrible happened here,' she said.

Coco resisted the urge to say, *no shit Sherlock!* Instead she nodded, but said nothing.

Madame Cross moved again, dragging her feet as if they were leaden weights. 'Nita was a very tidy woman,' she said. 'This mess would appall her.'

'You said you heard an argument,' Cedric interjected. 'What kind of argument?'

Her eyes widened. 'You must think me an old woman prone to eavesdropping if you expect me to answer that question, young man,' she snapped.

Coco smiled. 'On the contrary. I would imagine you're the sort of woman who looks out for her neighbours.' She stopped, pointing at the body. 'I know it's difficult for you, but at this point, you are the only person who knew her. Can you confirm this is Nita Bain, mother of Elliot Bain.'

Madame Cross turned, stared at the body and nodded quickly before turning away. 'That is Nita,' she said.

Coco nodded, nodding at Sonny and Ebba. She moved towards the old lady, placing a hand gently on her shoulder. 'Let me get you back to your apartment,' she said. 'This must be very difficult for you, and my colleagues here need to take care of Nita.'

Cross nodded, stumbling forwards, her hands reaching out, slapping onto a sideboard, knocking a row of photographs and a fruit bowl to the ground. Coco lurched forward, pulling the woman to a chair near the deceased. 'Are you okay?' she gasped.

Madame Cross nodded, reaching over and touching Nita Bain's hand. 'Poor dear, Nita,' she whispered.

'You look very pale,' Coco said. 'Let's get you home and we'll call your doctor and have them check you out. You've had a terrible shock.' She gestured to Cedric. 'Give me a hand, Lieutenant.'

Cedric joined her, and between them they manoeuvred Madame Cross into an upright position. She looked back once again, her head shaking. 'Poor dear, Nita,' she repeated. 'Poor dear, Nita.'

14H00

Coco poured herself a café from the pot on Shlomo's desk in the corner of the cramped, dingy morgue and sat. She slowly sipped the lukewarm drink which vaguely resembled coffee, her eyes following Sonny as he continued getting ready for the autopsy. The remains of Nita Bain lay on the gurney, washed and cleaned and waiting for examination. With a positive identification from her neighbour, Madame Cross, they could at least try to understand what had happened to Elliot Bain's mother.

Madame Cross was safely settled in her own apartment. Her doctor had given her a sedative and said she would sleep until morning, and he would look in on her then. Her reaction had stabbed at Coco's heart because she suspected the elderly woman had little in her life. Her apartment was sparse and contained very little. A small television, an aged sofa and love seat, and a sideboard filled with the sort of trinkets found in a one-euro store. Coco made a promise to look in on her. It was a promise she knew she would most likely not keep, but she intended to try.

The comparison between them bothered her. She could see herself ending up like Madame Cross. An old woman alone in a crummy apartment. Coco hoped it would not be true. After all, she had four children. But then so perhaps did Madame Cross. Coco realised having a family, in the end, did not necessarily mean you would not end up alone. Coco's own parents and her only sibling, a brother, lived on the opposite side of France and none of them seemed to ever have a burning desire to visit the other. A weekly call was all they could manage, and the disappointment was always clear in the voices of her parents.

There was much Coco felt sure they would never, could never, really forgive her for. She was not sure she could blame them. They were a proud family, visible and respected in their insular Jewish community, and she had disgraced them. Two children before she was twenty-one, to two different fathers, neither of which had been a part of the children's lives and neither of which had placed a ring on Coco's finger. Not that she had ever wanted either of them to do so, but the disgrace was something her parents had never really gotten over. Coco's brother, Ari Jnr, on the other hand, had always been the favourite child. A child who brought no disappointment and was a shining beacon of light in the Brunhild family. It made Coco crazy because she knew the actual truth. The stench of hypocrisy ran deep through the Brunhild family line. Coco's father, a Rabbi, had been conducting an affair with his secretary for decades, with his wife's knowledge. Their pride and joy son, had his own set of problems and secrets, all of which, it seemed, were accepted and forgiven, because, like his father, he was a man.

Ebba Blom, the forensic tech, stepped in front of her, enveloping Coco in a heady scent, causing her to wrinkle her nose. 'What are you wearing, Ebba?' she asked. 'Eau de bat piss?'

Ebba shot her a poisonous look, before crossing the room towards Shlomo's direction. 'I've finished my examination of the deceased's clothing, and they are clean. No signs of blood or anything out of the ordinary. A few strands of hair, but they're long and brown, most likely hers. A few grey ones, but that's probably the old lady. I'll check the DNA to make sure.'

Coco raised an eyebrow, surprised at the politeness of her tone.

'Merci, Ebba,' Dr. Bernstein answered.

The automatic doors swished open, and Cedric entered, his heavy-footed steps echoing around the room. He waved, winking at Ebba, causing her to mutter something sounding like a Swedish curse under her breath. 'I've run checks on Nita Bain. No criminal record. She used to work as a seamstress, but she's been sick for the last few years with back problems. She was married to Antoine Bain, but he died in a car accident three years ago. That's where she hurt her back. They had one kid, Elliot, he was in the car with them, but he doesn't seem to have had any serious injuries.'

'Was there an investigation into the accident?' Coco asked.

Cedric nodded. 'Oui, but it didn't go anywhere. The traffic cops ruled it an accident. Nita spent some time in rehab for her back. She moved into the apartment when she came out and Elliot joined her. He'd been staying with his maternal grandparents, down South somewhere.'

'What about Elliot?' Sonny asked. 'Have you still heard nothing?'

'I called the hospital again,' Cedric said. 'He's still in surgery and as far as they know, it's touch and go.'

'Poor kid,' Sonny replied.

'Or bastard murderer,' Ebba added.

Coco ignored them both and scratched her head. 'Didn't Madame Cross say something about Elliot being on a scholarship to some fancy school?'

'Si,' Cedric reported. '*École Privée Jeanne Remy*. It's in Saint-Germain-en-Laye.'

'Saint-Germain-en-Laye,' Coco repeated. 'I don't think I know it.'

'It's about twenty miles outside Paris,' Sonny answered. 'It's a pleasant area, if you like the countryside and don't want to travel very far, it's perfect.'

'And what about the school?' Coco asked Cedric.

'It's named after its directrice, Jeanne Remy,' he replied. 'Quite small, only about twenty-five students and it specialises in science.' He whistled. 'And get this, the cost of admission for a term is €35,000.'

'A term!' Coco exclaimed. 'But our boy was there on a scholarship?'

Cedric nodded. 'Yeah, they enrol one student a year on a scholarship. They must be super smart and come from a disadvantaged background. Because of what Madame Cross said, I called up the school and asked about Elliot Bain. All some snooty receptionist would tell me was he was no longer a student in the school.'

Coco raised an eyebrow. 'Hmm, interesting. Why would the kid give up a cushy number like that?'

'Maybe he didn't,' Cedric reasoned. 'Maybe he got kicked out.'

'Private schools are notoriously competitive,' Sonny added. 'He'd have to be really at the top of his game to last. Just because someone is smart, doesn't always mean they have what it takes to succeed in an intense environment, the sort fostered in that type of school.'

Coco nodded. 'And if he got kicked out, we might just have a motive for what he did.' She stopped and stared again at the body of Nita Bain. 'But what does his mother have to do with it? I'm not sure why his anger would manifest itself in her direction.'

Sonny shrugged. 'If he makes it through the day, maybe you can ask him. In the meantime, why don't we open her up and see if that tells us anything?'

Coco blew her nose. She was still forcing herself to look at the remains of Nita Bain. The cutting, the skill and deftness of the pathologist was something she could understand, especially when dealing with the artistry shown by people such as Dr. Bernstein. Sonny was careful and methodical, but more importantly respectful when a person came into his morgue. On and off, Coco had been a cop for most of her life, and she had become acclimatised to most of the monstrous behaviour of her fellow humans. But she still had not gotten used to the smell emitted from dead bodies.

Occasionally, at night, when she finally slept after another terrible day, the smell would follow her into her dreams. She never saw the faces, just the smell of rotting, decaying bodies.

She would awake with a start, the darkness throwing ominous shadows at her. The only way she could get the darkness to disappear was to move quickly and to reach across the bed she shared most nights with her two youngest children - Cedric and Esther. She would press her nose to their warm scalps, and inhale the soft, sweet odour, instantly dissolving the nightmare remnants in her nostrils. Coco realised that soon, Cedric and Esther would do a full one-eighty like their older siblings, Barbra and Julian and grunt and growl at her whenever she approached. It filled her with an overwhelming sadness that someday none of her children would reciprocate her affection. It was an unbearable thought after everything she had been through in her life.

'Charlotte?' Dr. Bernstein called out.

Coco gasped. 'Désolé, Sonny, I was a million miles away.'

He smiled kindly at her. 'Probably the best place to be, when there's a body on the table.'

She stood quickly, pulling her woollen coat around her as if she had suddenly felt a chill. She moved closer to Nita Bain. 'What do we have?'

The doctor finished washing his hands. He turned slowly. 'We have a very sad case, that's what we have. Our poor femme, here, has lived a very chequered existence. She would have almost certainly been on some pretty strong medication for her back. The blood tests will clarify that when they come back from the lab. It's clear she has had multiple operations to repair the damage to her back from the car accident. I can't imagine she walked without being in constant pain.'

Coco stared at Nita's body. It appeared to her as if her entire body bore the remnants of a serious and grave accident. 'All of this was because of a car accident?'

Sonny considered his answer. 'Certainly the back injury, mais non, there is altogether something different here. Because, as you can see, there are most certainly newer injuries. Injuries which cannot be explained by a car crash several years ago.' He pointed to Nita Bain's stomach. 'These are bruises, which I imagine were caused by punches, or some kind of altercation. I can't be sure, but what I can tell you is that most of them are little more than a few days old, perhaps a week at the most. Some are older and healed, but we're looking at something extremely depressing here.'

'Wouldn't she have been in a lot of pain?' Cedric asked.

Sonny nodded. 'Oui, almost certainly, mais my examination of her back suggests she would have been on medication. We'll get the results in a day or two, but if she was on the sort of medication I imagine she was, then she may have been able to bear the pain from the other injuries.' He looked at Coco. 'It's a grim picture, Captain.'

Coco shuddered. 'A week, you say. About the time young Monsieur Elliot Bain came back from school,' she mused.

'And that's not all, I'm afraid,' Sonny continued. 'The stomach contents clearly show there are no recent pills in her system. So, I can't imagine this was a suicide.'

'Putain,' Coco groaned. 'She looked so peaceful. There was no sign of violence. How the hell did she die?'

The doctor moved across the room and pointed to a photograph on the monitor. 'This is her spleen. You can clearly see it has been ruptured.' He pointed at a second photograph, a closeup of a bruise on Nita Bain's stomach. 'This blow here, on her left upper abdomen, not more a week old, caused what I believe was a catastrophic abdominal trauma.'

Coco shook her head. 'What are you saying? She bled to death? Wouldn't she have known?'

Sonny nodded. 'She would have certainly felt pain in the abdomen, probably stretching to her left shoulder. There may have been several other symptoms, such as dizziness, disorientation, blurred vision, confusion, tachycardia, pallor, hypotension…' he trailed off. 'It wouldn't have been nice for her.'

'Then why the hell didn't she get help?' Coco countered.

'I can't answer that,' he replied. 'The scenario I'm offering you is extreme. She may not have had all of those symptoms, but what I can say, is she would have been in pain, even if she was taking medication for her back. Had she sought help, most physicians would have quickly assessed her condition as a blow to her spleen and acted accordingly. It may not have been enough to save her, but if she had sought help in the last few days, she may not have died.'

Coco began pacing. 'I can only think of one reason she wouldn't have sought help.'

'She didn't want to get her attacker in trouble,' Cedric concluded.

She nodded. 'Her son.'

'Or her "ethnic" boyfriend,' Cedric added, 'remember the old lady told us about him.'

Coco sucked her teeth. 'Unfortunately "ethnic" isn't a lot of use in actually helping us track him down.' She turned back to Sonny. 'What would her death have looked like?'

The doctor cleared his throat. 'When her spleen ruptured, it would have spewed its contents into the cavities of her body. It quickly turned into septicaemia, bacterial infection spreading to her vital organs - her heart, her brain. It would have been painful, but it should have also been quick.'

Cedric shook his head. 'And the kid didn't even help her? He was so worried about getting busted he didn't even try to save her? So, she's dead, and what does he do, he poses her body and makes it look as if she had died naturally. If he was such a smart kid, he'd have to know we examine any suspicious death.'

'Maybe he thought the bottle of pills would be enough,'

Sonny reasoned. 'And she could have died that way. Her injuries were catastrophic, she could have just passed away as she sat.'

Coco continued pacing. 'The question is - where was he going? What was the plan? And why did he change his mind when he saw me?'

'And why did the kid take the lift when he was only four floors up?' Cedric posed.

'If I lived on the first floor, I'd take the lift,' Coco reasoned. 'Not everyone is all about the fitness regime.'

Sonny frowned. 'Could he have known you were in the lift?' he asked. 'You told us he knew you were a flic. Maybe he saw you and asked for your help.'

'Then why did he try to kill himself?' she reasoned. 'Unless guilt hit him and he realised when he saw me, no one was going to believe the bullshit suicide theory and he didn't want to go to prison.' She shook her head. 'The trouble is, unless he wakes up, all we really have is a shitload of supposition.'

'And what about the scalpel?' Ebba interjected. 'He didn't kill his mother with it, he didn't attack you. Perhaps he had it because he was on his way to finish off the actual murderer.'

Coco regarded her with surprise. 'Good point, Ebba,' she said. She flopped heavily into a chair. 'We're just finding more and more questions we can't answer.' She tapped her chin. 'Ebba, can you go back to the apartment and do a more thorough check? See if there are any other prints, or sign of anyone else who may have been in the house recently. I want to make sure there's nothing we're missing.'

Ebba looked at Sonny for approval. He nodded. 'You don't have to ask me, what Captain Brunhild says goes.'

Ebba huffily moved to the corner of the morgue and began filling a bag with equipment. Sonny took a tentative step towards Coco, reaching into his pocket and retrieving a folded piece of paper. He handed it sheepishly to Coco.

'Really, Sonny, aren't we a little old to be passing notes to each other,' she laughed, 'sure, I'll go to the dance with you.' She opened the paper, her eyes widening. 'A cheque for ten thousand euros made out to me.' She stared at him. 'What is this about?'

Sonny lowered his voice. 'It's nothing, and it's not much. I know it isn't. But I also know times are tough for you right now. I just want to help in some way.' He raised his hands in an attempt to fend off any forthcoming protest. 'Call it a loan if you want, but it doesn't have to be. What's the saying, something about paying it forward. Well, this is mine. You pay it forward every day in one way or another, so think of it as a bit of good fortune pointing back at you.'

She shook her head, her cheeks flushing. 'Sonny. I don't know what to say, but I can't take your money. You work too hard for it.'

'So, do you, and you need it more than I do.'

She laughed. 'I need a lot of things, but you know, the one thing I don't need is charity,' she said with a sigh. 'My life is shit right now, but it will get better. I will get through this. I have so much, money is the least of my worries.'

'Coco, don't be stubborn, s'il te plaît,' he pleaded.

She touched his arm. 'What I was trying to say is, keep your money. I don't need it, but I do need you. My kids need men in their life. Real, decent, honourable men. Barbra and Julian will never admit it, but they're devastated by losing Morty, and Cedric and Esther aren't really ever going to get to know him, and my family are pretty useless…'

Sonny's face crinkled in confusion. 'You mean, you want me to be their daddy?'

Coco guffawed. 'What is it about men that makes you think a woman always wants rescuing? I don't want rescuing. I want my kids to have some good, male role-models. And I certainly don't want a daddy in my life.' She touched his arm again. 'But we're friends, aren't we? Friends without the yucky benefits?'

It was the doctor's turn to laugh. 'I'd love to spend time with your kids.'

She handed him back the cheque. 'Then keep your money. You can buy us all pizza and beers instead tonight, okay?'

He nodded. 'I'd like that.'

Coco turned around, realising Cedric had been listening to their conversation. His face was pale, and there was something about it she did not recognise. Was he hurt? 'And as for you,' she said with bravado. 'You look like you're good with a hammer. If you want to eat Sonny's pizza and drink his beer, you're going to have to work for it. There's a ton of stuff needs doing in my shitty apartment, because the damn landlord certainly is not going to.'

Cedric smiled. 'I can teach my godson all he needs to know to impress the chicks.'

Coco shook her head, surpassing a smile. 'Or the dudes, no judgement in my house,' she corrected. She watched as Ebba picked up her bag and headed for the door. 'Hey, Ebba! Sonny's buying, why don't you join us? It would be nice to have some decent female company in the apartment for once.'

Without looking back, Ebba called over her shoulder. 'I'd rather poke my eyes out with a needle.'

Coco watched her leave, shaking her head in amazement. 'Your assistant is a piece of work, Sonny,' she said.

Sonny nodded. 'I know, désolé. I'll have a word with her. She's very good at her job, but her social skills leave a lot to be desired.'

Coco shrugged her shoulders. 'Don't bother, I like her. She's not afraid, and I like that she hates everyone, so do I. It means she'll be good at her job. She won't judge and she won't care who she offends. She'll just do what she has to do and not be led by whatever anyone wants her to say or do. Keep her, damn it, promote her!' She smiled at Cedric. 'And she keeps the Lieutenant on his toes, which isn't such a bad thing!'

16H00

Commander Imane Demissy threw the report onto her desk and tutted. She sat on the edge of the desk, picking a piece of fluff from the trousers of her pale green Armani suit. Coco lowered her head, sinking into the chair. She hated the fact Demissy was now occupying the same office the former Commander, Mordecai Stanic, once used. Mainly because they had not replaced the desk, because Coco was fairly sure they had conceived her youngest child on it.

'Look at me, Captain Brunhild,' Demissy ordered, as if she was talking to a child.

Coco slowly lifted her head, resigned she was about to be told off about something.

'This is a mess,' Demissy continued. 'A big mess. And all I see is your name all over it.'

Coco pursed her lips. 'I'm not entirely sure that's fair. I got in a lift. The end. Nothing else which has happened today has anything to do with me.'

'And yet, your name is all over it. A boy slit his own throat in front of you. A boy who we now suspect had something to do with the death of his mother.'

Coco pressed her chin downwards. 'Well, that was not entirely down to me. It's not like my B.O. has the power to make people kill themselves rather than have to smell it.'

The Commander tutted again and tapped the folder. 'What are we missing?'

Coco shrugged. 'Beat's the shit out of me,' she raised her hand upon seeing Demissy's frown, and Cedric's smirk in the corner of her eye. 'Désolé. What I meant to say is.' She cleared her throat and when she spoke again, her tone was even and clear. 'At this stage, your honour, the facts of the investigation are eluding me.'

Demissy stared at Coco, evidently assessing whether she was being flippant. She narrowed her eyes, coming to no conclusion either way. 'Well, let us pretend we are police officers. We have one dead body, one attempted suicide, and a lot of supposition. Tell me, Captain. Where do you think this began?'

'The school,' Coco answered.

'The school?' Demissy questioned. 'How on earth did you come to that assumption?'

'Because it's all we have,' Coco retorted. 'We know from Madame Cross that Elliot Bain came back from school in the last week or so. Cedric has confirmed with the school he is no longer a pupil there. Madame Cross also confirmed since his return, there has been a lot of animosity in the Bain household.'

Demissy flashed a doubtful look. 'And why would that have anything to do with his school life?'

Coco smiled. 'When I was thirteen, my father sent me to a summer camp in Jerusalem. It was meant to be my introduction to the,' she stopped to make air quotes, '"promised land." What it actually resulted in was me being deflowered by the son of the tour guide. I was sent home on the first flight with a scarlet letter over my head for evermore.' She shrugged. 'When I say deflowered, what it actually amounted to was some creepy man copping a feel of my boobs. He said it would help them grow into the correct shape. I thought, well, perhaps he has a point. My boobs are a bit uneven. Perhaps that's what it takes, like a baker moulding a dough…'

'Arrete!' Demissy cried. She turned to Cedric. 'Tell me she isn't always this way?'

Cedric shrugged. 'I'd like to, mais… this is a good day.'

'Captain,' Demissy responded warily. 'Get to the point while I still have the ability to tolerate you, I beg of you.'

'My point is,' Coco continued, 'is something happened to Elliot Bain. A scholarship kid. He came back last week from a snobby school, for whatever reason, and it kicked up a shit storm in his home life. His mother is dead. Probably murdered. Someone may have attempted to make it look like suicide, we can't know at this moment. All we know is Elliot Bain is in hospital. I haven't even had the chance to see him yet, even though I spent an enormous amount of energy trying to stop him from dying. And all I know for sure is, I'd like to understand why. The school may be a dead end, but as far as I can tell, it's all we have to go on at the moment.'

Demissy pursed her lips. 'So, you're asking me to send you on a day trip to Saint-Germain-en-Laye?'

'What else do you suggest?' Coco retorted. 'You said it yourself. We've got a stiff and we've got a kid teetering on the edge. No clues. In my experience, in circumstances like these, all we can really do is take a step back.'

Demissy pointed. 'Well, getting the two of you out of the Commissariat for a day isn't such a bad thing.' Her eyes narrowed angrily. 'But if you go to Saint-Germain-en-Laye, make sure you behave yourself.'

Coco smiled. 'I always do, Commander. Trust me.'

The Commander raised an eyebrow.

Coco stood up and moved towards the doorway. 'Say, we're having a bit of a pizza party at my place tonight.' She moved her shoulders. 'Maybe you'd like to join us…'

Demissy rocked her head, her eyes widening. She said nothing.

Coco smiled. 'I get that. I like it. I respect a woman who can say all she needs to with her eyes. I'd give you the same look if you asked me to come to your house for a fancy fiddle-playing party.'

Demissy suppressed a smile. 'The doctor called from the hospital. She will see you first thing and give us a better idea of

Elliot Bain's prognosis. So, enjoy your party, but not too much, d'accord?'

Coco nodded, her face clouding.

19H00

Coco threw open the door, gesturing wildly. 'Welcome to my gaff!' she cried excitedly, spilling wine from the glass in her hand.

'Your *what?*' Cedric gasped, stepping into the hallway, pronouncing *what* as if she had just uttered something foul.

'Calm your britches, young fella,' she laughed, 'it's not like I said, welcome to my vagina!'

'Will you stop saying that!' Cedric wailed.

Sonny passed him and moved into the living room, lowering himself onto a small sofa, a squeak emitting from beneath him. He reached under and retrieved a child's toy. He placed it carefully on a coffee table already overflowing with books, magazines, cups and various takeaway boxes. 'Cedric, you really have to stop reacting,' he laughed, 'the more you react, the more she'll continue to wind you up.'

Cedric flopped huffily onto a worn dining table. 'It's easier said than done. She told Commander Demissy the other day, and she really wasn't impressed.'

Coco closed the door and moved into the living room. 'I just wanted to make sure the Commander understood that whilst I named my son after you, it's only because you have seen my vagina, not entered it.'

He threw his hands in the air. 'You don't need to tell her anything, and if you did, you could say, "Cedric helped me deliver my third child when he decided to be born in the middle of a chase."'

Coco shrugged nonchalantly, suppressing a smile. It amazed her still that ten years had passed since Cedric, on his first day as a police officer at the **Commissariat de Police du 7e arrondissement**, had been her only help when her baby was born. The labour was fast and brutal, on the filthy ground of a dingy warehouse. She wondered whether it was why the now ten-year-old Cedric was one of the filthiest, grubbiest children she had ever seen. She ensured he bathed regularly, but it somehow seemed as if he came out dirtier than he was when he went in. His face gave the constant impression of being covered in snot and chocolate. He was, however, she considered, a beautiful boy, with a mop of blond hair, blue eyes and filled with affection. He hugged his mother constantly, and Coco was sure it was one of the few things which kept her going. She hoped puberty would not change him.

'I'm going out, mother,' a raspy young woman's voice called out from the hallway.

'Me too,' a softer, but surlier young man's voice added.

Coco turned her head to see her two oldest children, Barbra and Julian. Barbra was curvaceous, her ample bosoms squeezing out of the leather bustier she was fond of wearing. She had never quite forgiven her mother for calling her Barbra, after her favourite singer, Barbra Streisand, nor the fact she had the same figure and hair as her mother. Unlike Coco, Barbra did not dye it blue, rather jet black. Julian, on the other hand, was tall and slight, with floppy brown hair he wore long on one side.

'Hi, Cedric,' Julian said with a self-conscious wave of his hand.

'Hi, Cedric,' Barbra mocked, repeating the greeting in a high-pitched camp manner. 'Why don't you just lick him? Mop up some of that drool dribbling down your chin, you perv,' she added tartly. Julian responded by punching her arm. She repaid him with her own punch, much harder and firmer, which caused him to cry out, turning his head away in obvious distress but not wishing to show it.

Coco sighed. 'Mes enfants, s'il te plait, I have guests, show some restraint, won't ya?'

'Guests?' Barbra sniffed. 'The steroid cop and the doctor who follows you around like a puppy dog?'

'Don't be so rude!' Coco bristled. 'Anyway, I need to talk to you about something. Did you hear what happened in the elevator today?'

Barbra tutted. 'Yeah, the creep killed himself and we've all been having to walk up the shitty staircase which stinks of piss.'

'The creep?' Coco asked sharply. 'You know Elliot Bain?'

'Bien sûr, I don't know him,' Barbra retorted. 'The delusional idiot asked me out on the stairway and when I said, are you serious? He stared at me, like he was some hotshot, and said, *ah, so you think you can do better, do you? Well, think again. You don't even know who your real dad is, and your pretend dad is a pervert who is going to die in jail.*'

Coco's eyes widened in horror. 'And what did you do?'

Barbra shrugged. 'I kneed the creep in the balls and pushed him out of my way.'

Coco ignored Cedric's snigger behind her, suppressing her own smile. 'Well, Cherie, you shouldn't have done that, but he had no right to talk to you like that.'

She shrugged again. 'I could not care less about the creep.'

Coco turned to Julian. 'Et tu? I got the impression you knew him.'

Julian appeared aghast. 'I don't know what you're talking about,' he blurted.

Barbra laughed. 'I saw the two of you talking and he was all flirty with you.' She turned to her mother. 'He's one of those types of boys. Thinks he has to appeal to everyone, even fuck them if he thought it would get him something.'

'I hate you,' Julian mouthed.

'I hate you more,' Barbra retorted. She moved to the door before giving Coco a chance to admonish her. 'I won't be back tonight, so don't wait up for me.'

'You most certainly will be back tonight!' Coco yelled.

'You're not sleeping over at your gangster boyfriend's place,' she hissed through gritted teeth.

'Get me my own bedroom, and I might actually want to spend some more time here,' Barbra replied opening the door.

'Get a job and give me some money, and I just might be able to afford to!' Coco retorted, but her daughter was already gone. She turned to Julian. 'And you, cheri? Are you staying at Matthieu's tonight?'

Julian's face clouded angrily at how she spoke Matthieu's name, as if she was implying something by it. 'Non,' he mumbled, 'we're just doing homework, I'll be back by ten.'

Coco watched the door close behind him. She turned back to Sonny and Cedric. 'My kids, folks. A sure sign of the importance of birth control.'

'They're good kids, Coco,' Sonny reasoned. 'They've just had a lot to deal with lately.'

'So has she, and it's not as if any of it was her fault in the first place,' Cedric retorted, his eyes widening as if he had surprised himself by defending his boss.

'Except it was,' Coco sighed. 'I brought Morty into our lives.'

'But you couldn't have known who he was, WHAT he was,' Sonny interjected. He stood and handed her a beer from the pack he was holding. She took it gratefully. 'Morty was an evil man, who did some terrible things,' he continued, 'all before you and all nothing to do with you.'

She gulped the beer. 'Maybe. Let's not waste any more breath talking about the *former* Commander Stanic.' She looked around the cramped living room. 'Barbra's also right about this. We're living in a two-bedroom tiny hovel because it's all I can afford. If I were her, I'd spend my nights with my criminal boyfriend too.'

'It's not tiny, it's bijou,' Sonny offered.

Coco snorted. 'It's a shithole, that's what it is.' She paused. 'But it's my shithole, and it actually feels good to me, that it's all mine, I owe nobody a thing for it. This,' she spread her arms about, 'may not be much, but it's all down to me.'

'Where does everyone sleep?' Cedric asked.

'Barbra and Julien share one room, and the rest of us have the other,' she replied.

'The rest of you?'

She nodded, sinking into a beanbag. It wobbled and threw her onto the ground, causing the contents of her beer to splash on her face. She wiped it and licked her fingers. Noticing Cedric's appalled face, she said. 'Hey, don't judge, beer is expensive! What was I saying? Oh yeah, you've met Helga, the au pair. She sleeps on a rollout at the bottom of my bed. Cedric sleeps with me,' she paused winking at Cedric, 'not big boy Cedric, little boy Cedric.'

Despite himself, Cedric laughed.

'And Esther is in her cot next to me,' she continued. 'It's very cosy, but actually quite comforting. Luckily the kids sleep through anything. So come bedtime Helga and I get comfy and watch some sappy TV movie until we fall asleep.' She smiled. 'Not such a terrible life, all things considered.'

'Doesn't Helga mind?' Sonny asked.

'Let me tell you about Helga,' Coco replied. 'She's in her fifties. She fled Germany after being with her husband for over twenty years. He beat the crap out of her most days, and when he was out, he locked her in the house. She only got away from him because he had an accident at work and the police came to inform her. She lied and said, she'd lost the key and locked herself in, so they broke the door. She went to the hospital to see the son-of-a-bitch, and he had the audacity to be mad at her for leaving the house. I guess something broke in her then, and she realised she was going to die if she stayed. When the doctor told her that her husband was going to be in hospital for at least a week, she knew it was her chance. Her only chance.' Coco took a sip of beer, wiping her nose with the sleeve of her jumper. 'She had no money, barely two hundred euros she'd squirrelled away, but she'd always dreamed of coming to Paris. They had a painting of the Eiffel Tower in the hallway, and she says it was what kept her going. So, she got on a train and came here. Obviously, she didn't know at the time how little two hundred euros was. She had to get a job, but with no qualifications and no French ID, there was little chance of that happening.'

Sonny shook his head. 'The poor woman. How did you meet her?'

'We busted her,' Cedric answered.

Coco nodded. 'She stole a baguette because she hadn't eaten for four days.' She gulped. 'A fucking tuna fish baguette. She ended up in our cells, but she wouldn't talk, especially to men. Every time one came near her, she punched them.'

Cedric rubbed his chin. 'She's got a hell of a right hook.'

'So, I talked to her. I knew her story before she even told me. Women only flinch like that for one reason and one reason only,' Coco continued. 'It was a slow night shift, there wasn't much going on. We talked, and she told me her story and I suppose, one thing led to another.'

She turned her head, staring at the row of photographs on the mantelpiece. 'She told me she loved kids, but had lost her own when her husband beat her so badly she miscarried at seven months. She held her baby for a few seconds before he died.' She took a long gulp of beer. Sonny handed her another.

Coco shrugged. 'Anyway, she needed a job, and she had no real chance of getting one. I needed help and haven't got a pot to piss in, so we struck a deal. I helped her with the paperwork to stay in France and she moved in with us. In our old place, she had a room of her own but when I told her I felt bad about her having to share my room here, she laughed and told me she used to sleep on the floor in a damp cellar when she was "disobedient." As far as she was concerned the rollout bed is her heaven.' She wiped her eyes with the back of her tattered jumper. 'It's a win-win. I don't have to pay her what I would another full-time nanny, because I couldn't. So, instead, when I'm here she gets to go out. As far as I can tell, she just walks and walks. She goes to museums, the cinema, whatever she feels like, because she can now. *She's allowed.* And the thing is, she's come out of her shell. She's stroppy and runs the house like a… like a… well, like a German. But she loves us really, and we love her. It won't always be like this. As you saw, Barbra's itching to leave, Julian won't be far behind, so Helga will have her own room soon and we can grow old together.' She took another gulp of beer. 'Aint that something to look forward too?'

Sonny smiled at her. 'You're a wonderful woman, Coco,' he said.

She pulled back her shoulders. 'Not really, it works for both of us. I'd just like to think if it was me in trouble, or one of my kids was, someone in a foreign country might take them under their wing and give them safe haven. That's all I've done.' She noticed from the corner of her eye, Cedric wiping his eye. 'Cedric?' she gasped. 'Are you… are you crying?'

He glared at her. 'Non, I'm not crying, you lunatic. It's the stench of baby shit in here.'

She reached over and punched his arm. 'My gaff doesn't smell of shit, you asshole.' She wrinkled her nose. 'Not much, anyway.'

'Where does this "gaff" word come from?' Sonny asked.

Coco smiled. 'Hugo Duchamp,' she replied. Hugo Duchamp was also a police Captain, working in a small town in Western France. They had worked together on a case a year or two earlier and had become friends. 'Apparently it's something they say in London when talking about their house.'

'Ah, how is Hugo?' Sonny asked.

'He's fine,' Coco replied. 'He calls once a week or so. Makes up some kind of excuse to talk, and he sends me a GIF once a day, usually a picture of a cute dog.' She smiled. 'Typical Hugo really. He doesn't know what to say, so he says nothing, which of course means he's saying everything.' She shuddered. 'The worst part of everything that happened is that people look at me differently, usually with pity, and that's a bitch.'

Cedric shrugged. 'I don't pity you,' he said, 'I just couldn't give a shit.'

Sonny laughed. 'I don't pity you, either,' he added, 'but I COULD give a shit.'

Coco lowered her head, blue hair falling over her face. She threw it back. 'Anyway, enough of this wallowing. She picked up her cell phone. 'I'm going to order the pizzas, and,' she winked at Sonny, 'because you're paying, I'm super-sizing it!'

MARDI (TUESDAY)

10H00

Dr. Stella Bertram opened the door and beckoned Coco inside. Coco walked slowly, hands stuffed into the ripped pockets of her woollen overcoat. Her hair was frizzy and unkempt, the shadow of a hangover on her face.

Dr. Bertram smiled. Her own hair was black and short, her eyes alert but with clear kindness. 'Tough night, Charlotte?' she asked.

Coco grimaced. Bertram had delivered her last child, and she always struggled dealing with people when they had seen her at her worst. She vaguely recalled the delivery, but with the help of copious amounts of painkillers, the details were a little lost in the cloudy recesses of her drug-addled brain. However, Coco clearly remembered that at some point, she punched the kindly doctor in the face, giving her an ugly black eye. Dr. Bertram, to her credit, had seemingly borne no ill will following the incident.

'Every day is a tough night,' Coco grumbled.

The doctor nodded. 'Occupational hazard, I suppose,' she agreed.

Coco stopped at the foot of the bed, raising her head slowly. Elliot Bain appeared even smaller and younger than she remembered him, his paleness and fragility stabbed her heart. She was not sure of his involvement in his mother's death at that point, and she really did not care. *Find out who made me do this.* She knew the words would haunt her, no matter what the outcome of the investigation. The only sound in the room was the omnipresence of the life-support machine. Elliot's eyes were taped shut, his mouth spread wide by the breathing tube, his neck swathed in bandages. The top half of his chest was exposed and devoid of any hairs. He was pale, his nipples small like a child's and he was thin. He reminded Coco of her own son, and it squeezed her heart. *Find out who made me do this.*

'How's he doing, doc?' she asked finally.

Dr. Bertram gestured for Coco to follow her to the corner of the room. 'I've been a doctor for a long time, and while patients who do come around from comas often tell me they have no recollection, I'm not entirely convinced there isn't some part of the brain which is listening.'

Coco nodded. 'I get it. Then it's not good news?'

Dr. Bertram stared at Elliot. 'He made it through the night,' she gave by way of an answer. 'That's a start. We operated and stabilised him. But I believe the damage to his vocal cords is likely irrepairable.'

Coco's eyes widened. 'You mean, he'll never speak again?'

She shrugged. 'Being unable to speak is the least of his troubles, if he wakes up at all. We're still running tests, but the prognosis isn't great. I should know more in a day or so.'

Coco sank into a chair. 'Poor kid, and with his mother dead, he has no one.'

Dr. Bertram nodded. 'Oui, I heard about his mother. Do you imagine he's responsible?'

Coco considered. Ebba had completed her examination of the Bain home and found nothing to indicate there had been anyone else in the apartment. It seemed the only three people who had been there were Nita Bain, her son, and their elderly neighbour, Madame Cross. As for the mysterious potential boyfriend, she had found no trace. An oddity in itself, but it meant they had very little to go on. If there was a boyfriend, and a potential second suspect, they had nothing on him. Madame Cross herself had confirmed she had never actually seen him. She based her assumption on him being "ethnic" simply on hearing his voice, which may or may not have come from a television. It was a mess, Coco concluded, and a mess with no obvious solution. 'I certainly believe he knew his mother was dead,' she answered, 'but whether he had anything to do with it…' she shrugged. 'What can you tell me about him?'

'Not a great deal, I'm afraid. Pretty normal, average seventeen-year-old, a little thin, perhaps, but isn't that the way of the youth of today. My niece keeps telling me she can't eat pastry anymore because she has to be,' she gulped, forming her fingers into air quotes, '"insta ready," whatever the hell that means.' She shook her head. 'Mais, non. There are no signs of anything untoward on his body. His blood, urine and toxicology screens both came back clean. I performed a hair follicle test, and everything points to him being a clean, seemingly healthy young man.' She tapped her head. 'Bien sûr, I can't commit on his mental health, particularly considering what brought him here. I sent his clothes off to your forensic lab.'

'Will he wake up?'

'He should,' Dr. Bertram replied. 'If he wants to. Maybe he doesn't want to. Trauma is a powerful weapon. If he has no reason to wake up, he may just not.'

Coco laughed. 'Cheery soul, aren't you, doc?'

'I gave up cheery a long time ago.'

'So he really won't be able to speak?' Coco asked again.

'The damage to his vocal cords is too severe,' Dr. Bertram answered. 'Poor kid.'

'Poor kid, indeed,' Coco repeated. 'When can I talk to him?'

'Today, tomorrow, the day after, never…'

Coco frowned. 'Can't you wake him up?'

'He's in an induced coma,' she replied. 'All we can really do is monitor his vitals. He may come around himself, or we may be able to do it. But not yet, not now. He's got a long way to go. There's no way to know what he's going to be like if or when he wakes up. Once we have a better idea what we're dealing with, we may be able to come up with some sort of plan. I also have the psych department on standby. They'll need to assess him before they'll even agree to you talking with him. I'll call you,' she added.

Coco moved back to the bed. 'What the hell happened to you, kid?' she mused. She turned back to Dr. Bertram. 'The second he wakes up, I want to be the first to know, okay?'

The doctor nodded. 'I hope you find out what happened to this kid. It might just help what happens next to him and his recovery.' She cleared her throat. 'Listen, I know… I mean, it isn't…'

Coco stepped back. 'Spit it out, doc.'

Stella Bertram glanced awkwardly at her feet. 'Paris is a big place, but in our world, it's pretty small.' She shook her head. 'What I'm trying to say, badly, is I know how tough it can be, being the subject of gossip. And I also know how tough it can be to have a social life, girlfriends to talk to, when you work crazy shifts and are always on call. Hell, my last relationship was four years ago.' She exhaled. 'All I'm saying is, if you need someone to talk to, get wasted with, then,' she spread out her arms, 'you could do worse than me.'

Coco turned her head away. 'I don't play well with others, doc.'

Bertram smiled. 'I know, that's why I like you. You're never dull. I hate dull.' She stepped past Coco, noticing the aghast look on her face. 'Don't look at me like that. I know you don't play for my team. Shame though, I have a feeling you'd be rather good at it.'

Coco's mouth fell open as she watched Bertram leave. 'Bien sûr, I'd be good at it,' she shook her head, running after the doctor. 'But, wait. What makes you think I'd be good at it? Wait, Stella, wait!'

12H00

'You drive like an old woman,' Coco commented, throwing a shady look at Cedric.

He tutted. 'I drive like a cop obeying the speed limit,' he shot her his own withering look, 'not like an old lady on crack.'

Coco turned her head and shrugged her shoulders as if acknowledging he had a point. 'I've always seemed to be in a hurry to get somewhere, beats the shit out of me where or why, but hey, what can you do?'

'How was the kid?' Cedric asked.

Coco grimaced. 'Not good. Best-case scenario is if he even comes around at all, he'll never be able to speak again.'

Cedric pursed his lips. 'You know, I've been thinking about the whole mess…'

'Steady, Cedric, too much thinking and smoke will start coming out of your ears!'

He ignored her and continued. 'I get the kid kills his mother and then makes a run for it, but why try to kill himself in the lift?'

'I've been thinking about that too, going over and over it in my head, and maybe it's just as simple as the fact I saw his face,' Coco answered. 'He had to have known she would have been discovered eventually, and I could place him at the scene. Once she'd been discovered, we would have gone looking for him, anyway.'

Cedric shook his head. 'But, it still makes no sense. No offence, but why cut his own throat? If you were the only witness, why not kill you, make a run for it and act shocked when the police found him later? He could have faked an alibi, par example.'

'He could have done a lot of things,' Coco responded, 'but he may just be a messed-up kid. He killed his mother after an argument, and he couldn't live with it. He saw me, knew I was a flic and realised he was going to prison, or the nuthouse, and thought better of it.'

'*Find out who made me do this*,' Cedric repeated. 'How does that fit into this?'

Coco did not answer, because she did not know how it did. Instead, she said. 'As I've just said, the kid was most likely messed up in the head. He wasn't making sense.'

'There it is,' Cedric said, pointing ahead of them.

Coco narrowed her eyes. They were approaching the end of a narrow road. It was a dead-end, finishing with a forty-foot cobblestone wall, with a small red door in the middle. Only a small gold plaque indicated what might lie behind the wall. Cedric drew the car to a halt, and they climbed out, Coco dragging her oversized bag behind her. She dropped it on the roof of the car, causing Cedric to tut with irritation. Coco turned around, looking back into the street. It was narrow, lined with trees on either side, and there was no sign of anyone or anything nearby. She moved towards the sign.

École Privée Jeanne Remy.

Above the sign was a bell and a camera. Coco pressed the button, a loud bell ringing, causing her to start. Barely a moment passed before a woman's voice crackled through the intercom.

'Oui?'

'Ah, Bonjour, Je m'appelle Captain Brunhild from the Commissariat de Police du 7e arrondissement in Paris.'

No response.

'And this is my colleague, Lieutenant Degarmo.'

The woman still did not respond.

'Are you there, Madame?' Cedric asked.

'Hold your identification cards up to the camera,' she said

briskly.

Coco and Cedric held up their ID cards.

The woman barely suppressed a sigh. 'What is this in connection with?'

'We need to speak with whoever is in charge.'

'What is this in connection with?' she asked again.

Coco's nostrils flared. 'We are investigating a murder,' she snapped.

'A murder?' The woman retorted, her voice rising sharply. 'Here at the École?'

'Non, in Paris,' Coco replied.

When the woman replied, the relief was clear in her voice. 'Then, what does it have to do with us?'

Coco clicked her teeth. 'I will explain that to whoever is in charge,' she snipped.

'Wait there,' the woman retorted, before the line went dead. A minute passed, and then another. Finally, the door buzzed and began to slowly swing open.

'Go up the stairs and someone will meet you at the top.'

Coco and Cedric moved through the narrow red door. Coco took in a sharp intake of breath. It was as if they had walked from a barren land into an enchanted forest. As the red door closed behind them, they were suddenly thrown into darkness. Lights flickered on, illuminating a narrow walkway between the dense undergrowth.

'What the hell is this place?' Coco asked, moving cautiously. 'It gives me the creeps.' As much as it pained her to admit it, it relieved her to have the sickening scent of Cedric's aftershave close behind her.

As the walkway ended, they came to a stone staircase which rose steeply. Coco strained her head and she could finally see what she imagined was the Gothic building which housed the *École Privée Jeanne Remy*. It appeared vast, with huge turrets lining either side.

'Tell me we don't have to walk up all these stairs,' she wailed. 'There must be… there must be.'

'Two hundred at least, I'd say,' Cedric said cheerfully, stepping in front of her.

'I swear to Dieu, if you run up them two at a time, I'll…' Coco said as Cedric began doing exactly that.

She placed her foot on the first step. It was cool and felt damp underfoot. She shook her head and pulled her body up via the handrail. After what seemed like an eternity, particularly after being peppered with several rest-stops, she finally made it to the top, wheezing in a way she thought might make her pass out. 'You think there'd be a damn lift,' she grumbled.

'We like our privacy,' a woman called out from the shadows of a marbled arch doorway.

Coco strained her eyes to see who was speaking because the voice sounded different to the one they had just spoken to. The woman stepped forward. She was tall and thin, with grey, high swept hair. Her face was pinched tight with only blood-red painted lips to make her appear less pale. She outstretched her hand. 'My name is Jeanne Remy. Welcome to my school.'

12H30

Directeurice Jeanne Remy gestured for Coco and Cedric to take a seat. Coco dropped her bag and took a chance to look around the office they had just been ushered into. It was vast. A bookcase lined an entire wall, filled from floor to ceiling with books, books which appeared to Coco to be ancient. Not the sort of paperbacks lining her own shelves, but rather ancient and dusty manuals, most likely technical and medical. A second wall contained numerous trinkets, which appeared to be valuable antiques and awards. It was not lost on Coco that the directeurice's office was most likely larger than Coco's entire apartment. The directeurice took a seat opposite them. The chair seemed as if it had been deliberately raised, positioned to look down upon whoever she was addressing. Coco had immediate flashbacks to the number of times she had sat in just such an office, being looked down upon by someone - be it a teacher or a Rabbi, as they began what was inevitably a long and tedious lecture. She had passed the time imaging them naked and it had left her very cold indeed.

'My secretary said something about a murder,' Jeanne Remy began. Her voice was soft, but there was a coolness too. Perfect for telling people off, Coco thought. 'I can't imagine what you think this might have to do with us,' she added.

'It has something to do with one of your students, a young man by the name of Elliot Bain.'

'Ah,' Remy nodded. 'My secretary also told me someone had inquired about him.'

Coco leaned forward, studying the directeurice's face. It was stoic. *You'd make an excellent poker player*, Coco thought.

The directeurice's eyes narrowed to slits. 'Are you telling me he is dead?' she asked with no trace of surprise or concern.

'Non, it is his mother,' Coco replied. She held back on Elliot's condition for a moment or two, then explained he was unconscious in hospital. 'You didn't sound surprised, why is that?'

Jeanne Remy did not reply, instead stood up and moved to the window. It was wide and had a breathtaking panoramic view of the city of Saint-Germain-en-Laye. 'He was a troubled child… *is*, a troubled child,' she corrected herself quickly. She did not turn around, so Coco could not see whether the mistake had affected her stony face, or if it had just been a genuine slip of the tongue. As far as Coco knew, there had been no names mentioned in the newspapers or online, and certainly no specifics had been released.

'It's my understanding, Elliot Bain was recently suspended from your school,' Coco began. 'Is that correct?'

The directeurice spun around. 'School records are confidential, Captain Brunhild.'

'Non, they are not,' Cedric interrupted.

She turned her head slowly to him, a smile twisting onto her blood-red lips. A smile reserved for pity and thinly veiled condescension when dealing with a child who had tried, but ultimately failed. Cedric lowered his head, cheeks flushing.

Coco smiled. 'The kid's got a point. Murder trumps taking a sneak peek at someone's test results.'

Jeanne Remy laughed. 'Do you even know what the *École Privée Jeanne Remy* is?' she questioned.

Coco lowered her head. 'A posh school named after you,' she answered.

The directeurice smiled. 'My father, Maxim Remy, won the Nobel prize for his work in the field of physics.' She moved from the window, stopping in front of the shelf filled with awards, her finger trailing slowly across them. 'He was a brilliant man, but he was devoted to his work. My mother used to joke that science was his wife and children. Obviously, it wasn't really a joke. Don't misunderstand me. He wasn't a bad man, but I was a young girl, and evidently was not enough to compete with science for his attention.'

'I understand,' Coco said, as if she did not understand it at all.

'When he died,' Jeanne Remy continued, 'I inherited his wealth, his name, and his reputation, mais, not his intellect. Alors, I did the next best thing.'

'You opened a school,' Cedric said.

She smiled at him. 'The only thing I could do to honour his name, was by using his name, his legacy… *his money*, to find the next Nobel prize winner.'

'And have you?' Coco posed.

Jeanne Remy smiled sweetly. 'Not yet. But we will. We are a very exclusive school. We take very few admissions. Only twenty-five students, not just from France, from every country all around the world…'

'If they can afford it, that is,' Coco muttered. 'Thirty-five grand a term is a "little" out of most people's budget…'

'We are expensive, and we are exclusive,' the directeurice responded, 'because we provide a world-class education, with world-class professors.' She moved back to the window. 'I chose this place for the school for many reasons. The main was it is remote. It is secure and it is impossible to access without permission.' She smiled, pride clear in her tone. 'I don't mean to brag, but we have students here who belong to royalty, to dynasties. Security is paramount.'

'And then you have the scholarship kid?' Cedric snapped. 'The poor kid, with the big brain, huh?'

She smiled at him. 'I see your reticence. Therefore, let me tell you a story. A young boy, born in India, to parents unknown, was left on the steps of a convent and by the age of ten he was already smarter than the orphanage could cope with. He ended up on a scholarship in Mumbai, and from them he came to our attention. We enrolled him for free and he studied here for four years.' She moved her head to the side. 'He now works for the CDC and he has been involved in the progression of vaccines. His work has saved thousands of lives.' She stepped across the room. 'And it all started here. You see, we teach, but more importantly we encourage. The brain is a fragile organ. It must be used. But it must also be trained. We must teach the geniuses of the future to tap into what,' she tapped her head, 'is in here. That is why we began the Scholarship in his name.'

Coco frowned. 'Then you're saying, Elliot Bain was as smart as this Mumbai kid?'

Jeanne Remy exhaled. 'Elliot Bain could be whatever he wanted to be. He's smart, obviously, that is why he came here, but unfortunately he's undisciplined and prone to distraction.' She exhaled. 'I loved my father dearly. He was, the measure by which I compared all other men, unfortunately none of which matched.' She shook her head. 'He had exceptionally high standards. Don't get me wrong, it wasn't his own fault. I believe with superior intelligence, it is often necessary to negate other parts of the brain. My father was angry and treated people close to him as if they were an inconvenience. I admit to not understanding it at the time, but as I age, I understand his intentions. And that is why I am here. We must uphold his legacy. We must nurture genius.' She paused and moved her shoulders slowly, her face clouding. 'However, it is not always easy. Sometimes the brain of a child matures quicker than it can cope with.'

Coco glanced sideways at Cedric. 'And that was the problem with Elliot Bain?' she asked.

The directeurice moved slowly back towards her desk. She sat down. 'My earlier statement stands,' was all she said. 'I can't discuss students, whether they be past or present.'

Coco glared at her. 'Non, it does not. If you want to do this dance we can. I can go back to Paris and get a Juge to give me a mandate. And then I'll come back here, no doubt with the press on my heels, because they'll be wondering which of the rich kids it is we're investigating.' She paused. 'I wonder how that will go down with your exclusive clientele?' She paused again, giving Remy a moment for the most likely baseless threat to sink in. 'Or, you could quit being a pain, tell us what we need to know and we'll be on our way. I have no interest in sitting in traffic jams on the way back into Paris. So, how about you answer our questions, and I can file my report to my Commander and we'll all be happy. Good plan?'

Jeanne Remy studied Coco with a burning intensity. She sucked in a breath. 'I expelled Elliot Bain from my school last week,' she said.

'Because he couldn't cut it?' Coco asked

The directeurice shook her head. 'On the contrary, Elliot was, is, a very exceptional student. The reason for his,' she trailed off, 'expulsion, was,' she trailed off again, 'behavioural.'

Coco's eyebrows knotted. 'Behavioural? As in, serial killer sort of behavioural?'

Jeanne Remy laughed. 'Bien sûr, non,' she responded. 'He, in the end, resorted to type.'

Coco continued to frown. 'What do you mean, he resorted to type?'

Jeanne Remy tapped long, thin fingers on her desk. 'He allowed his emotions to get the better of him. He allowed himself to be swayed by a girl.'

Coco snorted. 'He's seventeen. I'd be more surprised if he didn't constantly walk around the place with a hard-on.'

The directeurice's face contorted with disdain. 'That's not what this is about, Captain Brunhild,' she spat. 'These children are more advanced than their peers. Usually,' she added. 'The girl in question was Manon Houde.'

'Manon Houde?' Cedric interjected. 'Why do I recognise the name?'

'Her father runs Houde Industrial,' Jeanne Remy replied. 'They make equipment for rockets.'

Coco nodded. 'And Manon was smart enough to be sent here?'

'She was certainly smart enough,' the directeurice bristled, 'but I would suggest, not interested enough.' She sighed. 'Regarde, she is an only child, set to inherit a multi-billion euro business. She is smart, but she is also lazy, et...' she did not finish her sentence.

'She's also a seventeen-year-old girl,' Coco concluded.

Jeanne Remy nodded. 'Studying wasn't always her top priority,' she replied.

Cedric leaned forward in his chair. 'You said she swayed Elliot Bain. What do you mean by that?'

She stood again, moving back to the wide window. 'As you have probably already worked out, there is only one way in or out of this school. It is one of our unique selling points. However,' she took a deep breath, 'such regulations often serve as an incentive to those who wish to break the rules.'

Coco waggled her finger. 'Yeah, we get it. Kids like to bunk off school and go party in the nearest town. Is that what you're saying happened?'

Jeanne Remy nodded slowly. 'We aren't sure how it happened exactly,' she began cautiously, 'but our security team has since pieced together the likely scenario. Elliot Bain wrote a hack to the CCTV cameras, which turned them off for a period of approximately ten minutes. It was all it took for Mademoiselle Houde to leave the school.'

Coco frowned. 'How? She walked down the stairs and opened the door?'

The directeurice lowered her head, her cheeks flushing. 'I can't say I understand the entire system. But in any event, the door opens by button. And the button is situated by the front door. The fact is, we've never had trouble keeping people out, because they can't get in. But the fact Elliot Bain could bypass the security protocols meant he enabled the young lady to make her escape without being noticed.'

'Where is she?'

Jeanne Remy turned her head, gazing out of the window. 'We don't know.'

Coco looked at Cedric. 'When was this?' Coco asked.

'Last Lundi,' Remy replied.

Cedric scratched his head. 'So, she's been missing for seven days now? Does her family know she's missing?'

Jeanne Remy tutted. 'She's not "missing," she simply left.' She sighed. 'I can't go into too many details, but when we noticed Manon was missing, we checked her room. Her iPad and her computer were still there. We looked at them and by checking her emails, we realised she had been talking to a boy. A boy from outside these walls. And between the two of them, they had imagined a scenario of love and lust away from the confines of school and family.' She shrugged. 'I'm sad to say, this isn't the first time such a thing has occurred, as I'm sure you must know.' She raised her hand. 'Not at this school, bien sûr, but she found a student who was willing and able to bypass our security protocols.' She stabbed her fingers on the desk. 'Such a mistake will not happen again, I can assure you of that.'

'When did you discover she was missing?' Coco asked.

'The following morning. Mardi,' Jeanne Remy answered. She sighed again. 'I'm afraid it was all carefully planned. You see, the school is rather empty at the moment. Most of the staff and students leave the premises at this time of year. The students are taken on trips to various sites around the country, sometimes even further afield, to expand their education. Manon left the evening before she was due to leave for her trip. Her teachers discovered her missing the following morning, by which time she was long gone.'

'You didn't answer my question earlier,' Cedric interrupted. 'Does her family know she is missing?'

The directeurice took a deep breath. 'Once it became clear, she had left the school, we began an investigation. Elliot Bain came forward and admitted his part in it. He was immediately expelled and told to leave the school.' She noticed Coco's surprised face. 'I understand that may sound a little harsh to a layperson. But as I have said, this school is very important, not just to me but to the scientific community as well. What do you think would happen if the parents of our charges discovered we had a student who was helping their children to run rampant?' She snorted. 'We'd be closed within a week, I can assure you. Later that day, we reported Manon as missing to the local police and also to her father. I can't really tell you any more than that. But it is my understanding she is believed to be somewhere in the South of France with her boyfriend.'

Coco looked at Cedric again. *Something stinks here.*

Jeanne Remy stood again. 'Je suis désolé, but I must ask you to leave. I have a lot of work to get through, and I have told you all I can.'

Coco nodded and raised herself from the uncomfortable chair she had squeezed into. 'Merci, Directeurice Remy, for your time.' She gestured for Cedric to follow her towards the doorway. She stopped and turned back. 'It's fortunate Elliot Bain is going to come around soon, don't you think?' She was not sure it was true, but she wanted to see Remy's reaction.

Jeanne Remy did not respond, her face revealing nothing.

Coco nodded again. 'It will be interesting to hear his version of events, non? Merci for your time and au revoir.'

14H00

The first thing Coco noticed about Captain Tomas Wall of the Saint-Germain-en-Laye Commissariat de Police was his unfathomably square jaw and wavy blond hair. It hit his shoulders and made it appear he was auditioning for a shampoo commercial. Instinctively she reached up to touch her own blue-dyed tips. She immediately felt self-conscious. Her hair was frizzy and dry, probably in no small part due to the fact she was using bubble bath instead of shampoo to wash it, in yet another attempt to save money so she could feed her children.

Captain Wall rose from behind his desk, broad shoulders straining against an unreasonably tight, crisp white shirt. Coco glanced down at her green-checked wool coat, the tell-tale sign of a McDonald's breakfast prominent on the lapel. Wall outstretched his hand. 'Captain Tomas Wall,' he said. His voice was deep and manly, and she hated it. *Why couldn't you have had a squeaky voice?* she thought.

Coco closed her eyes for a moment. Wall had the sort of voice which had resulted in at least two of her pregnancies, and the looks to follow it through. She cursed, *you've certainly got your type, girl,* she chastised herself. *They might all look good, but each one was worse than the last.* 'Captain Charlotte Brunhild, I'm from the Commissariat de Police du 7e arrondissement in Paris.' She paused, tongue flicking across her lips. 'You can call me Coco, just as long as you call me,' she added with a wink, realising how bad she was at flirting.

'Mon Dieu!' Cedric cried out behind her.

Coco tipped her head backwards. 'The surly one is Lieutenant Cedric Degarmo.'

Captain Wall sank back into his seat, seemingly flustered.

'Could I get you something?' he began before quickly adding, 'like a café?'

'Non, merci,' Coco replied, sinking into an uncomfortable chair. 'We have to get back to Paris. I just wanted to stop and ask you about Manon Houde.'

Tomas Wall's face clouded. 'The student,' he nodded.

'The *missing* student,' Cedric corrected.

Wall shrugged. 'Missing in the sense she's shacked up with some kid in the South of France?'

Coco leaned forward. 'Then it's true. You know where she is?'

He shrugged again. 'We checked her emails. It seems that was the plan all along. I mean, why study when you can spend the summer in Nice having sex and partying on your rich daddy's dime.' He stopped, turning his head between Coco and Cedric. 'Wait, what does this have to do with Parisian cops?'

'Have you heard of Elliot Bain?' Coco asked.

'Sure,' Wall replied. 'Weird kid.'

'You spoke with him?'

Wall nodded. 'Yeah, right after the school reported Manon missing. Directeurice Remy was livid. Hell, if I'd offered it, she would have gladly have me arrange a firing squad for the kid.'

Coco and Cedric exchanged a look.

Wall continued. 'But there was nothing there. The kid was a punk, I guess, but he didn't really do anything wrong. The punishment from Remy was a little extreme if you ask me. The poor kid left town with his tail between his legs.' He studied Coco's face with enough curiosity it forced her to turn away. 'I still don't get what this has to do with Paris.' he repeated. 'Hell, it's nothing to do with us here. The school was doing their due diligence because Manon Houde has some big shot for a father, but it's just a kid gone wild. Honestly, if it wasn't because of Monsieur Houde, we would probably not have touched it.'

'Because he's rich?' Cedric asked.

'And determined,' Wall responded. 'He's been screaming down the phone to my Commander daily for us not doing anything to find his daughter.'

'But you said she was in the South of France,' Coco interrupted.

'That's what the emails said. Look, the truth is, we don't have the time, or the resources to look at this. I don't know about Paris, but I'm fairly sure it's the same for you. We don't have time for this sort of nonsense.'

Coco frowned. 'A seventeen-year-old girl has been missing for a week, and you're basing your investigation on emails sent between her and some supposed boyfriend?'

Wall's jaw flexed. 'I'm a cop too, Captain Brunhild,' he snapped. 'I know my job. Tell me, how concerned would you be if you discovered it wasn't the first time, or the second time even, that Manon Houde had snuck out of private school. She's run off before - at least two times, as far as I can tell.'

Coco tipped her head. 'She has?'

'The last time was last year in her previous school,' Captain Wall replied. 'Seems she took off with some greasy, spotty Spanish guitar player and was found in Barcelona high as a kite in a squat. Her father no doubt read her the riot act, threw her into some posh rehab and hoped they'd deal with the problem. He's only mad now because she's done it again. She lied and she's gone. Again. We've issued missing person reports, and that's about the best we can do.'

'Well, Directeurice Remy certainly mentioned none of this,' Coco conceded.

'Why would she?' Wall shrugged broad shoulders. 'Listen, as far as I can tell, Manon Houde's a clever kid who has just spent her life isolated in a bubble. She wants to taste freedom from time to time, and who can blame her?'

Coco closed her eyes for a moment. When she was

seventeen, she had felt as if she was suffocating under the expectations her family had placed upon her. She could understand Manon Houde wanting to break free, to breathe the air she chose for herself. She continued. 'You said Manon is in Nice, how can you be sure if you haven't been looking for her? Is it because of the emails?'

'Oui,' he responded. 'The emails were quite clear and explicit, the intentions of both parties were blatantly clear.'

Emails can be faked, Coco thought.

Wall took a deep breath. 'That's also part of the problem and why Monsieur Houde is jumping up and down, giving us all a hard time. It appears he's had private detectives searching for her, but they've come up with nothing.'

Coco's face crinkled. 'Rien? A kid in this day and age leaves no trace?'

Wall shrugged. 'It seems her cell phone is off and she has used none of her cards.'

Coco's eyes widened. 'She hasn't used her credit cards? Doesn't that strike you as odd? As far as I know, a girl like her generally only knows one thing to say, and it's "charge it."'

'You may have a point,' Wall reasoned 'but it's also what got her caught last time,' Wall reasoned. 'She racked up a hell of a credit card bill and it led her father right to her. If she's as smart as everyone says she is, she wouldn't get caught out the same way twice.'

'And she could have been hiding money for Dieu knows how long,' Cedric reasoned.

'Let's talk about Elliot Bain,' Coco said. 'What did he say about it? You said he was weird. What brought you to that conclusion?'

Wall considered his answer. 'You're going to have to level with me, if you expect me to do the same.'

Coco shrugged. 'We'll see. Talk.'

'His response was weird,' Wall responded. 'But enough for alarm bells to ring. Sure. He had a few choice words when I questioned him about Manon. *Bitch. Whore. Manipulator.*'

Cedric shook his head. 'Those words would ring alarm bells for me,' he said.

'And me,' Coco agreed.

Wall took a deep breath. 'Listen. He's just a kid. I got the impression he had the hots for her and that she played up to it. She flirted with him because she only wanted his help to bust her out of the school. Once he realised that, once he understood the consequences, I think he felt like a fool. His choice of words were harsh, but I'm not sure I would have felt differently myself when I was his age.'

Coco pursed her lips. 'Me too,' she agreed. 'The kid probably felt like a fool. Not only did Manon Houde ditch him, he ended up being expelled because of her. That would make the most even-tempered person mad.'

'As I said, I thought expelling him was a little extreme, if I'm honest,' Wall noted. 'But I suppose Directeurice Remy needed a scapegoat, and who better than the scholarship kid with no one to fight his corner. A shame, unfair, but...' he trailed off. His eyes narrowed. 'I've told you what I know, isn't it your turn?'

Coco took a deep breath. 'Yesterday morning, we believe Elliot Bain's mother was murdered.'

'By Elliot?'

Coco did not answer directly. 'Shortly afterwards, Elliot Bain tried to take his own life. At this stage, we don't know if he's going to make it.'

'Wow!' Wall gasped. 'Poor kid. Did he do it?'

Coco shrugged. 'It's hard to say. We've not really met anyone who knew him, and of course we can't interview him. What were your impressions of him? Other than weird, that's a filler word. And it seems to be the only thing anyone has to say about him, and it means very little.'

'But it fits,' Wall replied. 'He was just a weird kid. D'accord, give me a moment and I'll try to recall more of our meeting.' He took a deep breath before responding. 'I wouldn't describe him as shy, or reserved, but he's perhaps both of those. He's confident, he's awkward, he is a…' he threw his hands in the air. 'A seventeen-year-old kid. Hell, I have a seventeen-year-old. All I can tell you is they are a melting pot of emotions. One day they're up, one day they're down, one day the devil, the next an angel…'

'Tell me about it,' Coco murmured. She leaned forward in the chair. 'I'm sure your wife must be grateful for your support.'

Cedric muttered something under his breath.

'My *ex*-wife is anything but grateful to me for anything,' Wall replied with a grimace.

Cedric cleared his throat. 'If there's nothing to see here, perhaps we can head back to Paris, Captain Brunhild?'

Coco shot him a disparaging look. 'Sure, sure.' She stood up. 'What is it about the school? I mean, why is it like some fucking Norman Bates psycho house at the top of a hill.' She covered her mouth. 'Excusez-moi, for my foul language. I wash it out myself every day,' she added, before cackling, 'bugger all difference it makes, though!'

Captain Wall suppressed a smile, ignoring Cedric's tut. 'The Remy family have always had a lot of influence in this town,' he began, 'and the fact the school attracts the children of millionaires, billionaires even, from all around the world, means they have an enormous amount of influence. Ask the Mayor. These families are a crucial part of the economy. We've been told to make sure we never upset them.'

'And how does that translate?' Coco asked. 'You let them do as they please?'

Wall smiled. 'I may not be a big-shot Paris flic, Captain Brunhild, but I still hold a badge. Ecouté, a couple of kids might get drunk when they come down into town and they might kick up a fuss, cause some trouble. Instead of throwing them in a cell, we send them back to Directeurice Remy.' He smiled. 'I guarantee you, that's probably a far scarier prospect than what we can do for them.' He stared at her. 'I'm sure it's the same in your world. We pick our battles, and we choose sensibly.'

Coco nodded. 'Mais, a seventeen-year-old girl is still missing, and as far as I can tell, no one is really bothering to look for her.'

Wall continued to stare at her. 'And if I thought there was something untoward, I would be investigating. I'll send you the emails, if you like, and you can see for yourself. This kid is just out for a good time.'

'Merci,' Coco responded. She reached into her oversized bag, rummaging for a while before finally extracting a card. 'This has my email and my... personal cell phone number, *s'il te plait*, use it.'

Wall took the card with a smile. 'Merci, I will. Au revoir, Captain, Lieutenant.'

Coco moved towards the exit, without looking in front of her, banging her head on the doorway. She cried out, clutching her skull. 'Au revoir,' she winced.

Cedric ushered her out of the room. 'You really are the world's worst flirt.'

MERCREDI
(WEDNESDAY)

07H00

Coco awoke from a fitful sleep, filled with dreams where she had been wrestling with several burly men, one of which bore a striking resemblance to Captain Tomas Wall.

'Here, answer your own damn phone,' Helga shouted, tossing Coco's cell phone from the bottom of her bed. Coco ducked, sending the cell phone bouncing off her pillow and onto the ground, landing with a thud which immediately woke Coco's almost three-year-old daughter Esther. The screams began immediately. Coco groaned, pressing the pillow over her head to drown out the monotonous ringing and her daughter's early morning protests. She moved her hand around the floor, scrabbling to retrieve the cell phone.

'Allô? Allô? Captain Brunhild? Are you there?'

Coco's eyes widened in horror when she realised who was calling her. She pulled her body over the side of the bed and grabbed the phone she had inadvertently answered. 'Bonjour, Commander Demissy,' she shouted, trying to compete with Esther's increasing screams. She gestured to Helga to get out of her rollout bed and deal with her. Helga did so, with obvious reluctance, muttering curses under her breath as she swept the child away in the swiftest of movements.

'Désolé, Commander,' Coco repeated. 'What time is it?'

'Early,' Demissy snapped. 'I got a call, because apparently you didn't want to answer your own damn cell phone.'

Coco glanced at the screen, realising she had five missed calls. *Merci Helga*, she thought.

'I was sleeping,' she offered, 'Esther is snippy at the moment and Cedric's started peeing himself. I've spent most of the night trying to avoid the deep end of the bed.'

'Captain, I beg you, no more!' Demissy sighed. 'The reason I am calling is because Dr. Bertram has been trying to get in touch with you. Elliot Bain has come around, and she's not sure how long he has. So get your ass out of bed and get over there as fast as you can. Take a statement and close the damn case. Have I made myself clear?'

'Toujours,' Coco said with a yawn, listening to the suddenly disconnected line.

Dr. Stella Bertram gestured for Coco and Cedric to follow her into the room. 'He is awake,' she said, 'but he's very groggy and we haven't been able to communicate with him.'

'But he's aware? He's conscious?' Coco asked.

'I can't say what he is aware of,' the doctor replied. 'He's staring at the ceiling and that's about as far as we've got.'

'Will he make it?' Cedric asked.

'He lost an awful lot of blood,' she answered. 'I've spent the last day going over his vital signs with my team here. I'll try to explain it to you without getting too technical,' she said.

'Music to my ears,' Coco said, 'treat me like I'm stupid but do it in such a way I don't realise you are,' she wagged her finger. 'Begin.'

The doctor suppressed a smile. She took a deep breath. 'Following yesterday's events, Elliot's body went into hypovolemic shock, which in effect means the most important organs are not getting the blood, oxygen, and nutrients they need to survive. It also means that the body cannot get rid of waste products, like acids. If we can't get control of it, he will die. It's that simple, I'm afraid.'

'Then how are you treating him?' Coco asked.

'With fluids and blood products via an intravenous line,' Dr. Bertram replied. 'We're trying to replenish the blood he lost and improve circulation. We're attempting several transfusions - blood plasma, platelet, red-blood cell, etc. At this stage it's all about getting the heart's pumping strength to improve, maybe then we can get the blood where it's needed. He's also on a high dose of antibiotics, primarily to try to ward off septic shock and bacterial infections.'

'None of that sounds good, Dr. Bertram,' Cedric said.

She shook her head. 'It isn't. That's why I wanted to get you here as soon as possible.' She sighed. 'Getting him through this stage is one thing, but even if he makes it, he's looking at potential real long-term damage to vital organs such as his kidneys.' She took a deep breath. 'The fact he is young and strong will help, mais…'

Coco stared again at the young man lying in the bed, and it crushed her. She saw her own sons, and the thought terrified her. 'Can I talk to him?' she asked.

'You can try,' the doctor replied. 'Don't get your hopes up. He can't talk, and he's not conscious enough to respond to you. He won't be able to write his responses to you on a piece of paper, if that's what you're hoping for.'

'I'm expecting nothing and hoping for the best,' Coco said as she plodded across the room, stopping by the end of the bed. Elliot Bain's eyes were open, staring straight ahead, not blinking or moving. 'Elliot,' she whispered. 'C'est moi. C'est Coco.' She gasped, stumbling backwards. He had blinked. 'Did you see that?' she asked.

Dr. Bertram ran to the other side of the bed, running her fingers across the medical equipment, before turning to Elliot, shining a penlight in his eyes. His pupils dilated. 'Talk to him again, Captain.'

Coco leaned forward. She picked up Elliot's hand and held it between hers. She did not know why it surprised her, but it was warm. 'Elliot. It's Captain Brunhild. Coco.'

Elliot Bain's eyes flickered again.

'Keep going, Captain,' the doctor said quickly.

'Elliot...' Coco began, unsure as to what exactly she could say to the young boy lying helpless on the hospital bed. *Hey, your mother's dead, but don't ya already know it? Did you kill her?* There were too many questions and no way of getting the answers. 'What happened to you, Elliot?' She asked desperately. 'The last thing you said, was *find out who made me do this*. I want to do that for you, Elliot, but I don't understand what happened.' She paused. 'Was it something that happened at *École Privée Jeanne Remy*?'

Elliot's eyes widened, a gargling sound began emitting from his throat, his body convulsing angrily. Dr. Bertram waved her hands as she pressed an alarm button on the console, filling the room with an angry siren. 'Step outside, s'il vous plait.'

12H00

Coco stared at the clock on the office wall, the hands appeared to move deliberately slowly. It felt as if she had been staring at the telephone on her desk for hours and it had never rung. She still did not know whether Elliot Bain was alive or dead, and it troubled her in ways in which she did not understand.

All her instincts were telling her he was, most likely, a murderer. Until she knew for certain, she only saw the young boy who could be her son lying on a bed, fighting for his life, with no one in the world to care for him. And all that meant was she had to be the one to care for him for as long as she could. But then what? What if she uncovered the extent of his crimes? But even then... Could she stop caring? She bit her lip, angry at herself for allowing the whole situation to trigger something in herself she was desperately trying to bury. She had to let it go. She had to let the memories of Mordecai Stanic disappear into the darkness. He was the father of two of her children, but he was lost to her and them now. He had to be. There could be no reconciling what he had done, and more importantly the hand grenade he had thrown to her and her family. *Love has a limit.*

She looked up, her eyes widening when she realised Commander Demissy was there, staring at her as if she was something she had just stepped on in the street.

Cedric ran into the room. 'I've finally tracked down Manon Houde's father. He's on line two.'

'Merci, Cedric. Get back on to the hospital. I want to know how Elliot Bain is doing,' Coco said.

Cedric nodded and ran back into the principal office.

'Put it on speaker,' Commander Demissy said.

Coco picked up the telephone. 'Bonjour. This is Captain

Brunhild. I'm here with Commander Demissy. Are we speaking with Monsieur Houde?'

'Yes, you are,' the reply came. It was curt and spoken in broken English. 'This is Pieter Houde.'

Coco took a deep breath, trying to remember everything she could to speak to him in English. 'Hello. How are you?'

'Is this about Manon, have you found her?'

'I'm sorry,' Coco replied slowly. 'Your daughter's disappearance is being handled by the Police Nationale in Saint-Germain-en-Laye…'

Pieter Houde scoffed. 'Handled? Try mishandled, Captain Brunhild.' He stopped. 'If you are not investigating my daughter's disappearance, then why are you bothering me? And where are you, exactly?'

'I'm in Paris,' she replied. 'And I'm calling because I'm investigating another matter. A matter involving a young man by the name of Elliot Bain.'

'The pervert?' Houde hissed.

'Pervert?' Coco asked with a frown, unsure what he was suggesting.

'My daughter told me he kept pestering her,' Houde replied. 'Always following her, giving her gifts, writing her notes.'

'That doesn't exactly make him a pervert,' Coco interjected.

'She caught him… she caught him *touching* himself outside her room,' Houde interrupted. 'I'd consider that would make him a pervert, wouldn't you?'

Coco considered her response. 'And yet, it's my understanding your daughter asked Elliot Bain to assist her in escaping from the school…'

'Says who?' Pieter Houde roared. 'Jeanne Remy? Or that sycophant, Captain Wall? They've created a narrative which suits them.'

'Monsieur Houde, this is Commander Imane Demissy,'

Demissy interrupted. 'What do you mean exactly by, "a narrative?"'

'What I mean, *exactly*,' Houde responded, unable to hide his irritation, 'is that nobody will tell me anything. They say Manon left the school of her own free will, but then there is nothing. There are no records of her going anywhere. Directeurice Remy waited twenty-four hours before reporting it to the police, and even then it was only a throwaway. She provided them with the "narrative" of a rich wild-child running off to party.'

'With no offence,' Coco said, 'it's my understanding Manon has done this before.'

Houde sighed. 'Yes, she did. And she learned from it. We all learned from it. Manon was contrite, but more importantly, she was practical. She knew the implications of failing again.'

Coco smiled. 'You'd cut her off.'

'Exactly,' Houde replied. 'My girl is smart, she's not stupid, and she's not cut out to be poor. She can have her fun, as long as she has the funds to back it up. No credit cards, no fun,' he gave a sad laugh. 'She would not run away again.'

'I've read Captain Brunhild's report,' Commander Demissy interrupted. 'And there are emails, are there not? Emails which show a direct correlation between her life at the school and her relationship with a boy outside of the school.'

'I didn't say Manon was completely reformed,' Houde replied. 'She may have been having fun, but walking away, *disappearing*, it wasn't an option.' He took a deep breath. 'The last time she did it, I believe the anxiety killed her mother. I was angrier about that than her disappearance, and I believe Manon was too. She understood what her selfishness had done. To think she would do it again, so soon, is something I cannot accept. And then there is the matter of her not having any money. After the last time, I limited her access to her trust fund. She may like to suggest otherwise, but Manon is used to the finer things in life. I don't buy the whole scenario she's been hiding money. She has no money to hide. Certainly, no money from me.'

Coco and Demissy shared a look.

'What do you know of Elliot Bain?' Coco asked.

'Nothing,' he replied. 'Only what Directeurice Remy told me of his involvement. Just that he was the kid who busted her out. I asked to speak to him, but they wouldn't allow it. Remy told me she had dealt with the matter in private and that I had her assurance Bain did not know what happened to Manon after she left the school.'

Coco frowned, unsure how Remy could make such an assumption.

'Monsieur Houde,' Coco continued. 'When was the last time you spoke with Manon?'

'A week or two before her disappearance,' he answered, the pang of guilt clear in his voice.

'And is there anyone else she would be in touch with?' Coco continued.

'The only person she is close with at home, is Marta. Marta is our housekeeper,' he answered. 'Marta has been like a mother to her. They are very close.' He laughed. 'Marta considers herself a little too long in the tooth for emailing or texting, so once a week, like clockwork, Manon would call Marta. Even when she was away the last time, she still took the time to call Marta.'

Coco nodded. 'And when was the last time Marta spoke to your daughter?'

'Five days before her disappearance, which means…'

'She missed the call,' Commander Demissy concluded.

'And she wouldn't do that, she just wouldn't,' Houde said forcefully. 'Manon would ignore me, I accept that. I'm not the world's best father.' His voice cracked. 'But she wouldn't ignore her, not Marta. I'm sure of it. Will you help me?' he asked, the desperation clear in his tone.

Demissy stared at Coco. She cleared her throat. 'Désolé,

Monsieur Houde,' she replied. 'It is out of our jurisdiction. Our only involvement is the crimes committed here in Paris. Your daughter's disappearance is being investigated by the Police Nationale in Saint-Germain-en-Laye. We have no jurisdiction to investigate that.'

'Haven't you got it yet?' Houde hissed. 'The Remy family owns the authorities in Saint-Germain-en-Laye. Whatever happened to my daughter, Jeanne Remy will make sure it has no lasting effect on her precious school. Well, damn you all. I'll do whatever I have to do, to find my daughter. But if she's hurt, you'll all pay. I'll damn well make sure you do!' He stopped, the crackle of the line echoing around the room. 'Listen, I'm in Australia right now on business, so it will be at least Thursday before I make it back to France. I want my daughter found by then, or there'll be hell to pay.'

He disconnected the call; the buzz vibrating around Coco's tiny office. Demissy stood up and moved to the door. She turned to Coco. 'I started this week hoping for peace. A gentle transition of power. They warned me you would bring trouble to my door, and it didn't even take you a day.' She left the offices, slamming the door behind her.

Coco threw her hands in the air. 'How the hell did this all become my fault. AGAIN!' she shouted into the air.

23H59

Helga threw the cell phone at Coco. 'Your damn phone again!'

Coco's head jerked upwards, knocking her ten-year-old son's head from her chest. She grabbed the cell phone. 'What is it with people lately? Don't they know it takes eight hours for me to look like a hot mess?' She answered the call. 'Whoever the hell this is, I hate your guts.'

'Captain Brunhild, this is Captain Wall from Saint-Germain-en-Laye.'

'Captain Wall,' she gasped. 'I was just dreaming… thinking… I mean, I was just sleeping.' She glared at Helga, who had sat up on her rollout bed and was pulling her hair rollers back into place and cackling. 'What is it? It's a bit late for a booty call, isn't it?' Coco continued.

Wall snorted. 'Maybe in Paris, mais not necessarily, Saint-Germain-en-Laye…' he trailed off. When he spoke again, he was all business. 'I'm sorry to call you so late, but I've just been called out to *École Privée Jeanne Remy*. A cleaner accidentally unplugged a deep freeze in the kitchen while she was vacuuming. When she plugged it back in, she realised her mistake and she checked to see if everything was okay…'

Coco took a deep breath. 'And everything wasn't okay?'

'Not if you're Manon Houde, non.'

Coco gasped. 'What are you saying? Manon Houde is dead? In a damn freezer?'

'It would appear so,' Wall replied.

'And it's definitely her?'

'Directeurice Remy has identified her,' he answered. His voice was soft. 'I have no other information at the moment. I'm on my way to the school now, I'll secure the scene until morning and…'

'Why are you securing the scene until morning?' Coco interjected.

'The local pathologist is out of town. He'll be back by lunchtime tomorrow, so I just need to make sure everything is…'

'Tomorrow isn't good enough,' Coco retorted. She shook her head. She lifted herself up. 'I'll be there in an hour and I'll bring help.'

'Captain Brunhild, there really isn't any need. I just thought you would want to know,' Wall retorted.

Coco nodded. 'And I did. I'll still be there in an hour. Au revoir, sailor.'

'Sailor?'

'It's the outfit you wore in my dream,' she answered before disconnecting the call. She shot Helga a withering stare. She was smiling. 'Don't judge me. I may be off men, therefore my dreams are all I have.' She pressed some buttons on her cell phone.

Sonny answered his cell phone. 'Whoever this is, I hate you.'

Coco smiled. 'That's my boy. Pull on your pants. We're going on a road trip.'

JEUDI
(THURSDAY)

02H00

Cedric's head banged against the side window. 'You'd think if you dragged someone out of their bed in the middle of the night, you'd at least have the decency to drive like a sane person,' he grumbled.

Coco shook her head. 'I never drive like a sane person. I live in Paris. Driving there isn't for sane people.'

Sonny laughed. 'I'm still not sure what I'm doing here. This isn't my area, I really shouldn't be involved.'

'So, if a body turned up in your area at midnight and you were away, you'd be happy for me to leave the stiff for you until you got back, or would you rather I drag another handsome pathologist from another jurisdiction out of bed to help?' Coco posed.

'Non, évidement, non,' he responded. 'Mais...' He looked to Cedric, mouthing *handsome* in his direction. Cedric sighed.

'Anyway, don't worry about it. I left a message on Demissy's voicemail. She'll sort out the jurisdiction pissing contest,' Coco retorted. 'As far as I can tell, she has bugger all else to do.' She grimaced as the lights of the illuminated wall encasing *École Privée Jeanne Remy* appeared in front of them. 'I hope you had a good night's sleep,' she said, 'cos you've gotta lotta steps to climb.'

'CaptainWallthisisDr.SchlomoBernsteinoneoftheforemostpathologistsinParisandweshouldbeverygratefulhehasagreedtoofferhisexpertiseinthissituationconsideringtheholyhellPieterHoudeisgoingtostartkickingupatanysecond,' Coco said to Captain Tomas Wall, without taking a breath.

Cedric turned to Sonny. 'She is ridiculous when she's in heat.'

Coco stabbed a finger into his arm. 'Don't be a bitch, darling,' she spat.

Tomas Wall smiled. 'My Commander will not be happy about me handing over an examination to an out-of-towner.' He looked at Sonny. 'No offence, Dr. Bernstein.'

'None taken,' Sonny replied, 'and I can't say I disagree,' he added, yawning in Coco's direction.

'Let your Commander and my Commander duke it out,' Coco sniffed. 'I spoke to Pieter Houde. I'd bet my last cent, as soon as he hears about this, he's going to be jumping up and down on us all. And I for one, don't want to feel his wrath. So, I'm doing what I do best - covering my own ass.'

Wall nodded. 'I know what you mean. I've been on the receiving end of a few of his rants myself, and I don't fancy becoming a traffic cop. So,' he gestured for them to follow him down a narrow, winding staircase. 'I'd be grateful for your help, Dr. Bernstein.'

Coco pulled her bag close to her chest, pulling herself in as she stepped down into the darkness. She had barely made it up the steps to the school a second time, and now it seemed they were going down again, but this time into the bowels of the building.

'Why the hell do we break our backs climbing up to get here, just to have to walk down again,' she groaned.

'Because the only people who have to walk down these stairs are paid to do so,' Wall reasoned.

'"The staff," you mean,' Coco responded in an affected English accent.

They continued their descent in silence. The only sound was feet clacking against the stone steps and Coco's laboured breath. Eventually they made it to the bottom, the staircase opening into a large kitchen with several doorways leading into other rooms.

'This kitchen is bigger than my entire apartment,' Coco mused. She crept across the room, eyes flicking carefully as she took in her surroundings. She pulled open the first door, shocked to see a row of frozen pigs lining the walls. 'Where's the body?'

Wall pointed to the second door. They followed him in silence into a room filled with tinned goods on one side and a vast deep freeze on the other, a uniformed police officer standing sentry next to it. Coco took a step backwards, gesturing for Sonny to pass in front of her. He did, flicking forensic gloves on his hands. He lifted the lid to the freezer, Coco and Cedric peering over his shoulder.

Coco could not help herself. She gasped. 'Goddamn it,' she hissed through gritted teeth.

Manon Houde was lying in the freezer, her knees folded towards her chest, ice covering most of her body, face and hair. Her eyes were white and open, frost clear on her eyelashes. Sonny began a cursory investigation of her remains, his hands moving swiftly but carefully. Coco said nothing. She knew there was nothing she could say. Death was often instant, she reasoned. But discovering why it had occurred was often a very different matter.

After a few minutes, Sonny lifted his head, flicking off the forensic gloves. 'Before you ask, I have no proper answers to give you. Not here, and certainly not yet.'

'Blah, blah,' Coco replied, 'tell us what you can. Murder?'

Cedric snorted. 'Well, she certainly didn't crawl into a deep freeze for a nap, did she?'

Coco twisted her head to him. 'There could be several explanations for that, which might not indicate murder. She could have died naturally and someone panicked, wanted to get rid of the body for some reason. I once investigated a case where a woman died "on the job" so to speak. Her married John panicked, threw her body in the basement, and left her there for a week. It was only when she started to smell her neighbours complained. The John didn't kill her, but he also didn't want to risk being exposed. We still locked him up.' She narrowed her eyes. 'Now, if it's all right with you, Lieutenant, we'll let Dr. Bernstein finish, d'accord?'

Cedric lowered his head.

'Sonny?' Coco continued.

The doctor pursed his lips. 'As I said, I can't tell you a lot, right now. Murder, or otherwise.' He noticed Coco's scowl, and he smiled. 'Let's begin with what is evident,' he said. 'There are no obvious signs of cause of death, no obvious blood loss, or entrance wounds from a knife, or a gun even. I see no evidence of trauma at this stage. The skull seems intact, as does most of her body.'

Captain Wall stepped forward. 'You're making it sound as if it was a natural death.'

Sonny shook his head. 'Oh, non. There's nothing natural about this. What it is, is unexplained. The explanation should come when I have her in a morgue and can examine her properly.'

'What about time of death?' Coco asked.

Sonny stared into the freezer. 'I haven't performed the tests yet, because I believe it will be extremely hard to pinpoint. She's been frozen. What I can tell you is I believe she has been here for some time.'

'She disappeared a week ago,' Wall said.

'She could have been here for that long,' Sonny replied.

Coco looked around. The rest of the freezer contained what appeared to be frozen joints of meat and bags of vegetables. 'Someone must have noticed there was a dead girl nestled amongst the bags of frozen peas,' she offered.

'Not necessarily,' Wall countered. 'Most of the students are away at the moment on various excursions. As far as I could tell, there is only a skeleton staff on the site at the moment. There may have been no reason to come down here.' He pointed into the main kitchen area. 'Especially because it appears there's a freezer in there too, which seems to be for everyday use. This one here is probably a backup.'

Coco stepped across the room, tapping her chin. 'How very

convenient,' she muttered. 'I hate it when things are convenient, because sometimes they just are and other times someone has just seized an opportunity. Very annoying.'

'Worse for her,' Cedric interrupted, tipping his head towards Manon Houde.

'What about the cleaner who found her?' Coco asked.

Wall pointed upwards. 'She's upstairs in the staffroom, she's taken it very badly. She's also only an agency worker. The usual cleaner is on vacation, like most everyone else in the school. I've taken a statement from her.'

Coco stared at him. He smiled. 'And non, I don't think she had anything to do with it. But I'm happy for you to satisfy yourself.'

'No need,' Coco sniffed. 'I'm not here to tell you how to do your job.' She moved into the main kitchen area, turning her head slowly around the room, appraising the surroundings. It was clean and nothing seemed out of place. Other than the doors to the storerooms, she saw no actual entrance other than the staircase. 'How the hell did she even get here?'

'What do you mean?' Sonny asked.

She pointed at the spiral staircase. 'I can't imagine anyone dragging a corpse down those damn stairs, can you?'

'Not really,' he answered, 'and certainly not without leaving some kind of impression on the body.'

Coco frowned. 'Then what else could it be? She walked down here willingly and then was offed and chucked in the deep freeze?'

'It could have been the dumbwaiter,' Captain Wall interjected.

Coco raised an eyebrow. 'That's rather rude of you, Captain Wall. Just because they're a part of the working class, we shouldn't really call them dumb, they work just as hard as you and I, surely?'

'Non, non… that's not what I mean…' he replied, obviously flustered.

'Ignore her,' Cedric reasoned, 'she's messing with you. You'll start to notice the signs, eventually. The giveaway is her mouth is moving.'

Wall laughed. 'Follow me,' he said.

'Anytime,' Coco said, falling into line behind him.

Wall pressed a large red button on a wall next to a pair of steel shutters. Moments later, a loud metallic grinding noise filled the room, followed by the tell-tale sound of a descending elevator. With a ping, the steel shutters opened revealing a large square cupboard.

Coco peered inside. 'It's big, mais… is it big enough?'

Sonny extended his arms horizontally and vertically. 'A small young woman like Manon Houde could probably fit in here,' he said.

'And would take it as a challenge.'

Coco spun on her heels to be greeted by the stoic presence of Directeurice Jeanne Remy. Although it was the early hours of the morning, she was already perfectly groomed. Her hair was set and her makeup carefully applied. Instinctively, Coco touched her own blue-tipped mess and realised she had forgotten to even run a brush through it when she had leapt from her bed.

'What do you mean she would take it as a challenge?' she asked.

The Directeurice frowned. 'We use the dumbwaiter to bring down supplies to the kitchen, and to transport meals to the dining room. However,' she grimaced, 'students like to use it occasion to…' She waved her hands, 'to behave like children.' She turned towards the freezer room. 'Would you like to follow me to my office?' she spoke finally.

'Bien sûr,' Coco replied. 'Cedric, can you stay with Sonny and help him?'

Cedric nodded.

'The forensic team should be here soon,' Captain Wall

addressed Sonny. 'They'll assist you here, and I've instructed them to take you to the morgue when you're ready.'

Sonny nodded. 'I'll do what I can here, but I can't perform the autopsy for at least twenty-four hours.'

Coco gawped. 'You're kidding!'

He shook his head. 'I'm afraid not. The body has to defrost naturally at room temperature before I can even begin to examine her. I'll wait and assist the forensic team.' He paused. 'I'd be grateful if we can move her to my own morgue in Paris. I have a lot of my own cases to deal with today and tomorrow, and I have more advanced equipment to hand.'

Coco nodded. 'Bien sûr, Sonny. I'm just grateful for your help.'

'Anytime, Coco, you know that,' Sonny said.

'And we'll meet you there, after...' Coco added, before noticing Jeanne Remy had already left the kitchen, the clicking of her heels showing she was already halfway up the staircase. 'The bloody woman must be on steroids.' She waggled her finger towards Captain Wall. 'You go first.' She watched him as he departed, clutching her bag to her chest, eyes locked on his retreating figure. 'And I'll watch you, make sure you don't fall,' she whispered to herself.

03H00

Jeanne Remy lifted a crystal decanter from a sideboard, Coco imagined it probably belonged in a museum. It bore none of the ring marks and scratches which covered all her own furniture.

'I know it's early, or,' the directeurice began, 'late, mais, I thought you might appreciate a whisky.'

'I'm a gin girl myself,' Coco said, 'but whisky will do the trick. It's been a long night and we've still got a lot of it to get through.'

Remy smiled, poured three tumblers and handed two of them to Coco and Tomas Wall. She drained the contents of her own glass with one swift motion and refilled it.

'A woman after my own heart,' Coco smiled, draining her own and slamming her glass in front of the directeurice. 'Fill 'em up, barkeep!'

Remy gave her a distasteful look, but refilled the glass and passed it back to her.

'So, now we've done the polite bit,' Coco began, 'we can cut to the chase. My doc is going to tell me very soon, that in all likelihood, last week Manon Houde didn't run off for her shag-fest in Southern France with some hunk. Instead she was murdered right here, in this school. Her body was most likely bundled into a dumbwaiter and then thrown into a deep freeze.' She paused. 'Correct me if I'm missing something?'

Remy tipped her head. 'Well, that appears to be the facts as they present themselves at this moment.'

Coco leaned forward. 'Then, what about Elliot Bain?'

The directeurice's forehead crumpled in apparent confusion. 'What about him?'

'I'm just confused, that's all,' Coco answered. 'As far as I know, Elliot Bain was expelled from your school for his part in

Manon Houde's apparent escape, and yet,' she paused as if for dramatic effect, 'it appears as if she never actually escaped.' She took a deep breath. 'I'm not a super-swot like the kids you have here, but even I can see there's a glaring discrepancy between those facts and what seems to have happened.'

'I don't know what you're asking me,' Remy shot.

Coco stared at her. 'I suppose what I'm really wondering is. What did Elliot Bain say?'

'What did he say?'

Coco nodded. 'Oui. What did he say? I mean, I don't know the kid, but I'm guessing he's pretty smart, smart enough to win a scholarship to,' she picked up a brochure from the Directeurice's desk, flicking on a pair of broken glasses and narrowing her eyes to read the blurb, *'one of the world's foremost scientific schools, specialising in nurturing the creators of the future.'* She threw the brochure back onto the desk. 'Well, it all sounds very impressive, but I come back to my point. Why would Elliot Bain accept being expelled from your world-class school for a crime he never actually committed?'

Remy sipped her drink, the ice slipping from side to side as she studied Coco. 'Elliot Bain is a troubled child,' was all she said.

Coco slammed her fist on the desk. 'I'm getting pretty fucking sick of everyone saying that, when they have absolutely no proof of any wrongdoing.'

Tomas Wall cleared his throat. 'What Captain Brunhild means,' he interjected, 'is it makes no sense for Elliot Bain to be expelled when there was no reason for him to be.'

Remy pursed her lips. 'It is now my understanding, Elliot tried to take his own life, shortly after murdering his own mother. I think,' she paused, 'we can assume, he was more troubled than I imagined.' She stood up and began pacing, her hands wringing the pearls around her neck.

'My question is,' Coco said, 'what did Elliot say about Manon's disappearance? I mean, it's one thing to be accused of helping her escape, but if he didn't do it, I can't think of a single reason why he would accept his expulsion.'

'I can,' Remy snapped. 'And it should be obvious to you too. I'm not a detective, but it's not so difficult to understand. He killed Manon. He disposed of her body and what was left? To make his escape. He confessed to helping her escape, knowing full well it would cause his expulsion. He was sent away from this school and therefore escaped his crime.'

Coco frowned. 'To do what? Return to Paris and kill his mother and then kill himself?' She shook her head. 'It makes no sense.'

The Directeurice sighed once again. 'I apologise for stating the obvious, mais, the explanation is surely logical; it's even scientific. He killed Manon, disposed of her body, then returned home. Presumably he could not bear for his mother to discover the truth about him, so he killed her and then killed himself because he didn't want to spend the rest of his life in prison.'

'It's all very neat,' Coco answered. She glanced down at her wrinkled shirt. 'And as you might guess, I detest neat.'

'There's nothing neat about any of it,' Remy retorted, her eyes flicking distastefully over Coco.

Coco nodded. 'Exactement, Directeurice Remy! Neat is wrong. Neat is not the world we live in. Neat is not Elliot Bain. The fact is, Manon Houde died in your school a week ago, and no one bothered to look for her because you convinced them they didn't need to.' She ignored the burning intensity of the look in her direction from Captain Wall. 'Pieter Houde is going to find that very alarming, as are most of the parents of your students.'

Remy continued to stare at Coco but said nothing.

Coco continued to hold her gaze. 'This isn't a game of chicken, Directeurice Remy,' Coco finally said. 'And it's not about blinking first. I have no interest in embarrassing you, or your school, and nor do I believe does Captain Wall.'

Wall nodded with determination. 'Bien sûr,' he answered.

'But that means nothing if you expect us to walk away from this without your cooperation. You have to understand your "brand" is going to come into question.'

'There is nothing I can tell you,' Remy said matter-of-factly.

Coco gawped at her. 'That isn't a response. At least, not one I'm willing to accept,'

Wall reached over and touched her arm. 'Captain Brunhild, s'il vous plaît.'

Coco pushed his hand away with more force than she intended. 'My point, Directeurice Remy, is that a young woman in your care, ended up squashed into a freezer and we have already wasted a week. There's no room left for covering your ass. Whatever happens next for you, as far as I can tell, is damage control.'

Remy regarded with her interest. 'Damage control?' she asked, raising an eyebrow.

Coco nodded. 'A young woman was most probably murdered in this school and her body disposed of. I don't need to tell you the press is going to have a field day covering it, and all those rich and important parents will not like that one bit.'

Remy waved her hand. 'The press are inconsequential.' She stared at Wall. 'Aren't they Tomas?'

Tomas nodded and lowered his head.

Coco watched him, her eyebrows knotting in confusion. She made a mental note to question him on it later. She closed her eyes for the moment, the headlines of several newspapers flashing before her. *Paedophile cop in Catholic Church dungeon sex slave scandal! Disgraced cop's wife returns to work!* Coco remembered the last headline particularly well because it had been accompanied by a photograph of her wearing her favourite coat covered in baby puke while eating a donut.

'I wish that were true,' Coco said finally. 'But it isn't. Ecouté,

Directeurice Remy. This is now only about one thing. I have no interest in embarrassing you, and I'm sure nor does Captain Wall, but we have a dead girl, and the fact remains you either help us investigate, or let it be known you don't want to help us.'

'That sounds rather like a threat, Captain Brunhild,' Remy shot back.

Coco smiled. 'I never make threats. They are pointless and redundant,' she responded. 'Instead, what I do, is to be as fucking annoying as I can until I get the results a victim deserves.' She smiled. 'And believe me, being fucking annoying is something I am very, VERY good at.'

Wall laughed, immediately covering his mouth.

'Perhaps I need to speak to your Commander,' Remy contorted.

Coco shrugged. 'Go ahead, she'll tell you exactly the same thing I am,' she said, not at all sure Commander Demissy would do any such thing.

Remy sighed. 'What do you want me to say?' she asked with obvious exasperation. She folded her hands in front of her. 'What do you want me to say?' she repeated, her voice softer the second time.

Coco leaned forward. 'Tell us what happened last week, and not the watered down PC version. The absolute truth.'

'We're a very small school,' Remy began. 'And what makes us prestigious is that we provide our charges with a world-class education…'

Coco wound her fingers. 'I've read the brochure, directeurice,' she said, 'alors…'

'I think what, Captain Brunhild is trying to say is we need to understand what happened to Manon Houde,' Tomas Wall interrupted, 'and the only way we can begin to do so, is to understand how she spent her last few days.' He glanced at his notepad. 'We know she disappeared eight days ago. Therefore, we need to begin there. What can you tell us about last Mercredi?'

Remy pulled a series of folders from one of the desk drawers. 'Our students are divided into pièces. Five to a room, with a teacher and a teacher's assistant. Manon was part of the group in the East Wing.'

'Who were the other four members of the group?' Coco asked.

Remy consulted the files. 'Elliot Bain, Ada Fortin, Fabian Auch and Enzo Garnier.'

Coco nodded. 'And where are they? We need to speak with them.'

'They're not here,' Remy responded quickly. 'I've already told you, our students are all on various field trips. It's something we do regularly as part of the curriculum.'

'Where are they?' Coco interrupted.

'They are in the North of France at a site of historical importance,' Remy retorted.

Coco scoffed. 'This site is more important than anything else right now. So do whatever you need to, but get them back here today.'

Remy shook her head. 'That's not something I can do, Captain. And I don't appreciate you giving me orders.'

Coco stood, pulling a scrap of paper out of her pocket. 'This is the telephone number of Pieter Houde. I'm fairly sure he has a private jet. If you have any doubt as to how quickly those four kids can be back in Saint-Germain-en-Laye, then I suggest you ask him to arrange it. If you don't like me giving you orders, I suggest you talk to him and see if you prefer it that way. In the meantime, I would like to speak to the teacher who was involved in Manon Houde's education.'

The directeurice looked at her watch. 'Captain Brunhild, it's the middle of the night. Surely they don't need to be dragged out of their beds at this hour? They'll be up for breakfast soon enough.'

Coco shrugged. 'I'm up, I'm happy to do it myself.'

Captain Wall stood up next to her. 'We can do this later, Charlotte,' he said. 'Long day tomorrow, why don't you lie down for a couple of hours?'

Coco gurned at him. She nodded at Remy. 'What time is breakfast?'

Remy appeared confused. '07H00, usually.'

Coco lifted her arm and looked at her watch. 'D'accord. Show me a couch, somewhere out of the way, I snore like a hog apparently.' She moved towards the door. 'Just one thing, I don't want my breakfast to have come from the deep freeze. Is that possible? And as the kitchen is out of bounds, you might want to order in.'

'The kitchen has been closed all week,' Remy snapped. 'As most of the staff and students are away, there is no need. We have thé and café making facilities in the staff quarters, and we have food delivered daily from town.'

'That's good to know,' Coco said, 'and somewhat convenient.'

Remy turned her head away. Her eyes staring into the darkness outside the window.

07H00

Coco chewed happily on the egg and bacon baguette, tearing at the warm bread as if it was the first food to have touched her lips in a long while. She was not even sure if she had eaten the previous evening. She had returned home late, and Helga had already fed the children and put them to bed. Helga had then gone out to the cinema, leaving a meal for Coco in the oven, but Coco was unsure if she had touched it. Her memory most probably clouded by the bottle of wine she had finished instead. She took another bite, unaware she was being studied by Directeurice Jeanne Remy with barely hidden irritation. They were seated in a large dining room, lined with wooden tables and benches. A few students had joined them and were sitting in the furthermost corner of the room, watching with obvious anxiety. Coco pointed her baguette in their direction, pieces of egg falling to the floor.

'Were they here last week?' she asked.

The Directeurice shook her head. 'They returned from their trip yesterday and were away all last week.'

Coco tipped her head in Cedric's direction. 'All the same, they must have known Manon Houde. Take statements from them Cedric.'

Cedric nodded and moved across the dining room.

Coco finished the remains of the baguette, wiping her mouth with the sleeve of her coat. 'Wait, a minute. Are you sure the bacon didn't come from the deep freeze?'

Remy studied her, a faint smile on her face as if she was considering whether to lie to her. Finally, she shook her head. 'As I told you yesterday, with so many students away, we get the food sent up from town.' She stopped, her face clouding. 'I spoke with Pieter Houde.'

Coco nodded. 'I can imagine how well that went.'

'He's furious, but most importantly he's heartbroken,' Remy replied. 'A dangerous combination.'

'An understandable combination,' Coco retorted. 'Whatever happened here, it's all going to come out. You have to know that.'

'What did the autopsy show?' Remy asked. 'Was it natural causes?'

Coco leaned forward in her chair. If Manon Houde had died as the result of a fall, there would be only one reason for Jeanne Remy to know. She had somehow been involved. It made no sense for her to assume Manon's death was natural in any way, Coco reasoned. Remy, or whoever was involved, would have had to know the body would be discovered, eventually. Unless there had been another plan to dispose of the body, and an overly keen agency cleaner had disrupted the plan. There was something about Jeanne Remy she did not like. It was not just she was the complete opposite of Coco - poised, elegant, and draped in jewels and wealth. Coco had looked into her eyes and saw the truth. Jeanne Remy was as fake as anyone else. It was all for show.

'It's too soon to determine cause of death,' Coco answered. 'The autopsy will take place tomorrow morning in Paris. I hope to have something definitive then, but in the meantime we obviously have to treat this as a suspicious death.'

Jeanne turned to Captain Wall. 'And you agree with this, Tomas?' she asked, with the usual overly familiar tone of a teacher scolding a student. 'I mean, aren't you in charge of this investigation?'

Wall cleared his throat. 'Captain Brunhild and I are conducting a joint investigation, because it covers both of our jurisdictions.'

Jeanne sighed. 'Ah, here are the teachers.'

Coco turned her head to see two women had entered the dining room and were lingering by the doorway as if awaiting permission to enter. The Directeurice raised her hand, motioning her fingers, gesticulating for them to approach. Coco studied them carefully. The older of the two was small with mousy hair and an anxious, pinched face. The younger teacher was taller, with a pale, porcelain-like face and peroxide hair set into curls on either side of her face. They approached the table with clear reticence.

'Mademoiselles,' Remy said, 'take a seat,' she commanded.

The two ladies pulled out chairs and sat opposite Coco and Wall.

'May I present, Mademoiselle Caron Voland,' Remy said, gesturing towards the older woman. 'She is the East wing teacher.' She gestured to the younger woman. 'And this is Margot Tasse, her assistant.'

'Enchanté,' Coco addressed the two ladies. She had noticed the difference in Remy's tone whilst introducing the younger woman. It seemed antagonistic and surly and out of character for the normally poised directeurice.

Margot Tasse smiled at Wall. 'Good to see you again, Tomas.' Her voice was heady and sensual, her tongue moved slowly across her bottom lip as if she was appraising a potential catch.

Under normal circumstances, Coco would have been pleased to see a man like Wall squirm in his seat, but at that moment she was not, and it bothered her. There could be no man in her life. The only wall she would tolerate was the one between her and every man on the planet. The fact she was experiencing a pang of jealousy bothered her immensely.

Caron Voland raised her head slowly. When she spoke, her voice could not have been more different from Margot's. It was the voice of a woman who was not used to being listened to. A woman only familiar with talking about her speciality, not the type of woman able to engage in a social discourse more attractive to men. 'Did she suffer?' she whispered. 'Did Manon suffer?'

'We can't be sure, Caron,' Wall said, moving his hand slowly across the table. She studied it, but did not move her own.

Coco glared at him. It appeared as if Wall was familiar with most of the women at *École Privée Jeanne Remy* and she could not decide whether it bore any significance. She was sure it did not, but it bothered her all the same. 'She was murdered and bundled into a deep freeze,' Coco spoke. 'Not her best day.'

Remy twisted her head. 'This is Captain Brunhild. She's from Paris,' she snapped. 'And despite her assumption, Manon's death has not yet been determined as a murder.'

'Not *yet*,' Coco confirmed, 'but either way, the illegal disposal of a body is still a crime. Murder or not, a crime has been committed at *École Privée Jeanne Remy*.' She held Remy's gaze. 'And as uncomfortable and inconvenient as it might be for you, this isn't going away.' She turned to the teacher and her assistant. 'When was the last time either of you saw, Manon?'

Caron and Margot exchanged a look. 'Lundi Dernier,' Margot answered.

'C'est vrai,' Caron confirmed.

Coco made a note. 'And that was when?'

'It was after class, around 17H00,' Caron replied.

'And it was just before the trip planned for her class?'

Caron nodded. 'We had a light supper and then everyone retired to bed early because they were leaving early the following morning.'

Margot smiled. 'I imagined it was all very well planned,' she interjected.

Coco raised an eyebrow. 'What do you mean?'

'The trip was planned for Mardi,' she replied. 'I believe Manon had planned her… "excursion" to coincide with the trip we planned for her group.'

'Then what went wrong?' Coco countered. 'Because it's pretty fucking obvious something did.'

'Captain Brunhild, s'il vous plaît,' Remy interrupted. 'You are in a school, merci, show some decorum.'

'Désolé,' Coco retorted, staring directly at Remy. 'I forget sometimes. I suppose it's because I'm used to spending my days with drug dealers, gang-bangers, racists, rapists, murderers, and,' she smiled at Remy, 'people who look right at me and lie through their teeth.'

'And paedophiles?' Remy tipped her head. 'You missed that from your list.'

Coco sucked in her breath, her bosoms rising rapidly, knowing instantly Remy had researched her. 'You're right. I deal with all types of filth, but the one thing you have to know about me is I don't care whether it's a junkie off the street, or my… or someone I care about. Filth is filth.' She touched her coat. 'I don't care about filth on my clothes, because I'm too busy caring about the filth around me. I don't do favours for anyone.' She leaned forward. 'I may be terrible with social conventions and rules, but if someone you cared about died, I'd be your saving grace. Because no matter what obstacle was put in front of me, whoever lied to me or looked down at me, means nothing to me. I don't need love. I have four children who *practically* love me. I have Barbra Streisand to fill my nights. I don't need approval to do my job. But I do it for all the kids like Manon and Elliot Bain.' She exhaled. 'Alors, let's cut the crap and get to the point. I have no interest in dragging your precious school through the mud, but the longer you derail me, the longer you make it difficult for me, the more of a pain I'm going to become in your ass.' She turned back to Margot Tasse. 'You were telling me about the trip, and how Manon was planning to use it as a cover to go off on some sort of dirty vacation with some random garçon. Fill in the blanks. If it was all so carefully planned, what went wrong?'

Caron and Margot did not look at each other.

'This isn't the time to be silent,' Wall directed to the two of them.

'Finally,' Coco added, glaring at him. 'I thought I was the only cop on the case.' She pointed at the fading red circle on her coat. 'This here is the blood of Elliot Bain. It's the blood he spilled on me as he fought for his life in my arms.' She lifted her hands. 'These two, slightly chubby, yet still rather fabulous, hands were what I used to try to stop the blood spurting from his carotid artery three days ago. I want to understand why he chose to do that. And I'm certain the only reason I'm going to be able to do so is by understanding what the hell happened in this school last week.'

Caron took a deep breath. 'As Manon's teacher, I had begun to notice changes in her in the last few weeks.'

'Changes?' Coco queried. 'As in, changes related to a boy?'

She shrugged. 'Peut être. It's hard to say.' She frowned. 'There have been boys before,' she said finally. 'And she's usually very vocal about them.'

Margot snorted. 'She liked to brag about it, you mean.'

Caron turned her head sharply towards her assistant. 'You shouldn't speak like that, Margot. Manon is dead.'

'And that's very sad, but I'm not a hypocrite,' Margot snapped back. 'She was a spoiled bitch who made all our lives miserable.'

'Margot!' Directeurice Remy hissed through gritted teeth. 'You will not speak of a student in such a way.'

Coco covered her mouth to suppress a smile. She addressed Margot. 'Anything you say is for me to decide whether or not it is important. What kind of ways did Manon Houde make your lives a misery?'

'The usual,' Margot replied. 'Talking to us as if we were beneath her.'

Coco glanced around. 'This is a pretty snooty school, I would have thought you'd be used to that sort of thing.'

Caron nodded. 'Oui, but Manon seemed to...' the elder teacher trailed off as if she was searching for an acceptable way to finish her thought, 'derive great pleasure from causing conflict,' she added finally.

'Like threatening us with having us sacked and making sure we never worked professionally again,' Margot added.

Coco looked at the directeurice. 'And could she do that? Do the Houde's have that much influence?'

Remy glanced at her feet. 'Pieter Houde is a very influential man, and he is also one of our primary benefactors,' she gave by way of an answer.

'So, you're saying, he has a powerful reach,' Coco added.

'I'm saying nothing of the sort,' Remy spat back, 'and nor should you be.' She stared at the teachers. 'Any of you.'

'Yeah, yeah,' Coco retorted. 'I get the idea. He's a big powerful man with big powerful friends and if I don't watch it, I'll end up directing traffic on the Champs-Élysées, or worse.' She snorted. 'Do you know how many times really powerful men have threatened me, and as it stands, I'm still here.'

'You should be careful, all the same, Charlotte,' Wall said.

She ignored him, and she ignored the fact the way he spoke her name made her heart skip a beat. 'Tell me, as her teachers, what exactly you did to warrant such a threat from Manon Houde?'

Caron and Margot exchanged a look. 'I caught her having sex,' Margot said.

'You did what?' Directeurice Remy squealed, informing Coco it was the first she was hearing of it. 'With who? And when?' She stared at Coco. 'Those sorts of relationships are strictly forbidden in my school.'

'Sure they are,' Coco replied, 'but when you put a gaggle of teenagers together, unless you lock them in chastity belts, I'm afraid it's inevitable there'll be a bit of…' She formed the thumb and forefinger on her right hand into a circle and wiggled the middle finger from her left hand into the hole, 'rumpy pumpy.'

Wall snorted, immediately blushing and lowering his head,

seeing the look shot in his direction from Directeurice Remy.

'Who was it, and why was I not told?' Remy hissed.

Margot lowered his voice. 'It was Elliot Bain, and after what happened, well, there didn't seem to be much point.'

'That was not your decision to make,' Remy replied. 'Caron, did you know about this?'

Caron nodded slowly. 'Margot told me, and I have to say I agreed with her. We dealt with it between us.'

Remy glared at her. 'We'll discuss this further in private later.'

'When did you catch them?' Coco asked.

'The day before she disappeared,' Margot replied.

Coco tapped her chin. 'That's interesting.'

'It is?' Wall countered.

'Sure,' she answered with a smile, 'it could have been payment.'

'Payment?' Directeurice Remy gasped. 'I'm not sure what you think you're suggesting, but I can assure you, Manon Houde is a… was a good girl, from a good home.'

Coco narrowed her eyes. 'Do you know how many prostitutes start out that exact same way?' She raised her hand in an attempt to fend off Remy's protests. 'But to confirm, I'm not suggesting *anything* at this stage. I'm just trying to understand what led Manon Houde to be shoved into a deep freeze in your kitchen.' She stood, remnants of food falling from her coat, and began pacing. 'Let's go back to Lundi dernier, or rather the day before. Dimanche. The day Margot caught Elliot and Manon doing the dirty.' She faced Margot. 'Where was that, exactly?'

Margot's eyes flashed with concern, moving slowly in Remy's direction. Remy nodded. 'In the kitchen,' Margot answered.

'The kitchen?' Coco repeated, her voice rising sharply. 'The damn kitchen?'

Margot nodded. 'It was late. I was having trouble sleeping, so I went down for a glass of milk. And I saw them there, on the table.'

'Oh, mon Dieu!' Remy exclaimed.

'Beginning, middle or…' Coco smiled, 'the end?'

Margot coughed. 'I couldn't say,' she answered. 'Elliot was mortified, I think. He pulled up his trousers and ran up the staircase. I thought I would speak to Caron about it in the morning, which I did. Mais, as I said, it became pointless anyway.'

Coco nodded. 'We'll come back to that in a moment. What happened with Manon?'

Margot grimaced, running her hand through her perfectly coiffured peroxide hair and mussing it. 'She laughed at me, and she didn't even bother to…' she paused, 'cover herself. In fact, she made a big display of it.'

'We're not painting a very good picture of Manon,' Caron interrupted. 'The truth is, she was a good girl. A girl who was just lost, that's all. I know it sounds like a cliche, but in her case it was true. She grew up with everything, but she really had nothing except for one thing - her arrogance.' She took a deep breath. 'Her often downright cruelty, was the result of it all. She told me once since her mother had died she only ever saw her father once or twice a year at most. He sent her to one school after another and she escaped them all. But when she came here, I think she found her calling, for want of a better word. She was a very, very intelligent young woman.'

Directeurice Remy nodded. 'It's true, she was. Few women are equipped with a scientific mind, in my experience. It was my father's bitterest disappointment that I did not share his talent. I believed if we could convince her to focus, Manon Houde could have gone on to great things.'

Coco pursed her lips. 'Let's continue with the timeline,' she said. 'What did Manon say to you?' she asked Margot.

'The usual,' she shrugged. 'You can't stop me. I'll have you flipping burgers if you try. Blah blah. I told her to go to bed, and

I'd deal with her in the morning.'

Coco turned to Remy. 'When did you first realise she was missing?'

'At dix heures,' Remy answered. She pointed at Charlotte. 'Mademoiselle Voland informed me Manon had not turned up for her class and that she and Mademoiselle Tasse had searched her room and found no trace of her.' She shuddered. 'It soon became apparent she had left the school and who had helped her do so.'

Coco nodded. 'Mademoiselle Voland, earlier you suggested Manon Houde had somehow changed in the weeks preceding her death. What did you mean by that?'

Caron Voland considered. 'It's hard to explain.'

'Try.'

She shrugged. 'She was quiet.'

'Quiet?' Coco repeated. 'And that's a bad thing? I have four kids. Quiet is something I dream of on a daily basis.'

'But it was unusual for her,' Margot Tasse took over. 'And it wasn't just that she was quiet. I'd say she was being secretive.'

'Secretive?' Coco asked.

Margot nodded. 'The other people in her group kept questioning her about why she was always on her cell phone, texting or emailing and she snapped, telling them to mind their own business. That surprised me. I think she was keeping something secret because she wasn't bragging.'

'Maybe she was just being sensitive,' Captain Wall interrupted, 'especially considering she was in a relationship with someone, perhaps someone different to whoever she was communicating with.'

Coco laughed. 'You've obviously never dealt with a teenage girl,' she said. 'We're capable of huge deception when needed.'

Wall coughed, lowering his head. Coco frowned. She needed to speak to Wall in private because she was sure there was something he was not telling her, but she could not determine whether it was important to the case or just none of her business.

'I don't think it was that,' Margot said. 'As loath as I am to suggest otherwise, I believe Manon would have no problem talking about her love life. And nor do I imagine any teenager would be surprised to know there were other people in their lover's life.'

Remy blew her lips.

'Oh, you're not so old, Directeurice Remy. Times haven't changed so much. When you're seventeen, having one or two boyfriends or girlfriends is a rite of passage,' Coco said. She winked. 'I know I certainly did.' She sat down again. 'There's only one reason I can think of why a teenage girl might keep her mouth shut about a relationship.'

'What's that?' Caron Voland said.

Coco continued. 'He was older, or married, or both. Someone she liked, who told her she had to keep their relationship secret.'

'That is a lot of supposition, Captain Brunhild,' Remy replied.

'Peut être,' Coco responded. 'But it doesn't mean it's not true. And more importantly, it makes perfect sense. Manon Houde had a secret lover. She wanted to get away, but she knew her father would never let her, so she seized the opportunity when the rest of her group were going to be away on a trip. But she couldn't do it alone, so she roped in the scholarship student who most likely had a great big ole crush on her. She did whatever she needed to get him to help her.' She paused. 'Elliot admitted immediately what he had done to help her?'

Remy nodded. 'As soon as we noticed she was missing, it didn't take us long to understand how she had escaped.'

'And yet the fact remains, she probably never did,' Coco added, pursing her lips. 'She never left the school.' She shook her head. 'Then why the hell did Elliot lie about helping her bust out of here?' she said almost to herself.

A heavy silence descended on the room, the only sound the

scraping of plates from the students in the corner of the room. Coco pushed back her chair, the scraping against the tiled floor echoing, causing everyone in the room to stare at her. She looked at her watch. 'I really have to get back to Paris,' she said, gesturing for Cedric to come back from his discussion with the students.

Directeurice Remy rose to her feet. 'Bon. Captain Wall will continue with the investigation.'

Coco picked up her bag. She gestured towards Wall. 'No offence to the Captain, but I'm not done yet. There are too many questions which need answering. Au revoir,' she said, hurrying towards the exit without looking back. 'I'll be back,' she called. 'Let's go, Cedric,' she gesticulated towards her Lieutenant.

14H00

Coco's eyes scanned the forensic examination report, suppressing a yawn as she did. She was exhausted and still had not managed to sleep. Since returning from *École Privée Jeanne Remy* and Saint-Germain-en-Laye, she had only managed a quick shower after she made sure her children were ready for their day. As usual, she felt as if she was doing a whole lot of nothing, and doing it very badly. Barbra had begun working in a clothing store and was no doubt gearing up to leaving home once and for all. Julien, on the other hand, had become even more sullen than usual. Cedric was angry and combative, she assumed because he did not understand why his father had suddenly and so completely disappeared from his life.

Coco had trudged back to her tiny office in Commissariat de Police du 7e arrondissement, feeling even more dejected than usual. The files on her desk appeared to be multiplying, but the time to go through them seemed to be getting shorter and shorter. She gestured for Cedric to come into her office, cursing as Commander Demissy walked past and thought Coco was gesticulating to her.

'You want me?' Demissy asked.

Like I want gonorrhoea. 'Non, I was after Cedric. Captain Wall has just sent through the forensic report, I thought we'd go through it.'

'Ah, bon,' the Commander said, slipping into a chair. 'Lieutenant, take a seat,' she instructed Cedric.

Cedric sat down, folding his hands in front of him.

'Pieter Houde is hounding me,' Demissy said, 'even from his private jet.' She narrowed her eyes in Coco's direction. 'I'm still failing to see what any of this has to do with the 7e arrondissement, mais…' she spread her hands in front of her, 'seemingly it does.'

'The forensic report came in,' Coco told Cedric.

'And hopefully it will clear the whole matter up,' Demissy added.

Coco shook her head. 'Not really, in fact it raises more questions than it answers.'

'How come?' Cedric asked.

She handed him the file. 'There is no evidence of Manon Houde being murdered in the kitchen. The staircase was clean, the floors clean, the dumbwaiter clean. Someone did a pretty good job of tidying up if it was a crime scene.'

'What about her room?' Cedric asked.

'The same,' Coco replied. 'No evidence of a crime. It's a mess, but nothing unusual for a teenager, and certainly no sign of a crime being committed there,' she sighed. 'You've seen the school, it's huge. She could have been murdered anywhere. It would take a forensic team weeks to search the whole place, and the longer it takes, the more likely evidence is lost.' She paused. 'And then there's no guarantee Manon Houde was even murdered inside the school. It could have taken place outside in the gardens, and it's been raining on and off for most of the last week, so anything usable likely washed away.'

'I read your report,' Demissy interjected, 'what there was of it,' she added with clear admonishment. 'There is absolutely no indication the death was anything but natural causes.' She raised her hand. 'Oui, I realise she didn't place herself in the freezer, but a cover-up is something much different, and more suited to the police in Saint-Germain-en-Laye. It isn't too hard to imagine why someone must have panicked and tried to cover up what happened.'

'Then why leave her there for a week?' Coco posed.

'Because the kitchen staff were on holiday,' Demissy reasoned. 'And the freezer in question was in an ante-room, one which isn't used very often. The person who hid the body could have known that. And then you turn up, stomping all over the school, and the plans had to be changed. If the cleaner hadn't unplugged the freezer, the body could have disposed of and we may never have been any the wiser.'

Coco frowned. 'Then what are you saying, we forget all about this and leave it to Wall?'

The Commander tutted. 'It's a little late for that since you dragged us into this mess. Non, you'll return to Saint-Germain-en-Laye tomorrow morning, deal with Pieter Houde, and interview the students who knew Manon Houde, when they get back from their trip. You'll return to Paris tomorrow evening with the case closed, so we can get back to solving our own crimes,' she said as she stood.

'You have more faith in me than I do,' Coco mumbled.

'I doubt that, Captain Brunhild,' Demissy retorted. 'I *sincerely* doubt that. Close the case by tomorrow. Both of them.'

Coco watched her leave the office.

'She doesn't want much, does she?' Cedric exhaled.

Coco stared at the folder, a picture of Manon Houde staring at her. *What happened to you, Manon? What the hell happened to you?*

15H00

Coco spread the papers in front of her, carefully and deliberately. There were ten sheets, each detailing an email conversation between Manon Houde and her supposed lover. She looked at Cedric.

'Isn't Fritz an unusual name?' she asked.

He shrugged. 'Sure, *Coco*,' he answered with clear sarcasm.

'Merci, *Cedric*,' she retorted. 'Listen to this and tell me what you think.' She cleared her throat and began reading from the first sheet.

Heya Fritz. Great talking to you on the phone yesterday. It was awesome to hear your deep, manly voice. I imagined your hands moving all over my nubile body. It's crazy we can't be together physically, but we will soon, I promise, I'm working on it. I'll bust out of this place soon and we can spend the rest of our lives making love on the beach. Love'n'Hugs Manon xxx

'Well, what do you think?'

The Lieutenant shrugged again. 'It sounds like every soft-core porn.'

Coco clapped her hands together. 'Exactly, listen to the reply.'

Hey sexy. Can't wait to show ya what I got. Cos it's ready for you and has your name written on it. In BOLD. Haha. Love BIG Fritz.

Coco visibly shuddered. 'No man who suggests he has a big, you-know-what, has a big, you-know-what.'

Cedric narrowed his eyes. 'Is that true?'

She leaned forward, moving her head towards his jeans. 'Sure it is. If you've got it, you don't need to flaunt it...'

He coughed uncomfortably and crossed his legs.

Coco chuckled. She threw the remaining pages towards him. 'They're all the same.'

'What were you expecting, Dostoevsky?' he responded.

Coco regarded him with surprise. 'Go, Cedric. I'm impressed.'

He glared at her. 'I read. I'm not illiterate, you know.'

She smiled. 'Sure, honey. Non, my point is. This can't be how kids write. This is how I would write if I was sending fake emails using my vast knowledge of eighties and nineties American movies.'

Cedric stared at one of the emails. 'It doesn't mean it's not real.'

Coco gave him a doubtful look. 'How would you write to a chick?'

He grimaced. 'Well, I wouldn't call her a "chick" to begin with.'

'Exactement!' Coco exclaimed. 'And you wouldn't sign off as "BIG Cedric," would you?'

Cedric laughed. 'I can't believe you of all people haven't sexted.'

'Bien sûr, I've sexted,' she retorted, offended. 'What's sexting?' She scratched her head. 'Oh, you mean, *I got my boobs out and I'm wearing my crotchless panties*, kinda thing? Sure, I know how to do that.'

Cedric nodded. 'And you're *perfect* at it,' he laughed.

'My point is,' she interjected, 'Monsieur Rudey-pants, these emails don't seem real to me.'

'And you base that on what?'

'Everything I've heard about Manon Houde.'

'Didn't you tell me they caught her having sex with Elliot Bain, probably just to secure his help in escaping?'

'We don't know the reasons for it,' she retorted. 'The point is, I just don't buy these emails. These aren't the sort of emails which would make someone like Manon Houde up sticks and risk being cut off by her father. For what reason? Cos Fritz supposedly has a big…'

Cedric scanned the emails in front of him. 'They do seem a little too teenager, mais…' he shrugged yet again. 'There's nothing here to prove it one way or another.'

Coco pointed at the top of the sheet. 'The email address, BIGFRITZ1999 at GMAIL dot COM, is traceable, non?'

Cedric nodded. 'We can apply for a Mandate to access it, but pourquoi? Manon Houde never left the school. She never got to see BIGFRITZ. I can't imagine a Juge letting us invade his privacy based on what we have.'

'But it might be all we have,' she bounced back at him. 'And he might be the only clue we have. I'll ask Etienne Martine to see what he can find, off the record.'

Cedric shook his head. 'You shouldn't really drag him into this. It's not his job.'

'We need all the help we can get,' she replied. 'You heard Demissy. We have to close this case and fast.' She suppressed a yawn. 'D'accord. I have to follow up on the burglary in Rue De Castello and try to get home and see my kids. We'll look at this again later.'

Cedric stood and moved away from her desk. He stopped by the doorway. 'Are you okay, Captain?' he asked.

'Sure, why do you ask?'

'You seem a little fried,' he replied, 'even more than usual.'

She waved her hand. 'Merci for the concern, Lieutenant. I'll be fine. I just need a good night's sleep, and once we figure out what the hell happened to Elliot Bain and Manon Houde, maybe I will. See you later.'

Cedric nodded, evidently unconvinced.

'Close the door behind you,' Coco said, turning her attention back to the files on her desk.

20H00

Coco kicked off her boots and flopped her feet onto the coffee table, kicking off an assortment of toys and pizza boxes. She sighed contentedly as the white wine slid down her throat. She smiled, noticing the four large holes in her socks, held together by a large piece of brown plastic tape. Sewing had never been something she had any interest or aptitude with. She closed her eyes, nursing the plastic tumbler of wine on her chest. The apartment, for the first time she could remember, was completely silent. Barbra and Julien were both out and Cedric and Esther were already asleep, snuggled with Helga in Coco's bed, as she watched some old romantic movie badly dubbed into German. Coco realised once she had reached the bottom of the bottle, she would most likely be joining them. The loud buzz of the intercom jolted her back to reality and made her jump to her feet before it woke everyone up. She felt weary and wondered who the hell was bothering her now. 'Yeah?' she growled into the box.

'Ah. Allô. Bonjour... I mean, salut, bonsoir,' a man's voice called out through the crackles.

'Pick one,' Coco snapped. 'Who is this?'

'C'est moi, c'est Tomas.'

'Tomas?' Coco retorted.

'Tomas Wall,' he replied quickly. 'Captain Wall from Saint-Germain-en-Laye.'

'Captain Wall from Saint-Germain-en-Laye,' Coco repeated as if she did not understand what he was saying.

He laughed. 'Yeah, that's me. Ecouté, je suis désolé for turning up like this, but I wanted to see you.'

I wanted to see you. She shook away the happiness she imagined she was suddenly feeling. 'How do you know where I live?'

Sept Jours

'I rang the 7e Arrondissement and spoke to your Lieutenant. He gave me your address and said as long as I turned up with *pizza and beer*, you wouldn't be mad.'

Coco bit her lip. *I'll kill you, Cedric.* She sighed. 'What kind of pizza?' she asked wearily.

'Large stuffed crust pepperoni,' Wall replied. 'I'm good at following instructions.'

She sighed again and pressed a button on the intercom. 'Apartment 10a.'

'You're weird.'

'I'm *what?*' Tomas Wall replied.

Coco cracked open a can of beer. She reached across the table and grabbed a slice of pizza. 'You're weird,' she repeated.

Wall laughed. 'You're going to have to be more specific, Captain Brunhild.'

'And you're going to have to be *less* specific, Captain Wall,' she replied. 'And unless you want me to throw this,' she glanced at the pizza in her hand and shook her head, she looked around, smiling when she spotted a child's teething ring, 'this at you, then you call me by my name.' She stopped. 'And FYI, I've seen the movie,' she stopped before whispering, *'possibly gay son.* But more importantly, I don't eat fruit. Fruit bores me. Anything which says, *eat me, I'll make you happy and healthy,* is a bare-faced liar.'

Wall shook his head. 'I have no idea what you're saying to me right now.'

She laughed. 'It's very simple. Call me Captain when we have to look as if we know what we're doing. Any other times, my name is Coco, unless I've irritated you and you want to get my attention because I've gone off on a tangent, or,' she paused, 'I look like I'm going to punch you.'

Wall smiled. 'That's a lot of rules.'

'It's very simple,' she replied. 'Call me Coco. Or don't.'

Wall wrote an imagined note on his palm. 'Duly noted.'

Coco drained the contents of her beer and then opened another. 'Why are you here? You got nothing else to do in Saint-Germain-en-Laye?'

He did not answer. Coco took another drink.

'You got something to say, don't ya?' she asked.

Wall lowered his head, slowly sipping his beer. 'I saw the way you looked at me,' he answered finally.

Coco spat out the mouthful of the beer she had just slugged. 'Hey! Just because I imagined you in a sailor's outfit and then stripping out of it, means absolutely nothing. I had a dream about the old man who runs the Chinese takeaway. He's ninety, if he's a day, but mon Dieu, he's a good kisser.'

Wall shook his head. 'I'll say it again. I have no idea what you're saying.'

Coco frowned. 'Then what are you talking about?'

He stared at her. 'This morning. In the dining room. You looked at me and I knew you knew.'

'Ah,' Coco retorted. She sipped her beer. 'And what do you think I know?'

Wall took a deep breath. 'Saint-Germain-en-Laye is like any town, or village. It doesn't really matter the size of a place, or how many people live there. It's small.'

Coco stared at him. 'You shagged who, exactly?'

Wall's eyes widened in surprise. 'What do you mean?'

She laughed. 'You know exactly what I mean. You're correct, I saw the way you were with the teachers.' She paused. 'You bang them all?'

Wall glared at her, slamming his beer onto the table. 'That's a disgusting thing to say!'

Coco shrugged. 'It's a disgusting thing to have to think, but it's true, non?'

'My wife left me because she said, "I wasn't enough,"' he replied. *'Was not enough.* They're simple enough words, but in the dark of night, when the sheets in your bed are dry and lonely, they take on their own meaning. *Not enough.* What does it mean? In bed? In life? I don't earn enough? I don't do enough? I spent years going over and over it in my head. And in the end you realise it doesn't matter. Sometimes, you're just not *enough*.'

Coco opened her mouth to respond, but could think of nothing to say. She leaned back on the sofa, nursing the beer on her bosom, staring at Wall.

'There's a bar in town,' he said finally. 'Where saddos like me go.'

Coco nodded. 'Text me the address,' she laughed. She leaned forward again. 'You drove to Paris for a reason. I'd like to think it's because you are so intoxicated by me, you couldn't resist, mais, I know that's not true.'

Wall took a deep breath. 'I've gotten into something, something I shouldn't have.'

'Meaning?'

He sipped his beer. 'It's complicated.'

Coco nodded. 'I've got haemorrhoids. Luckily, I've just managed to get comfortable on this lumpy second-hand sofa, therefore, you have my complete, *relaxed* attention,' she said, wriggling on the sofa. 'Alors, talk.'

Wall exhaled. 'This bar, *La Fontaine*, is one of the busiest places in town. Friday nights are the most popular.' He shrugged. 'There's something about the impending doom of a weekend when you have no one to spend it with. It feels… it feels very empty and long.' He turned his head, taking in Coco's chaotic living room. 'You do not know how lucky you are to have such a… such a vibrant life.'

Coco laughed. 'Vibrant is a kind word for it!'

He shrugged. 'You are loved. This room reeks of love. My

home reeks of boredom, irritation, and a son who doesn't want to be there, *ever*. It's only because his mother wants him less that he's there at all.'

It was Coco's turn to shrug. 'My oldest two children wouldn't agree with you.'

'And yet they're still here,' he replied. 'Just because they complain means nothing.' He spread his arms. 'This is a room where people feel safe.'

Coco turned her head, unsure what he meant. The paint on the walls was peeling, some of them covered with prints and photographs. The rest of the room lined with sideboards and cupboards she had cobbled together from various charity shops.

He exhaled. 'I haven't felt so relaxed in a long time,' he continued.

'You have really low standards,' Coco laughed. She looked around the room again and realised despite the chaos, the room told her one thing. *This is a home. People live here. People love here.* She stared at him for the longest time, imagining him as part of the furniture and it broke her heart. *No man can live here.*

'Get to the point,' she snapped.

'I've had one-night stands,' he answered after a moment, 'one-night stands I'm not proud of.'

'You mean, Margot Tasse, the teaching assistant?'

He nodded.

'It was casual, and it was nothing important.'

Coco frowned. 'Then why did it become important?'

Wall pulled back his head. 'What do you mean?'

'You know exactly what I mean,' she replied quickly.

'We were seen.'

'Seen?'

He nodded.

'Seen?' she repeated.

'Seen?' she repeated again.

He sighed. 'Manon Houde was there one night.' He paused. 'And she saw us together.'

'Us?' Coco questioned. 'You mean you and the teacher?'

'Oui,' he replied.

Coco flicked her hair over her shoulder. 'How did she see you?'

Wall attempted a smile. 'With her eyes?'

'Now's not the time to be cute,' she bounced back. 'The question is, how the hell did Manon Houde see you in the first place? I may be missing something, but as far I can recall, Directeurice Remy said no one could leave the school.' She stabbed her fingers on the table. 'And unless I'm very much mistaken, the reason everyone claimed Manon Houde escaped was because Elliot Bain arranged it for her which resulted in him being expelled and then, moi,' she stabbed at her chest, 'becoming involved in this ridiculousness.'

'It wasn't the first time I saw Manon,' Wall added.

Coco cocked her head. 'It wasn't. In the bar?'

He nodded. 'It was only one other time, and she wasn't alone.'

'Elliot Bain?'

Wall shook his head. 'Non, at least I don't think so. I only saw him from behind, so I can't be certain, mais…'

'If you only saw him from behind, why do you think it wasn't Elliot?' Coco asked.

He shrugged. 'I've met Elliot, and he's a skinny kid. You can just tell he's a kid still. As I said, I can't be certain, but the man who was with Manon that night was bigger. He didn't strike me a kid, rather a fully grown man.'

Coco pursed her lips. 'A full grown man? That's an odd choice of words for someone you just saw in passing.'

Wall studied her face. 'You don't believe me?'

'I never said that,' Coco retorted quickly.

'You didn't have to do,' he shot back. 'I'm not...' he trailed off, biting his lip.

'You're not who? Mordecai? Is that you were going to say?' Coco hissed.

Wall did not respond.

She shook her head. 'It's good to see my reputation has made its way to Saint-Germain-en-Laye. Delightful.'

'Non, but I googled you.'

Coco smacked her head. 'I've been googled! I can just imagine how that turned out.'

He smiled at her. 'It's not as bad as you might think. In fact, there's a lot of sympathy and support for you and your kids.'

She glowered at him. 'I'm not sure that's better or worse. Life in a goldfish bowl sucks, no matter how you ended up in it.' She sucked the remains of her beer and cracked open another, draining most of its contents in one go. She continued to glower at him. 'I wasn't calling you a liar, but I don't buy your story. To start with, why didn't you mention any of this to Directeurice Remy?'

He took a sip of his beer. 'I don't blame you,' he responded. 'I didn't tell her, because firstly, it was none of my business.'

'And you didn't wanna get busted for schlepping the teaching assistant,' Coco concluded. 'It's not really a federal crime, although peroxide perms went out of fashion in the eighties,' she snapped.

He lowered his head, his cheeks flushing.

Coco's eyes widened. 'Unless... unless,' she gasped. 'You're schlepping more than the teaching assistant!' she exclaimed. 'You dirty dawg,' she laughed, sounding impressed. 'Who? Caron Voland?' Her eyes widened. 'Don't tell me you're doing the dirty with Directeurice Remy? How does she even do it? Doesn't she have a stick stuck up her ass?'

Wall snorted. 'I'm not "schlepping" the directeurice, but merci for the mental image.' He sighed. 'But I have had a dinner or two with Caron over the last few months.'

She nodded. 'And you didn't want one finding out about the other, huh?'

'Something like that,' he shrugged. 'There's not a lot to do in the evenings in Saint-Germain-en-Laye.'

'D'accord,' Coco said. 'Why did it matter about Manon Houde seeing you with Margot Tasse? You're both consenting adults.'

He sighed again. 'Manon told Margot if she let on about her being out of the school, she'd tell the directeurice about our affair.'

Coco frowned. 'I go back to my original point. It's hardly a federal crime.' She paused. 'A glaring indication of distinct lack of taste, but also hardly a crime.'

'Margot is married. Her husband works out of the country a lot of the time, et…'

Coco mustered fake outrage. 'Oh, you home wrecker!'

He smiled. 'I didn't want to cause her problems, especially over something so casual.'

Coco nodded. 'I get that. You're a caring adulterer.' She sipped her beer. 'You said you spoke to Elliot Bain. Did you ask him if it was the first time he had busted Manon out of the school?'

'I did, and he swore it was the first time.'

She frowned. 'But, you knew that wasn't true.'

'Non, I didn't,' he replied. 'All I knew was she had made it out before. The point is, why would he lie? Why wouldn't he just say he'd done it before? Especially since he got expelled, anyway.'

Coco nodded. 'You may be right. If he didn't get her out the previous time, the question is, who did? Her mysterious lover?'

'The thought crossed my mind,' Wall confirmed.

'Which suggests the possibility her beau was someone else who worked at the school.' She stared at Wall. 'Are you sure, you don't know who he was?'

'I promise you,' he replied. 'Why else do you think I'm here? Embarrassing myself in front of you.' He took a deep breath. 'I messed up, and it's going to come back to me one way or another.'

Coco gave him a surprised look. 'Hey, as far as I can tell, your ex told you a few things in the heat of a divorce to piss you off. It worked, so ever since you've been looking at ways to prove her wrong. You got caught out by one of the kids and kept your mouth shut so as not embarrass either woman, or find yourself named in a divorce case.'

'But I withheld a piece of information regarding a missing kid,' he whispered. 'A piece of information which could have helped.'

She shook her head. 'Or not. Hey, as far as I'm concerned, I never really bought the whole, "this is the first time a kid ever snuck out of boarding school," line. Do you know why?' She smiled. 'Because I once went to boarding school, and they said the same thing. There were exactly fourteen ways in and out of that school without being caught, most of them I invented myself.'

'I bet you were a hell of a fun kid to know,' Wall said. His eyes crossed. 'Désolé, that sounded really creepy.'

'Relax, sailor,' Coco replied. 'You're right, I was fun. I'm even more fun now,' she winked, before her face clouded. 'Or rather, I used to be.'

Wall's lips pulled into a sad smile. 'You will be again. You're just in a bit of a funk right now. It'll pass.'

'It's taking its own sweet fucking time,' she muttered. 'But, yeah, you're right.'

A moment passed. 'Then, you're not mad at me?' Wall asked finally.

'Of course not,' she replied. 'Merci, for telling me. I'm not sure what any of it means, but as I've said, I never quite bought the whole scenario.' She finished her beer. 'However, considering what we found yesterday, it's certainly interesting. We have a suspect.'

'You really don't think it was Elliot Bain?' Wall mused.

Coco shrugged. 'Peut être, pas peut être. Unless he wakes up, we might never know. But if you're right and there was someone else involved with Manon, why on earth did Elliot take the blame? Especially since we now know she never left the school in the first place.'

'What should I do?' Wall asked.

Coco contemplated. She stood and began pacing her living room. 'What can you do? The truth is, you can't swear you saw Manon at all. And you certainly don't know who she was with.'

'I'm sure it was her.'

Coco nodded. 'Mais, the only important part of it is. Who was the dude?'

'I've gone over this in my mind so many times,' Wall answered. 'And I paid so little attention. I'm fairly sure he was white and had dark hair and wasn't a kid, but I have absolutely nothing to back it up.'

'We need to find him,' Coco said.

'Je sais.' He sipped his beer. 'What about Elliot?' He shook his head. 'I just don't get it.'

Coco laughed. 'Tell me about it. I relive the incident in the lift in my head every day.'

'I can imagine,' he replied. 'I couldn't face it, so I walked up the stairs.'

'Me too,' Coco said. 'And it's going to kill me if I have to keep walking up ten flights every day.' She stared at him. 'I don't understand what happened to Elliot Bain, but we owe it to everyone involved in this mess to at least try to figure it out.' She continued to stare at him. 'And to do so, you might have to step outside your comfort zone. You might take a bit of heat for it, but trust me, because believe me, I'm the expert in these things. There is a light at the end of the tunnel. No matter how much of a mess things seem, they're not really. Each day is a new day and brings new opportunities.'

'You're very wise,' Wall said.

Coco smiled. 'Non, I'm not. I watch a lot of Oprah, that's all.'

He laughed before his face clouded. 'Can I see him? Can I see, Elliot?'

Coco moved towards the front door. 'Let's go.'

21H00

'He looks a waxwork dummy,' Wall said, before twisting his head. 'Is that an awful thing to say?'

Coco shrugged. 'Beats the shit out of me. If you said he looks like the elephant man, then perhaps we'd have a problem.' She moved closer to the bed, her finger tracing across Elliot's arm without touching it. 'He's a beautiful kid. I'd kill for olive skin and rosebud lips. It breaks my heart to think nobody might get to kiss them.'

Wall regarded her with curiosity. 'You say the oddest things.'

She shrugged again. 'It's true, though. Every time someone dies suddenly, whether it's suicide or murder, but especially when they're young, I think of all the missed opportunities. Not the long-term things, not the, oh, they might finally get married and have ten kids and blah-blah-blah. My first thought is always. Did they kiss enough? Did they get to fool around enough? Did they get to have that feeling where their hormones were beating out of control, making them feel like their entire body is going to explode if they don't get to do it with the pretty fille or garçon they crave. It's heartbreaking. I don't know what Elliot Bain did, and how it made him do this terrible thing to himself, but every time I look at him and see those lips, I can't help but hope he had a chance to put them to good use.' She laughed sadly. 'I realise that makes me a terrible cop.'

Wall touched her arm. 'Non, it makes you an amazing cop. But more importantly an amazing, caring person.'

She looked at him. 'Don't think you can sweet talk me, Tomas Wall.'

He smiled. 'I wouldn't dare.'

'Good, cos I'm not easy, no matter what you've heard,' she

responded.

'It doesn't matter,' he shot back, 'because as you know, I'm only into teachers, certainly not flics.'

Coco laughed, reaching over and punching his bicep with such force it caused him to wince. 'Don't think making me laugh will help you. That only helped on my last four pregnancies.'

Wall laughed, throwing back his head. 'Dieu. That felt good. I don't think I've laughed like that in the longest time. Merci, Coco.' He turned back to Elliot. 'Will he wake up?'

Coco lowered her voice. 'The doc's not sure,' she said. 'And even if he does, he's got a long road ahead of him.' She gestured for Wall to follow her into the hallway. 'I have to know your thoughts on this kid, because I'm getting so many mixed messages about him, most of which are coming directly from me. I don't know why, but there's something very wrong about it all. I just can't imagine he murdered his own mother and then casually walked into the lift and slit his throat.'

'I don't know what to say, Coco,' Wall said. 'The kid is a kid. I can't say it any better than that. I can't read them.'

Coco nodded. 'My eldest daughter, Barbra, looks at me, talks to me, and every word out of her mouth sounds sincere, but the only thing I know for certain is that when her lips are moving, she's lying.'

'Ha,' Wall snorted. 'That's a little extreme. I'm sure she's not that bad.'

'Maybe not, but young Monsieur Bain here, could be the same. Just because he has those lips, doesn't mean they're not cruel.' She took a deep breath. 'Let's just hope he wakes up so we can find out one way or another.'

Wall looked at his watch. 'It's after nine. I should get home.'

Coco nodded. 'You've had a lot of beers.'

Wall nodded. 'Yeah, I have, haven't I?'

Coco began walking down the hallway. 'You can sleep at my

place, but I swear to Dieu, if you try to climb into my bed, the only bed you'll end up sleeping in is the one next to Elliot Bain. Comprende?'

Wall smiled.

VENDREDI (FRIDAY)

07H00

Coco lifted herself slowly from the rollout bed, shaking her head in an attempt to wake herself up. The television was still on, playing some trashy American movie badly dubbed into German. Coco's eyes widened as the events of the previous evening slowly started to come back to her. Crawling up ten flights of stairs, two bodies falling on top of each other, laughing like schoolchildren, lips locking in a drunken haze.

'I'm not going to sleep with you tonight.'
'Pourquoi?'
'Because tomorrow would be better, and if we wait, I'd be doing it because I'm sober, and not lonely, and because I actually trust you. Not that it really matters, but it will determine what happens afterwards. All those things combined would make it a much better experience for us both, trust me.'
'You're putting an awful lot of pressure on a day.'
'That's what they're there for, they've got nothing else to do.'

She shook her head again, trying to remember what happened next. She vaguely recalled struggling to get her key in the door and then Tomas Wall wrapping his arms around her and helping her guide it in. And then… and then… Falling into the living room and then… and then. Her son's best friend Matthieu snoring peacefully on the sofa.

Coco shook her head again, trying to piece together the rest, cursing the extra bottle of wine they had consumed in the bar next to the hospital. Her eyes widened. She could remember going to the bathroom and then coming out to find there was no trace of Wall. In a panic, she had padded in a drunken stupor toward her bedroom. She lifted her head, turning it slowly towards her bed and it came back to her. Tomas Wall was still in the same position, his stocky body squeezed in-between Helga and Coco's two youngest children, his arms draped around them, his lips contorted into a deep sleep.

'Dieu, I should have just slept with him,' she muttered to herself, rolling herself into a crawling position. 'Wall! Wall!' she called out, the sound of her own voice hurting her ears. 'Get out of my damn bed. I've gotta go to the morgue. Sonny is ready for me.' She stared at him, shaking her head. 'Saying as you're already here, you might as well tag along.'

Tomas Wall's eyes snapped open. 'Where the hell am I?' he cried in obvious confusion.

08H00

Cedric smirked as Coco and Tomas Wall made their way through slowly into the morgue. 'Café?' he called out in a loud voice.

Coco glared at him. 'I hate you,' she mouthed. 'Mais, oui. Black and very strong.'

He laughed. 'Just like your men, huh?' he retorted, his eyes flicking over a dishevelled Tomas Wall. 'Apart from last night, it appears.'

Coco stopped, moving an outstretched arm between Wall and Cedric. 'He came to… we talked… we went…' she shuddered. 'I'm too hungover for this. He didn't sleep with me, he slept with Helga,' she said finally.

'Your au pair?' Cedric gasped.

Wall looked aghast. 'In the same bed, but that's all,' he cried, before adding, 'I think. I'm slightly vague on the whole evening.'

Cedric smirked, handing them both a café. 'You've been Coco'd,' he said.

Coco sank into her chair. 'I'm fairly sure I would have remembered that.' She took a gulp of the drink, immediately wincing at the heat, spitting it down her chin. 'We need to sober up before Commander Demissy finds us,' she mumbled.

'The Commander is in court this morning,' Cedric said. 'Lucky for you.'

The telephone on Sonny's desk began ringing. She screamed, covering her ears. 'Stop the damn bells!' she cried desperately.

Sonny laughed and picked up the telephone, speaking quickly and quietly. He replaced the receiver and moved quickly around the autopsy suite. 'Merci for letting me do the autopsy here, I would feel very weird about using someone else's morgue. Was there any problem with it?'

'Not at all,' Coco muttered, staring at the email on her cell phone. 'Commander Demissy cleared it with the Police Commander. She's also spoken with Manon Houde's father. He's trying to arrange his private jet to come and get him in Australia, but one way or another, he's going to arrive soon enough and he's going to want answers. If I didn't know better, I'd say Demissy actually sounds worried.'

'I bet it was an interesting conversation,' Captain Wall added.

Coco continued reading. 'He's also identified his daughter from the picture you took and given his permission for the autopsy.' She stood. 'So, it appears we have all our ducks in a row.' She moved across the tiled floor, stopping in front of the remains of Manon Houde. She was covered in a white sheet, but it was clear she was still in the semi-foetal position her body had been forced into in the freezer. Coco winced because she knew what was coming next in order to lay her flat.

'She's just a baby,' Coco muttered to herself. She faced Dr. Bernstein. 'Désolé, for dragging you into this, Sonny.'

He shrugged. 'It's my job.' He flicked on a pair of latex gloves and slipped a visor over his face. 'Let's get started, shall we?'

Coco imagined it would take a long time for the vison to leave her. Sonny had forced Manon Houde's body out of the originally frozen foetal position - it had been one of the most horrific things she had seen, and she knew the image would stay with her for a very long time. She looked to her right. Captain Tomas Wall was staring at his feet and she recognised the look on his face. *My child is seventeen.* It was the same thought which consumed her. Whatever Manon Houde had been in life, she had surely not deserved how it ended. Robbed of her future before she had really even begun living it. Cedric was staring at the young woman in a way she did not understand. It was as if he was willing her to wake up, as if her premature death was just too much for him to process.

Coco sighed. The truth was, they all had to deal with death in their own way if they were to stand any chance of making sense of it. The three of them had watched in silence as Sonny, one of the kindest, gentlest men Coco had ever known, went about the invasive and cruel act of exposing a person's body. But he did it with a dignity and reverence. Each slice of his scalpel was slight and it always appeared to Coco it was done with an apology. *I'm sorry for having to do this to you.*

Sonny stepped away from the gurney, flicking off his gloves and removing the visor. He stretched his arms in front of him, entwining his fingers, rolling his head from side to side. Coco understood the movements. He was detaching himself from the horror of what they had forced him to do. It was what made him such a good pathologist and such a wonderful man. It made her sad he had found no one to share his life with. She made a note to herself to see what she could do about it.

'D'accord,' Sonny said suddenly, breaking the silence and causing Coco to jump. 'Let me tell you what I do know.'

Coco pulled out a notepad from her bag. It was covered in stickers her children had placed all over it.

Sonny moved back towards Manon Houde. 'We have a well-nourished female, approximately seventeen years of age. She is of slight build and average height. I have recorded her exact measurements in the report, but there is nothing of significance or cause for concern. There is no obvious sign of sexual assault. She was not a virgin, but I don't see any evidence of recent sexual activity. Although, you have to understand, the freezing conditions we found her in will probably skew most of the readings I take.' He took a breath. 'The body shows no signs of trauma, nor assault, however an examination of the skull shows blunt force trauma.'

'She was hit over the head with something?' Wall asked.

Sonny mused. 'There is no evidence of that,' he said finally. 'If they hit her with something, I would expect to note it. Par example, a brick or a hard object would cause some kind of skull fracture which would be easy to spot.' He moved towards the monitor in the room's corner and pressed some buttons. Moments later, a closeup of Manon Houde's skull filled the screen.

'Jesus,' Coco cried, 'that's a hell of a lot of damage.'

He nodded. 'I've seen something like this before,' he said. 'And in that case, it resulted from a fall down a flight of stairs.'

Coco and Wall exchanged a look. 'Like the winding stone staircase in the kitchen?'

'Peut être,' he answered.

'I'll make sure the forensic team gives the stairs a thorough going over,' Wall added.

Coco returned to face Manon. 'She fell down the stairs and someone shoved her in the freezer rather than call for help?' She turned back to Sonny, pointing at the image of Manon's skull. 'And this? Would it have been fatal?'

Sonny studied the photograph as he considered. 'It would have certainly needed immediate intervention, mais…' he trailed off. 'C'est possible they could have saved her.'

'Pauvre fille,' Coco whispered. 'He let her die.'

Wall looked at her, obviously alarmed. 'We know nothing for certain yet, Captain Brunhild.'

She gawked. 'We know she hit her head in a pretty bad way, and rather than help her, someone bundled her up and threw her in a fucking freezer. That's the best-case scenario, because otherwise it means he smashed her over the head himself.' She glared at him. 'Either way, it's enough for me to want to string someone up by their balls.'

Cedric cleared his throat. 'How long has she been dead, doc?' he asked.

'A while,' he replied. 'She's been frozen for at least four or five days. That's why we had to wait for the autopsy.'

'Then it's possible she died on the day of her disappearance?' Coco asked.

He nodded. 'I'd say it's likely,' he answered.

'And there's nothing else you can tell us?' she asked with obvious exasperation.

'Désolé,' he replied. 'I've got all the samples ready, so we can send them off to the lab. Peut être, it will give us a better idea of what happened to her.'

'Good luck with that,' Wall interrupted. 'The labs backed up. We're still waiting on stuff from over a month ago.'

Coco shook her head. 'That won't do.'

'It's the same everywhere, Coco,' Sonny added. 'We're all backed up.'

Coco stared at the box on the table. 'Are those the samples?'

Sonny nodded. 'Oui.'

Coco pursed her lips. 'Send them to lab now,' she said finally. 'And tell them to put a rush on it.'

Sonny frowned. 'Why would they do that?'

She smiled. 'Because they don't have a choice.'

'Captain Brunhild, this is highly irregular,' Wall reasoned. 'And who's going to pay for it?'

'Does it matter?' she shrugged. 'A young woman is dead, and I don't give a shit who pays for it. If it bothers you, send me the bill.'

'That's not how it works,' he reasoned.

'That's how it works in my world,' she shot back. She pointed at the box. 'Get it to the lab now and I'll deal with the rest. Hell, her father will damn well pay for it, if he has to.' She tapped her chin. 'In fact, I'll give Etienne Martine in Montgenoux a call - if anyone can make sure the lab pulls their finger out he can.'

'Who's he?' Wall asked sharply.

'A friend who knows how to cut corners properly without wading through bullshit,' she retorted. She looked at her watch. 'Ah, it's almost time for breakfast, then shall we go back to the school?'

'We've got a day full of our own cases to get through in Paris,' Cedric interjected.

Coco glared at him. 'Bien sûr, we do. And I've got four kids to look after…'

'Then what are we doing with a case that's not ours?' he countered.

She pointed at Manon Houde. 'Because someone shoved this poor girl in a freezer, and,' she pointed at a red stain on her coat, 'a kid tried to kill himself in front of me, and I've still got his blood on me. Both of those things piss me off, and I don't have the patience to be patient, just because it happened in some provincial backwater where everything is done at a snail's pace.'

Wall watched helplessly as she moved towards the doorway. Cedric stood and rubbed Wall's shoulder. 'Best not to argue. In my experience it only prolongs the agony.'

11H00

Directeurice Jeanne Remy extended her arm, moving her fingers slowly. 'Take a seat,' she addressed Coco and Cedric. 'The students are already waiting.'

They moved into the office. Three students lifted their heads in unison, their faces pale and anxious, reminding Coco of every time she herself had been called into someone's office. She attempted a consoling smile, but it was met with nothing but a turn of the head.

Remy sank into her chair. 'Can I get you anything? Café? Thé?' She stopped, staring at Coco. 'Gin?'

Coco held the directeurice's gaze, resisting the urge to shout. *Oui!* 'I'm fine,' she answered demurely instead. She stood and made her way to the table and pointed at the three students. She guessed they were all more or less the same age, seventeen or so. The first, a large dark-skinned girl with black hair pulled into box braids; the second, a blond-haired boy with a long nose and keen, alert eyes. The third reminded Coco of herself. His hair was dyed green, his face paled with make-up and defiant eyes lined with kohl. She understood him immediately because it had always been her own mantra - if you can't fit in, stand out.

She turned to the directeurice. 'I'd like to talk with the students alone, if you don't mind,' she said.

Remy shook her head forcefully. 'That's out of the question, I'm afraid,' she snapped. 'These students are minors and they are in my charge. I will not allow them to be interrogated by the police, and their parents would be rightly furious with me if I did.'

Coco threw her hand to her chest, mock offended. 'I'm from Paris police nationale, it's not quite the Stasi,' she said demurely. 'D'accord, mais s'il vous plaît, don't interrupt.'

The directeurice flashed her a look which clearly said, *as if I would*.

'Bonjour kids,' Coco said. 'Je m'appelle Captain Charlotte Brunhild, and this is Lieutenant Cedric Degarmo. We're from Paris…'

'What does Manon's death have to do with Paris flics?' the blond student interrupted.

'Elliot,' the girl responded in a tone of voice which suggested to Coco she was most likely the self-proclaimed leader of the group. She wondered how that had gone down with Manon Houde. Everything Coco had heard about Manon suggested she was not the sort of young woman who can easily be friends with her own sex.

'Let's begin with your names,' Cedric said.

The girl swung her braids over her shoulder. 'Ada Fortin.'

'Fabian Auch,' the blond boy added.

The boy with blue hair met Cedric's gaze defiantly. 'Enzo Garnier. What's it to ya?'

Coco laughed. 'Ecouté kids. We're here because of what happened to your friend, Manon. So, let's not be smart asses and we'll all get along fine.'

'The only friend Manon had, was Manon,' Enzo interrupted.

'Enzo!' Fabian cried. 'She's dead.'

He shrugged as if he could not care less. 'What am I supposed to say?' he spat back at Fabian. 'She hated us all. She looked down at us, like we were beneath her. Hell, my father is probably worth as much as hers, so is yours, but it didn't matter to her. She still thought she was better than we were, and she convinced us all she was.' He paused, his cheeks flushing and his breath laboured as if he had realised he had said too much. He turned his head slowly to Coco. 'But yeah, it's sad she's dead.'

She held his gaze. 'I get it. She was a bitch. She made your life a misery, but in the end, it doesn't really matter. She's dead, and that's sad, and you're allowed to feel sad and conflicted.' She reached out to him. 'But you're not allowed to lie. That's what this has to with Paris.'

He pulled back from her.

'Is he dead?' Ada asked. 'Is Elliot dead?'

Coco frowned. 'What would make you think that? Have you heard from Elliot since they expelled him?'

The students exchanged a look but did not answer.

'Have you heard from Elliot?' Coco pressed.

'Not since he was expelled,' Ada answered finally.

Coco addressed the boys. 'And you two?'

Enzo shrugged. 'I don't even have his number.'

'I tried calling him a few times, left some messages, but he never got back to me,' Fabian said.

Coco turned to face Ada, fixing her with her best, don't mess with me, kid, expression. 'I'll ask you again, what made you think Elliot could be dead?'

Ada dropped her head. 'Because he didn't call me back either, and I thought…' she shuddered. 'I thought we were friends and the way he left here, the way he ran from the school, I was frightened that's all.'

Coco nodded. 'What about it frightened you?'

Ada shrugged. 'I don't know. He was just calm about it all. He didn't even try to defend himself, and he was desperate to get out of here. It made no sense, it still makes no sense. Elliot knew how this school was his big chance, his only real chance to make something of himself. All he used to talk about was making a fabulous life for his mother.'

'He was certainly a mother's boy,' Enzo agreed. 'It was a bit sickening, actually.'

'It wasn't sickening, it was sweet,' Ada scolded. 'He actually looked forward to spending time with his mother. When was the last time either of us even saw ours?'

Coco locked eyes with Cedric. Another piece of the puzzle which did not fit.

'Is he dead?' Ada asked again. 'S'il vous plait, I beg you, tell me.'

Coco paused, unsure how to answer. 'I don't know,' she answered honestly. 'You're not kids, so I'll level with you. Something happened to Elliot in Paris. I can't go into too many details right now. But he's in hospital, and I'm afraid he is in a very serious condition. At this stage we simply can't know if he's going to pull through. Even if he does, he's got a long, hard road ahead of him.' She paused. 'You seem like you cared about him. And that's all the more reason I need you to help me understand what happened. Namely, how and why Manon Houde died.'

'Well, it's obvious,' Fabian Auch said. 'Elliot killed her. He faked her disappearance and used it as a chance to get himself out of the school.'

'Except he didn't run,' Ada interrupted. 'He went home to Paris, and he ended up critically ill.'

Enzo looked up, holding up his cell phone. 'He's the kid who slit his own throat, isn't he?'

'Quoi?' Ada gasped, snatching the phone from him. She stared at the screen and began reading aloud. *'7e Arrondissement Police still are no further forward in explaining why a seventeen-year-old man attempted to cut his own throat in front of a police officer. A statement from Commander Demissy indicates the young man was troubled and may be also implicated in the death of his mother and another crime outside of Paris. She maintains there will be no further comment at this time.'* She handed the cell phone back to Enzo, turning back to Coco. 'They're talking about Elliot, aren't they?'

'We can't talk about an ongoing investigation,' Cedric replied.

'Bien sûr, it's Elliot,' Fabian interrupted. 'Why else would the Paris cops be here asking questions?'

'It makes no sense,' Ada cried.

'Exactly,' Enzo added. 'Elliot isn't an idiot. If he wanted to make a run for it, then he would have.' He looked at Coco. 'If he wanted to kill someone, he would have and he'd have gotten away with it. He's smarter than the rest of us, no doubt about it. And this entire throat cutting thing is…' he considered. 'Lazy and irrelevant.'

'Irrelevant?' Cedric questioned in surprise.

Enzo nodded. 'I'm not a flic, but if you ask me, you're looking at two different things.'

Coco frowned. There was something about what the green-haired punk was saying. Something which had been bothering her for days. She was missing something because she was looking in the wrong direction. She did not know what it meant, but it was a nagging thought she could not get rid of. 'What do you mean?' she asked.

He shrugged. 'I'm not a cop,' he repeated.

Coco studied him, trying to satisfy herself whether he knew more than he was letting on. She was sure of it, but she was also sure if she pushed him, he would most likely see it as a challenge and bait her. 'When was the last time any of you saw Manon?'

'Lundi,' the three students answered in unison.

'We had Monsieur Badeaux's class, and then supper, and we went to our rooms to get ready for the trip,' Ada added.

'Monsieur Badeaux?' Cedric questioned.

'He's the professor of biology,' directeurice Remy interjected. 'And the professor who accompanied the group on their trip. He alerted me of Manon's disappearance.'

Coco nodded. 'And did anything unusual happen in your last biology lesson?' she asked the students.

The three of them exchanged a brief look.

'She was being a bitch,' Enzo said, before adding. 'As per usual.'

'Enzo!' Fabian scolded. 'You can't say stuff like that.'

The green-haired young man shrugged. 'Sure I can. She was a

bitch. You know it, I know it, Ada knows, and Elliot knew it if he'd only admitted it to himself. She was a grade A using bitch.'

'Monsieur Garnier, I counsel you to use some decorum,' directeurice Remy interjected.

'Manon's dead, what does she care?' he retorted.

'I care,' Remy hissed, 'and so would her family. Therefore, I warn you, as I do on an almost daily basis, learn to conduct yourself as I instruct, or you will be returned to your parents in Tuscany. Do I make myself clear, *again*?'

He shrugged. Coco watched him and wanted to slap his constantly shrugging shoulders so it hurt every time he moved them. 'We were talking about the last time you saw Manon,' she continued.

'It was normal,' Fabian Auch said.

Ada Fortin nodded. 'Except…' she trailed off.

'Except?' Cedric asked keenly.

She chewed one of her braids. 'She was excited about the trip. TOO excited.'

Coco smiled. 'Because she knew she wasn't going.'

Ada returned the smile. 'That'd be my guess.'

'Then where was she going, and why didn't she go?' Coco asked.

'I don't know,' Ada replied. 'I'd be the last person she'd tell.'

Coco nodded. 'Then who would she tell? She must have had friends? When I was a kid,' she said with a wink, 'back in the dark ages, you understand. Popular girls were only popular because they travel in covens.'

'Not here,' Ada shook her head. 'No covens here. Our packs are small and full of swots.'

'It has always been our policy to have small groups,' directeurice Remy confirmed, 'for this exact reason. This isn't high school. The children are here because they are highly intelligent and destined to be the next generation of academics. They are not here to be in "cliques" or any such nonsense. I would not tolerate them, should they even try.'

Coco turned her head. 'But they're also young adolescents, and I've not met a single person in my life who isn't compromised by raging hormones in one way or another. Isn't that what happened here? Weren't Manon Houde and Elliot Bain consumed by what they assumed was love, but was really just lust. She with someone else, he wants to be with her. Isn't it how this all began?' She faced the three students. 'And you're telling me she never confided in any of you?'

They all shook their heads.

'And there was no one she would have confided in?'

'Manon was only really interested in men,' Ada Fortin sniffed. 'She didn't have time or interest in forging relationships with women.'

'There's no one in particular you can think of?' Coco pressed. 'No particular man?'

'She was close to Elliot,' Fabian Auch interjected. 'But I guess you've figured that out by now.'

Enzo scoffed. 'He was her puppy dog - no more, no less. He did her bidding, and she threw him scraps when it suited her to keep him interested.'

Ada laughed. 'You're only jealous because it used to be you.'

Enzo's face clouded, his mouth twisting into an angry pout, but he said nothing.

Coco studied him intently, realising there could be many people who had disliked Manon Houde. But were they angry enough to kill her? She could not be sure, but more importantly, she did not want to believe it. She nodded. 'Merci. D'accord, I think we're done here for the moment. But I'm sure I'll have more questions. But before I go, I'd like to speak with the biology teacher. What was his name, Monsieur Bordeaux?'

Remy's eyebrows knotted with irritation. 'His name is

Badeaux,' she snapped. Her face clouded. 'And he isn't here right now.'

Coco stared at her. 'What do you mean, he isn't here right now?'

Remy lowered her head. 'I'm afraid he took the news very badly, and he left the school when he heard what happened.'

'And went where?' Coco pressed, her nostrils flaring in irritation.

'Try *La Fontaine*,' Enzo Garnier. 'It's a bar where everyone goes when they want to forget.' He smiled. 'Or get laid.'

Directeurice Remy sighed wearily. 'Enzo, merci, behave yourself.'

Coco gave him a quizzical look and wondered whether it was the same bar Tomas Wall had entertained his lady friends, and been spotted by Manon Houde. She glanced at her watch. 'Well, it's after midday, so I'm allowed a liquid lunch,' she announced. 'Mais, before I do, I'd like to speak with the security guards.'

Remy's eyes flecked with anger. 'Why?'

Coco fixed her with her best, *do I really need to answer that?* stare and moved towards the door. She turned to Cedric. 'Take statements from the students and come get me in an hour,' she paused, 'or two.' She smiled at Directeurice Remy. 'Merci for your help,' she said with little conviction. 'I'll be back.'

Remy's lips pulled into a tight smile. 'I don't doubt it.'

12H00

Coco tightened her eyes, staring intently at the two security guards sitting in the anteroom immediately to the right of the entrance to École Privée Jeanne Remy. She was not entirely sure if her gaze was coming off as intimidating or suggesting she had constipation. Either way, she reasoned, they have to know I am not a woman to be messed with.

'I'd like to thank you for both coming in to speak with me,' she said. 'My name is Captain Charlotte Brunhild, and I'm from the *Commissariat de Police du 7e arrondissement* in Paris.' She turned her head slowly and deliberately. 'And your names?'

'Allain Muscrat,' replied a pimply-faced man in his thirties.

The second guard, a grey, much older man said. 'Martin Delan.'

'Bon,' she responded. 'Now tell me, which of you has been taking bribes?'

Martin Delan choked, his eyes popping. Coco reached forward, slapping his back hard. 'Steady on, old fella,' she cried, 'no need to get so upset. It's not the end of the world, is it?'

'What do you mean?' he spluttered. 'What are you talking about, bribes? I've never been so…'

She stopped him. 'I know, I know. I offend everyone, but it's the way of the world.' She turned to Allain Muscrat. 'And you, are you offended by my outrageous suggestion?'

'Bien sûr,' he answered gruffly. 'Anyway, you're crazy. That Bain kid admitted what he did and was kicked out of school.'

Coco nodded several times. 'You're a smart one, Monsieur, and you are indeed correct. But you see, the thing which is bothering me, the thing I can't quite my head around is - if this was a one-time thing, and Elliot Bain had somehow managed to trick his way out of here, well, that's understandable, non? I mean, a smart kid like him could have hacked into your system, I would imagine, or do it the old-fashioned way, distract you long enough to sneak someone out. However, there are two fatal flaws in that scenario. Do you know what they are?'

Martin Delan shook his head vigorously. 'Non, non, I don't,' he answered breathlessly.

'Well, since you're interested, I'll tell you,' Coco continued. 'Manon Houde never left the school last week. But she left before. Alors, it appears Elliot Bain confessed to something which didn't happen when he said it did, but had almost certainly happened on several occasions previously. Which just brings me back to one fact. Kids are lazy. He could do some fancy-schmancy work around of your computer system, and that might work long-term, but it runs the risk of getting discovered. There is a far better way. Good old-fashioned, lining someone's palms with cold hard cash.'

She began pacing, giving the words a chance to sink in. 'Ecouté,' she said finally. 'As far I'm concerned,' she paused before adding with dramatic effect, 'the police, that is. No crime has been committed. You might get into trouble with the old Directeurice, but you can get around that I'm sure.'

'We can?' Allain Muscrat said quickly, with evident keenness.

Coco smiled. 'Level with me, and I'll tell you,' she reasoned.

Martin Delan turned to his colleague. 'What did you do, Allain?'

'They pay us shit here,' Allain said after a few moments had passed. 'And all we see every day is rich kids rubbing our noses in it.'

'Directeurice Remy treats us very well,' Martin snapped.

'She treats us like we're servants. When was the last time she even spoke to you?'

Martin did not answer. He shook his head sadly. 'What have you done? *What have you done?*' his voice raised shrilly.

'Yeah, what have you done?' Coco repeated.

Allain hung his head. He lifted it slowly. 'Do you know how long it takes me to earn two hundred euros from one of the bratty kids who study here? Less than five minutes. I flick a switch. The door opens. I flick it again. I wait sixty seconds. I flick a switch. A door opens. I flick it again. Repeat a few hours later.'

Coco nodded. 'I'd have done it for fifty,' she said.

Allain smiled. 'I didn't see the harm in it. They're seventeen, eighteen years old. They're practically adults, anyway. What's the harm?'

'We're paid to protect them!' Martin exclaimed.

'We're paid to sit here and watch the front door,' Allain replied. 'I have a wife and three kids under the age of five. Two hundred euros isn't something I can afford to turn my nose up at.' He stared at Coco. 'How much trouble am I in?' He motioned behind him. 'Remy's going to fire me, isn't she?'

Coco shrugged. 'I can't answer that. What I can tell you is something you probably already know. This school is her life, and she will not want to be embarrassed.' She took a breath. 'And I suspect you both know a lot about the comings and goings of this school.' She paused. 'Manon Houde was murdered here. Of that, I am very sure.'

'I swear, we know nothing about that,' Allain replied. 'You see this room,' he extended his hands. 'We sit here, we open a door, we close a door, we do this, we do that, we basically do nothing other than sit in a starched uniform looking as if we are poised to protect precious brats from intrusion.'

'Allain,' Martin sighed wearily.

'We all wear uniforms,' Coco offered, 'in one way or another.' She pointed at her coat. 'I love this coat. It's ten years old, well, ten years old to me, at least. It's probably much older to someone else. But I bought it with a paycheque I couldn't afford to use. But I loved it. It's warm, it's kinda sexy, but I bought it. I saved up the entire month for it by having a cheese baguette for lunch - seventy-five cents from the local vendor. It was a good baguette, mais, I'd rather have had steak. But I made my choice. I wanted a second-hand coat I couldn't afford, and I didn't want it to interfere or take away from my kids, so I did what I had to do to make it work.' She tugged at the woollen lapels. 'This is my uniform.' She shook her head in confusion. 'What were we discussing?' She nodded. 'Ah, yeah. So, was it only students sneaking out?'

Allain frowned. 'Well, oui. This isn't a prison, although by the way the brats whine sometimes, you'd think it was. The students weren't allowed to go out without permission. As for everyone else, the adults, well, obviously they can come and go as they please.'

'And do they?' she asked.

Martin nodded. 'Most evenings the teachers go out into town.'

Coco pursed her lips. 'And do you record the comings and goings?' she questioned.

Martin pointed at a large open register on the security desk. 'Everyone has to sign in and out, for security and safety reasons. If there's a fire or something like that, we need to know exactly who is on the premises.'

'Ah-ha!' Coco exclaimed. She turned back to Allain. 'Did you watch who came and went each time?'

He shook his head determinedly. 'Non, not at all. I didn't want to know. I only ever saw the one boy.'

'Elliot Bain,' Coco said.

'Oui,' he replied. 'He paid me and told me when to open the door and when to close it. I never looked to see who was leaving.'

Coco turned her head, wondering what it could mean for her investigation. If students paid to leave the school in secret, then there was also the possibility so would a teacher. 'And the night of Manon Houde's disappearance, did you see Elliot?'

Allain nodded. 'Oui.'

Coco scratched her jaw. 'And you definitely didn't see who left?'

'Non, I told you. I didn't look. I never looked,' he responded.

'And what happened next?'

The security guard gulped several times. 'In the early hours of the morning, Elliot came to see me. He said Manon was gone and wouldn't be coming back. I went crazy, telling him she had to come back, that the Directeurice would be furious and we'd be in so much trouble,' Allain said. 'The kid just stared at me. He was so calm whereas I was freaking out. He said it would be fine, he'd sort it all out.'

'Sort it all out?' Coco repeated. 'What did he mean?'

'He said he would take the blame and tell Directeurice Remy it was all down to him, and that he had somehow got into the computer system and turned off the cameras.'

Coco frowned. 'And why do you think he did that?'

'What do you mean?' he asked.

'Well,' she continued. 'Why would he take the blame alone? I mean, unless he had some weird crush or soft-spot for you, all he had to do was tell the truth and you'd get most of the blame, non?'

Allain shrugged. 'I supposed I just thought he wanted to take the blame so that when it all blew over, we could go back to the same arrangement as before,' he reasoned. 'To be truthful, I didn't give it much thought. I was just relieved not to be dragged into it.'

Before Coco could ask any further questions, Cedric appeared in the doorway.

'The Directeurice is on her way,' he warned breathlessly. 'She says she wants to talk to you.'

Coco sensed the anxiety on the security guards' faces. 'I can't hang about. I'm off to the pub.' She smiled reassuringly. 'Don't worry, I'm sure you'll be fine.' She headed towards the door without looking back.

13H00

La Fontaine made Coco feel very sad, and very, very old. It was a bar which in daylight, echoed the shadows of the night before. She also instinctively knew that when evening came, it hid the shadows in fluorescent lights, obliterated by the cheap cocktails served. She found herself loving it and loathing it at the same time.

She turned her head slowly around the room. Despite it being early in the afternoon, it was already busy, filled with businessmen in suits, young women in very little and older women squeezed into outfits they really ought not to be wearing. She looked at an empty seat and table and wondered whether it was where Captain Tomas Wall had entertained some of his many women. She banished the thought from her head. It took her but a moment to spot the man she was looking for. She did not need to ask if it was him. His demeanour told everything she needed to know. Monsieur Badeaux, the biology professor at *École Privée Jeanne Remy* was nursing a whisky sour, and not his first judging by the line of them on the ring-stained table. *Great*, she thought, *he's already half-cut. I won't get anything sensible out of him.*

She waved her hand towards the admittedly unnaturally attractive young barman. Tight body. Blond hair pulled into a ponytail, blue eyes which could strip her of her clothes. 'Hey, sailor. Gin, lime, tonic, *heavy* on the gin,' she called out to him. He winked at her in acknowledgment in a way which made her want to both kiss him and punch him in equal measures. She flopped heavily onto the wooden barstool, struggling to get her feet above the ground. She stared at the man she assumed was Badeaux. 'Salut,' she said.

The man lifted his head slowly, his pupils dilated and he frowned with apparent confusion. 'Who are you?' he mumbled, the scotch breath crinkling Coco's face.

She took a moment to appraise him because it was all it took. Although he was crouched over the chair, she could tell he was tall, overly thin, with dull brown wavy hair and matching eyes. There was nothing wrong with him, she concluded, but he was most definitely nondescript. The sort of man who made a good roommate, but not one who would ever rock anyone's world. *I'd be happy with you, but you'd bore the tits off me.*

'What's your name?' she drawled, smiling at the barman as he planted her drink in front of her.

'Ruben,' he mumbled, 'Ruben Badeaux.'

She nodded. 'I'm Charlotte, but you can call me,' she paused as she considered. 'Charlotte.'

He nodded, seemingly confused. 'What you doing here, Charlotte?'

'What are *you* doing here?' she countered.

Badeaux considered his response. It took him some time. Coco drained her drink and indicated for her new friend behind the bar to refresh it. 'Tell me, Ruben,' she said, 'what's got you drowning your sorrows on a Vendredi afternoon?'

Badeaux stared at her. 'You're a cop, aren't you?'

Coco looked aghast. 'How on earth do you know that?' She pointed at her green-checked woollen coat. 'I hardly dress like one,' she sniffed, unsure how offended she should be.

He smiled. 'I saw you at the school.'

She nodded. 'Then you must have known I would have wanted to talk to you, and instead you came here and do what? Hide? Drown your sorrows?'

The teacher shrugged. 'I figured you'd find me eventually, and I realised I preferred it to be later.'

Coco frowned. 'Pourquoi?'

'Parce que,' he answered, but did not go further.

'Manon Houde's death has hit you hard then, has it?' Coco

asked.

He twisted his head, his hands flailing in front of him, knocking a glass over, the dregs and several ice cubes spilling. The barman appeared, handing Coco a drink with a sly wink. He wiped the table and left.

'I suppose it's only natural,' Coco continued. 'I mean, it would distress anyone to lose a student.'

'Manon was a lovely young woman,' Badeaux whispered.

Coco regarded him with surprise, because it was not the impression she had been given of the deceased. Could Badeaux be Manon's secret lover, the one Tomas Wall had seen her with. He certainly matched Wall's basic description of the man. She decided to risk the question. 'Did you ever bring Manon here?'

His face crumpled in confusion. 'What are you talking about?' He retorted, the slur of his voice not entirely covering the anxiety of his tone.

'Manon was seen in this bar,' she said, 'with a man, probably a secret lover.'

Badeaux snorted. 'And you think it was me?'

She shrugged. 'Why not? I find you here crying into your whisky glass. It's not difficult to put two and two together.'

'I'm sure Manon had many lovers,' he replied, but did not elaborate.

'Peut être,' Coco conceded, 'but how did she get out of the school?'

Badeaux laughed. 'You really don't think kids don't sneak out of the school all the time?'

'Not according to Directeurice Remy,' Coco replied.

He laughed again. 'Jeanne retires to bed after dinner each evening. By eight o'clock she's finished her fourth brandy and has passed out from the sleeping pills she takes for insomnia. She wouldn't know what the hell goes on in the school after dark.' He paused, laughing again, before adding, 'thank Dieu!'

Coco scratched her head. She needed to know if he knew about the security guards. 'But isn't there an elaborate security system to monitor who comes in and out of the school?'

'Sure there is,' he agreed. 'Monitored by a team of security guards who get paid a pittance to look after snotty-nosed brats who treat them like crap. You have to remember, Charlotte, most of the kids in that school have more money than the likes of us will ever see, and they're not afraid to splash it about when it comes to something like sneaking around.'

Coco considered this, realising there was something very wrong about it.

'It's surprisingly simple,' Badeaux went on, 'even if Remy checked the footage all she would see was a slight glitch while the guard turned the recorder off and on just long enough for whoever to sneak out and clear the reach of the security cameras.'

'And you knew about it, but did nothing?' Coco asked.

He shrugged nonchalantly. 'Why would I care? They're all over the age of consent. No harm, no foul, as far as I can see.'

'Except Manon Houde is dead.'

He took a sip of his drink. 'And if the rumours are to be believed, that wasn't because she left the school. It was because she stayed.'

He is right, Coco realised. And yet. And yet...

'How did she die?' he asked, as if he did not want to know the answer. 'There are some awful rumours going around the school about how she ended up in the freezer, and what they did to her body to get her into it.'

Before she could answer, Coco's cell phone buzzed. She picked it up, reading the screen. 'Can you wait here for a moment?' she asked Badeaux. 'I just have to make a call.'

Badeaux shrugged. 'Sure. I've got nowhere to go.'

13H30

Coco stepped outside the bar and pulled out her phone, quickly tapping in a telephone number.

'Etienne Martine.'

'Ah, dear Etienne. This is Coco. How's life in Montgenoux?' Coco asked. 'I miss you crazy kids.'

'It's okay. We've had a slow couple of days in Montgenoux,' Etienne retorted. 'No serial killers for a day or two. Hugo said to say hi, by the way.'

'He's not mad at me for asking for your help with the samples?'

'Non, bien sûr he isn't. He said he'd do the same, if he had to.'

'Give him a big kiss for me,' Coco said, 'and I mean it. It's good to keep Ben on his toes.' She took a breath. 'Alors, you can't have gotten my results already, can you?'

'Just preliminary, I'm afraid. But I managed to pull a few strings, and what they've found so far is certainly interesting. I scanned Dr. Bernstein's autopsy report, and it seems the deceased had some kind of catastrophic fall, which could have been accidental or the result of a blow to the head.'

'Something like that,' Coco answered.

'I can't be certain, but there may be an explanation why your girl may have fallen and hit her head.'

Coco's eyes widened. 'And what might that be?'

'The blood test indicates that she was poisoned,' Etienne replied.

Coco gasped. 'Poisoned?' she repeated.

'Oui,' he replied. 'There were high levels of compounds that would indicate ingestion of a plant called Belladonna.'

'Belladonna?' Coco questioned. 'Doesn't that mean "beautiful woman?"'

'Yeah,' Etienne replied. 'It's a plant more commonly known as "Deadly nightshade." It's been used for thousands of years for a lot of things like pain relief, a muscle relaxant, those sorts of things. Often it can be mistaken for the person being sexually aroused, flushed cheeks, dilated pupils…'

Coco closed her eyes, wondering whether she had imagined it, but she was sure when she had first seen Manon Houde in the freezer, it had appeared as if there was blusher on her cheeks.

'But more importantly,' Etienne continued, 'someone who has ingested Belladonna is likely to have a myriad of side-effects. For example, they may experience a loss of balance, staggering, and slurred speech. They could appear drunk or high, and they could certainly fall and hurt themselves quite badly.' He paused. 'All that being said, the other side of the coin is, the levels of Belladonna in the poor girl's system would have been enough to kill her, anyway.'

'Then she was murdered?' Coco asked.

'I can't answer that,' Etienne responded. 'All I can tell you, is all it takes is for a single leaf of it to be ingested for it to be fatal.' He took a breath. 'I'm not a pathologist, but as far as I can tell from the autopsy report, the fall killed her, but with those levels of Belladonna, she would have likely died, anyway.'

'And then someone threw her in the freezer,' Coco added. 'Where on earth would someone get this Belladonna?'

'It's surprisingly easy,' Etienne answered. 'It grows easily, and it's very hard to discern what it is, and how dangerous it might be.'

'It grows easily, you said?' Coco questioned, immediately thinking of the dense trees and undergrowth which lined the path to *École Privée Jeanne Remy* and enclosed it. She looked at Wall. 'There's a lot of trees and stuff around the school.'

Wall shrugged. 'Yeah, maybe.'

'Don't you work with Ebba Blom?' Etienne asked.

'Yeah,' Coco replied. 'She's a blast,' she said with as much cheeriness as she could muster with her hangover.

He laughed. 'Her manners could do with a little refining, but I've worked with her before. One of her many fields of expertise is botany. All I'm saying is, if you need someone to sniff out Belladonna, she might just be your girl. Do you want me to give her a call and ask her to come and assist you?'

'You're a doll, Etienne,' Coco said. 'Did they find anything else?'

'Non. There were the usual traces you'd find in Manon Houde's blood. A little bit of alcohol, even cocaine, but nothing which rings alarm bells or was excessive enough to have caused her death.'

'But she was poisoned,' Coco said. 'And we're sure of that?'

'You'll need to wait for an official report, but unless she picked the Belladonna herself, I can't think of how else so much of it would have ended up in her system,' Etienne replied. 'And it's not something people who choose to end their own lives would necessarily go for. It's not a pleasant end.'

Coco turned back towards the bar. 'Then let's go and find ourselves some weeds. Merci, Etienne, love to you all in Montgenoux. I may be in touch again, I could use your help.'

'Anytime, Captain,' Etienne responded. 'Au revoir.'

13H45

Coco moved her head to the side in an attempt to study the face of Monsieur Badeaux, to understand if he was asking a question he already knew the answer to. She had returned to the bar after her conversation with Etienne Martine and ordered another drink. She needed to understand what was happening, but there was little of it which made sense to her. She studied Manon's teacher, and perhaps lover. His eyes were already bloodshot and his face carried a shadow of guilt, but she had experienced enough to understand guilt and sorrow were emotions often inextricably linked. 'There's evidence which suggests Manon was poisoned, but I'm afraid at this moment, we can't be sure how directly it was involved in her death.'

His eyebrows knotted in confusion. 'Poisoned?'

She nodded.

'What kind of poison?'

Coco stared at him. 'We believe it was Belladonna.'

He nodded. His reaction surprising her because it was the opposite of Remy's. 'You don't seem surprised?'

He shrugged. 'It's quick, easy to administer and very effective. A very clean way to murder someone.'

'You sound almost impressed, Monsieur Badeaux,' she said.

His eyes widened. He pushed himself back in his chair. 'I'm drunk, my inhibitions are down.'

Coco laughed. 'Funny. When I'm drunk, I don't know my inhibitions are down until I end up in someone's bed, or pregnant, usually both.'

'Are you suggesting I'm lying?'

She shook her head. 'I'm suggesting nothing,' she shot back. 'I'm investigating a murder, that's all. And I have to wonder about everything people say to me.' She paused, deciding to try another tack. 'Tell me, where would a person go about getting some Belladonna?'

He shrugged again. 'It's easy enough. It grows easily, and it grows naturally.'

'At the school?'

His eyes flashed, and in that moment, Coco thought she saw something other than drunkenness. Was it concern? 'We grow lots of plants in the gardens,' he answered after he had composed himself. 'Mainly herbs for food, but sometimes other plants which we use for teaching purposes.'

'Poisons such as Belladonna?' Coco pushed.

'I couldn't answer that,' he replied quickly.

'Can't or won't?'

'What are you asking me, Charlotte?' he snapped. 'Are you asking me if I poisoned Manon with Belladonna?'

'It's a start,' she retorted.

He shook his head. 'Non, it isn't.'

Coco frowned. His head had dropped, and she realised she had hit a wall with him. 'What about Elliot Bain? How did he get mixed up in all of this?' she asked instead.

Badeaux finished his drink and gestured to the barman for another. 'Charlotte?'

Coco finished her own drink and nodded. 'Why not?'

'Deux,' Badeaux mouthed to the barman. 'Aren't you on duty? Shouldn't you be drinking water?'

She smiled. 'Probably. I'm not always good at doing what I'm supposed to do, and technically I'm only really on duty in Paris. Here I'm, well, I suppose I'm on a bit of a field trip.' She paused. 'So, about Bain?'

He nodded. 'Rumour has it, Bain was the middleman between the students with the cash, students who didn't want to risk getting caught. They paid Elliot, and he paid the security guards.'

'No doubt taking a cut for himself.'

'Oui,' Badeaux replied. 'I know money was tight for him at home, so he used to send money to his mother.'

Coco frowned again. 'Then how did it all go wrong? How did he end up getting busted and expelled?'

'Because we were supposed to be going on the trip the next morning,' he answered, 'and when she didn't turn up, I raised the alarm. Remy went berserk, of course, so Elliot came forward right away and confessed his involvement.'

'Except he wasn't involved, and Manon hadn't left the school. Why would he confess?'

'Because he murdered her,' Badeaux reasoned, 'and he wanted to make his escape.'

'That seems to be the popular opinion,' Coco retorted, reticence clear in her voice.

'But you don't buy it?' the teacher asked, confused.

She did not answer immediately. 'I don't know what I buy, other than something stinks about the whole thing,' she answered after a few moments. 'Why did he confess?'

Badeaux cleared his throat. 'Peut être he imagined Directeurice Remy would be lenient on him, especially when Manon came back unharmed. Remy is a bitch, but she's not stupid. The school is her world - she never married, she has no children, no family. The last thing she would want is a scandal of any kind.' He continued, warming to his theory. 'Non, it makes perfect sense. Elliot must have assumed Manon would come back and the two of them would get a rap across the knuckles, and the whole sorry business would have been swept under the rug.'

'You could be right,' Coco conceded. 'But I think with such a high-profile student like Manon gone, Remy had no choice but to blow the whistle, and scholarship kid Elliot was expendable.' She stared at Badeaux. 'Were you there when he was expelled?'

He nodded.

'And how did he seem?'

He appeared confused by her question. 'What do you mean?'

'I mean,' she continued, 'was he angry? Frustrated? Contrite?'

Badeaux considered for a moment. 'I wouldn't say he was angry, or sad even, he seemed almost…' he trailed off as if searching for the right word.

Coco leaned forward, believing what came next might just be important.

'I'd say he almost seemed relieved,' Badeaux concluded finally.

That's it, Coco exhaled. *Relieved.* She still was having trouble imagining the olive-skinned cherub capable of cold-blooded murder. Not that she was prone to naivety. The last year had told her not to trust anyone, and she imagined Elliot Bain was capable of a lot of things nobody would imagine, just like anyone else in the world. *We all wear masks to hide our true selves.* It was what happened next in his timeline which troubled her. Run. She got that scenario. Go home to mother, she got that too, but to kill her, and then to attempt to kill himself, did not fit for her. *Find out who made me do this.* It made no sense to her, but of course, she knew once she understood what she was missing, it would make perfect sense. She had to believe in the process, or else the bleakness of what she saw on a day-to-day basis would render her useless as a police officer.

'Relieved,' she repeated. 'What do you mean by that?'

'It's hard to say,' he replied. 'Other than he didn't try to put up a fight. He didn't try to defend himself, or make excuses. He was just resigned, eager almost to get out of here.' He sipped his drink. 'Which again makes you think, knowing what we do know, he had a good reason to escape.' He pushed himself to his feet. 'Gotta take a piss,' he mumbled, staggering away from the table.

The barman appeared with their drinks. Coco smiled gratefully. A thought popping into her head. 'Hey, sailor. Can I ask you a question?' she asked him.

The young man laughed. 'Sure, but my shift doesn't finish until midnight,' he said with a wink.

Coco's eyes widened with surprise. *You've still got it, kid.* She studied him. He was thin and slight, but with a firm body squeezed into a too-tight white t-shirt. He was also barely twenty-years old. 'As flattering and as appealing as the thought might be, I've got underwear older than you, jeune homme,' she added with the slightest trace of sadness. 'Non, what I wanted to ask you was. Have you seen this girl?' She reached into her bag, picked up her cell phone and scrolled through some pictures until she found a shot of Manon Houde.

He leaned forward, engulfing her in the scent of youth. She fought the urge to lean forward and inhale him.

'Yeah, sure,' he said. 'Not for a week or two, but yeah, I've seen her here before.'

Coco nodded. She was not really surprised. Wall had already confirmed he had seen her in the bar. 'And didn't you worry about serving a minor?'

He laughed. 'What are you, a cop?'

Coco pulled out her police ID and flashed it in front of him.

He laughed. 'A flic. Cool. That makes you even more interesting.'

'Every time I have sex, I get pregnant,' she blurted out, immediately biting her tongue.

He laughed again. 'There are ways to prevent that, y'know?'

'Not me. My ovaries see it as a challenge,' she countered. She shook her head. 'Back to the girl. She was a minor.'

He shook his head. 'Non, she wasn't. I checked her ID. She was nineteen.'

'Non, Manon Houde was seventeen,' Coco replied.

His eyes widened, staring at the photo again. 'That's the girl who was murdered at the fancy school? I had no idea. They mentioned her name on the radio, but that wasn't the name on her ID, so I didn't put the two together.'

'And I bet you don't remember the name on the ID?'

'Actually, I do,' he answered proudly. 'I remember it was Amélie. Amélie something. I don't remember the surname, and I only remember that because it was my grandmother's favourite movie,' he answered.

'And you're sure?'

He nodded. 'Positive.' He shrugged. 'It's not so unusual. People use different names all the time. Especially in places like this - lying about their age or their marital status, that sort of thing,' he added with a flirty wink. 'I'm single, by the way.'

Coco ignored him. 'And this girl Manon-slash-Amélie, did you see her with anyone?'

The barman pointed behind her. She glanced over her shoulder, Ruben Badeaux was staggering back from the toilet, his face a ghostly pallor.

'Ask your friend. He certainly seemed to know Amélie well. But he wasn't the only one. She was a fun girl, it seemed. Too young for me,' he added, 'my tastes run more vintage.' He smiled at her again. A perfect smile, with perfect teeth and a perfect face.

Vintage. Coco gulped. She shook the despair suddenly overwhelming her away, forcing herself to concentrate on what lay ahead of her. It did not surprise her to imagine Manon Houde had been a sociable young woman, but she could not reconcile how it would help the investigation. She rummaged in her bag, retrieving a piece of paper and a pen. 'Merci, for your help. Write your number down in case I have any more questions.'

The server grinned, bending over, the outline of his buttocks against denim causing her to swoon. 'Even if you don't have any questions, call me anyway.'

Don't bloody well tempt me, she thought but did not say anything, stuffing the number into her bag and watching him slink back towards the bar.

Badeaux sank back into his chair. 'Désolé for being gone so long,' he mumbled. 'I got sick. I guess I'm not used to drinking so much. I think I'd better go back to the school and sleep it off.'

Coco nodded. She wanted to question him, but she understood she would get little sense out of him until he had slept off the whisky. All the same, she made a mental note to make sure Captain Wall placed a police officer outside the school to ensure there were no more random wanderings.

'Let's go,' she said, 'I'll walk you back.'

He stood again, stumbling and almost falling. She linked his arm through hers and placed her arm around him. His body was a dead weight against her. 'Great,' she muttered, dragging him towards the exit.

14H30

Directeurice Remy gestured widely at Coco as she pulled Ruben Badeaux through the door, her eyes darting wildly around the foyer as if she was ensuring no one was witnessing the drunken teacher stumbling across the antique Chinese rugs, still nursing a drink in his hands and spilling most of it. Coco spread her hands as if to say, *nothing to do with me.* Remy glared at her with a clear message, *I don't believe you.* Coco looked around. They were not alone. A smattering of students were watching with clear amusement. Remy spun on her heels, placing hands on boney hips, sending a message which made the students leave the foyer in a desperate hurry. All apart from Enzo Garnier who lingered on the staircase, his gaze challenging.

One of the security guards ran into the foyer, pulling Badeaux to him and dragging him towards the staircase. Remy watched, her face stoic and full of irritation. She said nothing, but the way she looked at Coco, her feelings were clear.

Coco shrugged. She was used to disappointing people. 'What can you tell me about Belladonna?' she asked.

Remy frowned. 'You mean the plant, deadly nightshade? What about it?'

'Because that's what killed Manon, obviously,' Enzo answered with a smirk, 'or else she wouldn't be asking.'

'How do you know that?' Coco quickly asked, immediately regretting it. 'What makes you think that?' she corrected herself, realising it was too late. Enzo had turned and was making his way up the staircase. Remy sighed in despair.

Coco turned to her. 'Who is in charge of the gardens?' she asked.

'Jacques. Jacques Anders,' Remy answered. 'He comes in

once, twice, three times a month, depending on the season.'

Coco nodded. 'And when was he last here?'

She shook her head. 'I couldn't say, I'd have to check. I rarely see him unless there's a problem.'

'I'd like his address, if you would,' Coco said.

Remy pulled out her cellphone, her fingers moving swiftly across the keyboard. '125 Rue Moraine,' she answered after a moment. 'It's about a ten-minute walk from here.'

Coco nodded. 'Merci. D'accord, I think we're done here for the moment.'

15H15

The afternoon air hit Coco hard as she made her way from the school. She nodded towards the police officer who had been dispatched to stand sentry by the entrance. 'No one leaves without my permission,' she stated.

He nodded and moved in front of the red door.

'Do you know where I can find Rue Moraine?' she asked him. She had to wait for Ebba to arrive from Paris to assist in the search for Belladonna, so had decided she would try and track down the gardener, a man, she hoped, might just have some answers.

He pointed ahead. 'Just follow this road for about five minutes, take the first left, and then Rue Moraine is about another five minutes on the left. Small bungalows.'

'Merci,' Coco smiled. 'Don't take this the wrong way, but I hope you have a really boring rest of your day.' She moved away from him, stuffing her hands into her pockets, her fingers touching something sticky which she did not have the heart to check. Instead, she trudged along the tree-lined pavement, allowing her mind time to rest. She hoped it would give it a chance to reboot and give her the clue she so desperately needed. She could not bear the thought of an unsolved case. Not because she was worried about her career. That had never bothered her. She had spent a part of her career after maternity leave as an investigator for an insurance company, and she had enjoyed it immensely. However, despite the salary, the hours were unconscionable for a woman with children. But it had taught her one ridiculously important fact. She had choices and that had opened her eyes. *I can be a good cop, or I can be good at something else if I have to.* She had carried it with her and it had informed her choices. She would do her best to speak for the disadvantaged.

She continued walking, forcing her head back into the current investigation. She needed to understand what she was missing, because the only thing she was sure of was that she was missing something. And it was something important. Something crucial, which would blow open the entire case.

She took a moment to try to re-evaluate. Her instinct was telling her Manon Houde had been murdered. She could not extend it to believing Elliot Bain was responsible, not quite, not yet. She knew she should. There was evidence linking him, and yet, and yet… She felt weary. It was enough. She could not believe Elliot Bain was innocent based upon his rosebud lips and his physical similarity to her own son. But it was what it was. All she had was her gut.

Take a step back, girl, she told herself. *Do what you do best. Think.* What were the alternative theories? The Belladonna could be a potential red herring. A scientific experiment gone wrong? She understood the biology lessons may have led to experiments which could be dangerous, but if that had gone wrong, if Manon Houde had died because of a foolish experiment, then the resulting scenario was something she did not understand, because it had to have meant there was more than one person involved in the cover up. Other than that, there was evidently a very different scenario they could believe in. Manon Houde had left the school to disappear with one of her apparent lovers. It bothered Coco that Manon Houde's previous track record had included a similar scenario. Had she merely repeated her past, or had someone seized upon it, using it as a chance to cover up another crime. Coco shook her head. The only thing she was certain of at that moment was Elliot Bain was front and centre involved.

A woman stepped in front of Coco. 'Are you lost?' she asked. She was an elderly woman, with silver-grey hair and a kindly face, worn by the sun.

'Where am I?' Coco asked, confused by the sudden interruption to her train of thought.

'This is Rue Moraine,' the woman replied. She pointed over Coco's shoulder toward *École Privée Jeanne Remy*. 'Did you come from the school?'

Coco laughed. 'Non. I'm a police officer from Paris.'

Her eyebrows knotted. 'A police officer from Paris?' she repeated.

Coco nodded.

'Pourquoi?'

'There has been a murder,' Coco answered.

The woman nodded. 'I heard about the child. A tragedy.'

'Did you know her?' Coco asked.

The woman pulled her coat across her chest. 'Non, not at all. I heard talk of the rich kids running riot in town, mais non, I don't imagine I have met any of them, nor would I want to. Why are you here now? What are you looking for?'

Coco turned her head around the street slowly. There was nothing fancy about Rue Moraine, but it appeared to her to be a perfectly decent place to live. Quiet and unassuming. And boring, perhaps, but a home where a family could live in peace, comfort and safety.

'I'm looking for a man by the name of Jacques Anders,' Coco said.

She looked surprise. 'Aren't we all? Mais, why would a young woman be looking for Jacques?'

Coco's eyes flashed, enjoying someone calling her young, for once.

'I knew he'd end up in trouble,' she said, making the sign of the cross across her chest.

'Trouble?' Coco questioned.

She smiled. 'He's a man. They always end up in trouble, in one way or another.'

Coco chuckled. 'I can't say I disagree,' she said, 'but why did you say, "aren't we all?" Are you saying Jacques is missing?'

She shrugged. 'Peut être he's missing,' she agreed, before laughing, 'or he's at a bar, or a racetrack,' she moved her shoulders slowly. 'Who can say? I was friends with his wife, and on her deathbed she made me promise I'd look in on him, bring him the occasional meal to make sure the old fool eats properly sometimes. Which I do, mais,' she shrugged again, 'he's a man, and he's,' she laughed, 'a man. He keeps his own time, and he does what he wants and he has no interest in taking advice from anyone else.'

'I get ya, sister,' Coco replied. 'Men are pigs.' She scratched her head. 'The question is, is there anything untoward about it? I mean, are you worried? Is it unusual for him not to be around? And more importantly, how long has he been gone?'

The woman stared at her, fear clouding her face. 'Why do the Parisian police care about Jacques?' She was suspicious suddenly, and protective, Coco could tell.

'Hell, we care about everyone,' Coco responded. 'Ecouté, level with me. I have to get back to Paris. I just want to chat with the old man. If he's off on a jolly somewhere, then that's great; I'm happy for him. But if there's something off, I need to know so that I can try to help him.' She paused, waiting a moment for her statement to sink in. 'Do I make myself clear?'

'He comes and goes,' she responded.

'Which house is his?'

The woman turned, pointing towards a doorway a few houses down the road. 'The one that a woman hasn't touched in a long time,' she sniffed.

Coco nodded. 'And how do you know he's not been around for a while?' she asked.

The woman grimaced, pursing lips in irritation. 'He never thanks me, but whenever I make my own evening meal, I make extra and leave it on his doorstep. It's the least I can do. His wife was a wonderful woman, and I promised her.'

Coco looked towards the door. 'And he hasn't collected them?'

She shook her head. 'Not for a few days.' She shrugged. 'As I said, he's probably gone off on a fishing trip, he usually tells me, mais sometimes he does not. He thinks I interfere,' she added with a loud tut.

Coco nodded. 'Do you have a key?'

'Non,' the old woman replied. 'We're not *that* close. But there used to be one under the plant pot outside the front door. He never cleans, so it's probably still there.'

They moved in silence towards Jacques Anders' house, the old lady, surprisingly sprightly, a half-step behind Coco.

Coco lifted the plant pot, crying triumphantly after she spotted a key. 'Stay back,' she warned, 'just in case.'

'Bien sûr,' the neighbour replied as if she had absolutely no intention of doing so.

Coco placed the key in the door. It turned, and she pushed the door open, stale air engulfing her, causing her to take a step back. It told her the house had not been aired for several days. She took a deep breath, exhaling slowly because she knew her next breath could be difficult. She sucked in the air, and then again. There was nothing but staleness and a smell which reminded her of just men. Sweaty, dirty men who did little to cover the stench, they seemingly had no ability to register in their own nostrils.

'Jacques?' the old lady called out, inching forward, fear clear in her shaky voice.

'He's not here,' Coco said with confidence.

'Are you sure? He could be… he could be…' the old woman said. 'It happened before two doors down. He was dead a week before we realised. And oh, the smell! Mon Dieu!'

Coco nodded. 'He could be dead. But he isn't dead here.' She moved further into the small home. 'All I can be sure of, is he hasn't been here for a while.' She looked around the spare room. 'And I hate to say it, but it bothers me.'

The old woman suddenly looked teary. 'Where on earth is Jacques?' she cried.

Coco looked around the empty house. 'Let's just hope he's fishing.'

17H00

'Everything looks the same to me,' Coco moaned. 'Like weeds, or worse,' she grimaced, as if she could not bring herself to say the word, '*salad.*'

Tomas Wall tipped his head to towards his left shoulder. 'We've attracted an audience.'

Coco squinted to see what he was talking about. At the top of the staircase, a small crowd had gathered outside *École Privée Jeanne Remy,* led by the directeurice herself, arms folded angrily across her chest. Coco turned her back on them.

'Well, Ebba, you found the bellamanon?' she asked.

The Swedish forensic tech raised herself to her feet, face crinkling in Coco's direction as if she was assessing whether Coco was being stupid or just ignorant. She tutted, seemingly satisfied Coco was being both. 'I've only just began my examination,' she sniffed, 'and these things can't be hurried, not if you want me to do it properly.'

Coco glanced around, frowning. 'I mean, how would such a thing even grow, and why?'

Cedric held up his cell phone. 'I've been reading about it. It can grow naturally, or it can be planted. Even though it's highly poisonous, it can be cultivated for medicinal reasons.'

Coco turned back to face the school. 'Or for education purposes.'

Wall moved next to her. 'You think the school uses it?'

She shrugged. 'Why not? If it really is a super drug like everyone seems to think, what better place to use it than at a school specialising in the sciences?'

Ebba shook her head. 'It wouldn't just be grown like that. This sort of thing is highly regulated. It's not just the leaves. The berries are highly poisonous, and they're definitely an attractive nuisance for birds and other wildlife.'

Coco snorted. 'Attractive nuisance - that should be my dating profile description.'

'Well, the nuisance part of it, at least,' Ebba muttered under her breath.

Coco ignored her. 'The only thing I understand about the phrase, "highly regulated" is that if someone wants to break the rules, they can do so.'

'We can ask the school if they used it,' Wall offered.

'At this point, I'm not sure I'd believe a word of what anyone in the damn school has to say,' Coco retorted. 'Either way, if we find it, someone could have planted it to commit murder, or at least to experiment with it. As everyone keeps speculating, we know nothing for sure. This could be a whole sex-game gone wrong scenario.'

'Ah-ha!' Ebba exclaimed. She ran a stubby hand across her shaved head, her pupils wide with excitement. 'Look over there, where the staircase takes a winding turn, right in the corner, next to the old oak tree.'

Coco squinted to see what she was pointing at. 'More weeds.'

Ebba shook her head. 'Belladonna isn't a weed. It's something altogether more beautiful.'

Coco regarded the tech with surprise. 'Well, I never imagined something so mundane would rock your world, girl.'

Ebba moved away from her. 'On the contrary, anything which can be used to simply and effectively get rid of someone without them knowing what's coming, is right up my street. Something you can hide in a salad or other food, brilliant.'

Coco shuddered. 'Remind me not to go to your place for dinner.'

Wall stepped near the oak tree. 'What makes you think this is Belladonna, Ebba?'

She lowered herself onto her haunches. She pointed. 'See this long, thin branches, with oval-shaped leaves with smooth edges and pointed ends?'

He nodded. 'Oui, mais, it looks like anything else around here.'

'My point exactly,' Coco mouthed, 'but no one ever listens to me.'

Ebba ignored her and continued. 'The leaves are growing on the stalks in an alternate pattern and then look at those flowers. They're purple and green and bell-shaped, and then you have the berries, shiny and black. All of these together confirm we are looking at deadly nightshade. Right here, just next to the school.'

'Is there anyway to be sure Manon Houde died from this particular bad boy?' Coco asked.

Ebba shook her head. 'Not really, but I guess it's not too much of a stretch to assume we're looking at the murder weapon.'

Coco stared at the nondescript plant. 'We all know what assuming anything means.'

Ebba stared at her. 'I have no idea what you're talking about.'

Coco waved her hand dismissively. 'Something about you making an assumption about my big ass.' She sighed wearily. 'We have a plant, granted, a deadly plant. We have no way of linking it to Manon Houde's death, and unless we find any fingerprints, I can't see how we can prove who planted it, or even if anyone did.' She shook her head, blue tips falling over her shoulders. 'A defence avocat would have a field day arguing this one out of court.'

'Then we have nothing,' Cedric said.

Coco turned back to face the school. Directeurice Jeanne Remy was still watching them from the top of the stairway, her hands wrapped tightly around her body, her face pinched, and set in an angry glare. 'We have something,' she answered. 'We have someone in the school who knows what the hell happened.'

Tomas Wall's cell phone beeped. He looked at it. 'Pieter

Houde has arrived. He's waiting for me at the station.'

Coco gave him a sympathetic look. 'Good luck with that,' she said.

'Can you come?' he asked softly.

She tilted her head, a pleased smile appearing on her face. 'Sure I can.' She turned to Ebba. 'And what about you, are you done?'

Ebba smiled. 'I'll be here a while. I'll take some samples from this beauty just in case you have anything to compare it with later.'

Coco turned to Cedric. 'She actually sounds excited. About plants.' She shook her head. 'Can you stay with her and make sure she gets back to Paris okay?'

'I don't need a babysitter,' Ebba snapped.

'And I'm not a babysitter,' Cedric snapped louder.

Coco waved her hands. 'Oh, just have sex you two and be done with it, all this pent up sexual tension is making me…' she considered. 'Either nauseous or horny. Either way. I have no desire to get pregnant again.' She swept away, moving onto the stairs. She noticed Remy was still at the top, staring down at them. 'Anyway, let's get this show on the road and find out who's zoomin' who. I'll start with the old Directeurice.' She nodded at Wall. 'I'll meet you at the station, I just have a few things to take care of, okay?'

Cedric shook his head. 'I'll never understand you. *Jamais.*'

17H30

Coco made her way slowly up the stairs, all the time conscious of Directeurice Remy's irritated glare. 'You're looking swell, Directeurice Remy,' she called out, breathless.

Remy cleared her throat. 'I must express my concern regarding your unauthorised search of school property.'

Coco shrugged. 'We weren't searching school property, we were just making sure you follow the poop and scoop legislation.'

The directeurice's face crumpled in confusion. 'We don't have any dogs here.'

Coco clapped her hands. 'And that's why you're going to get a big gold star for exemplary scooping.'

Remy sighed. 'You really are the strangest woman, Captain Brunhild.'

Coco smiled. 'I get that a lot, Directeurice Remy.' She tapped the side of her head. 'Which has got me to thinking. What if I'm the only sane person and y'all are the strange ones?'

Remy shook her head in disbelief. 'What were you looking for?' she questioned.

'I think you know the answer to that,' Coco replied.

'Is this about Belladonna?' the Directeurice asked. 'You can't be saying you found it here?'

'It would appear so,' Coco said. 'Does that surprise you?'

'Bien sûr, it does,' she shot back. 'As you know, we are a science based institution. We do work with poisons for educational purposes, but it is highly controlled and regulated.' She considered. 'Although it is possible it grew naturally, in point of fact.'

'Maybe, but that wouldn't explain how did it ended up in Manon Houde, would it?' Cedric interpreted.

'I can't answer that, obviously,' Remy countered.

Coco exhaled. 'I don't think there's a thing that goes on at this school that you're not aware of Directeurice Remy,' she stated. 'And nor do I think for a second you are being completely honest with me.'

Remy glared at her. 'I think I have been more than patient with you and your… *ways*, Captain Brunhild,' she said with clear contempt. 'And I find that I have reached the end of my patience. This would not have been allowed to progress this way if Tomas was in charge, as he should have been.'

Coco took a step back. There was something about the way in which Remy spoke his name which bothered her. It was not just in the obvious way, it was something else. Something altogether different. It was not necessarily the tone of a lover, more from someone who clearly thought she was in charge.

Remy cleared her throat again. 'Again, I ask what you were doing on my land?'

Coco shrugged. 'I'd love to, mais I'm afraid I have to go the police station. You see, Pieter Houde is waiting to see his daughter.'

'Pieter is here?' Remy asked, her voice rising shrilly. 'Why wasn't I informed?'

Coco shrugged again. 'Beats the shit out of me. Maybe he's pissed at you.' She stepped back down the stairs, waving cheerfully at the Directeurice. 'See you soon!'

18H30

Coco leaned against the wall outside *Commissariat de Police Saint-Germain-en-Laye* and reached inside her oversized antique Chanel bag, retrieving a packet of cigarettes. She opened the lid and counted. *Quinze*. She had rationed herself to no more than four a day. To hell with it, she thought and lit one. She opened her cell phone and searched for a number. She found it and hit the call button.

'Coco,' Etienne Martine answered.

'Etienne,' she said, sucking on the cigarette, closing her eyes to stop the smoke from getting in them. 'I was just calling to say merci beaucoup for your help with the forensic reports. You really saved me there.'

Etienne laughed. 'Always a pleasure. What else do you need?'

'What makes you think I need anything?' she replied, not entirely convincingly. She sighed. 'How busy are you? I don't want to piss off Hugo, by hogging you.'

'I don't think it's easy to piss off Hugo,' he replied, 'and anyway, as I said earlier, believe it or not, all is quiet in Montgenoux at the moment. What do you need?' he asked again.

She paused, unsure she should say aloud what she was thinking. 'You know I'm investigating a murder at *École Privée Jeanne Remy*? Well, a couple of things have come up, and I need some background checks. In particular the teachers, especially one by the name of Ruben Badeaux. There's also a gardener, Jacques Anders. I've just been to visit him and he seems to have gone off the radar. Bearing in mind Manon Houde's cause of death, his disappearance is certainly suspicious. And then there's an email address, BIGFRITZ1999 at GMAIL dot COM. Can you see if you can find out where that came from or who it might be? I realise I'm asking a lot of you, but Hugo always tells me he couldn't do his job without you, and I don't really have my own Etienne yet.'

'As flattered as I am,' he reasoned, 'can't Cedric do any of this for you?'

'He could,' she replied, 'and he should, except…'

'Except?'

'Except, I was rather hoping for your special knack of discovering secrets people don't want discovering,' she answered. 'And, one of them is a little delicate.'

'You mean it's a cop?'

'Oui, and I feel foolish even asking, but because I am asking, I wanted to make sure nothing came of it, if nothing comes of it, if you know what I mean. If I asked Cedric, it would sort of become official and I don't want it to, unless it has to.'

Etienne took a deep breath. 'We both know how gossip can get out of hand,' he said. 'I'm glad you came to me. I'll run background checks on anyone I can find who has any connection with École Privée Jeanne Remy.' He paused. 'And the flic?'

Coco looked towards the *Commissariat*. 'His name is Captain Tomas Wall, and he works at *Commissariat de Police Saint-Germain-en-Laye.*'

'Leave it with me,' Etienne said quickly. 'Take care, Coco. Au revoir.'

19H00

Pieter Houde extended his hand. Coco took it. It was ice cold and firm, and he squeezed hers with too much pressure. It was like the rest of his body, wide and muscular. 'It's good to put a… a face to the name,' he addressed her as if he was sure of no such thing.

Coco nodded, wishing she had run a brush through her hair but relieved she had at least had the foresight to eat half a dozen mints. 'I'm very sorry for your loss,' she said.

He waved his hands as if the words bothered him. She nodded. 'But I'm more sorry that there's nothing more useful I can say, other than what has happened to you is shit, and no parent should ever have to go through it. No matter how annoying our kids might be. Because in the end, all we have is regret for every cross word, every irritated comment we exchange.'

His mouth twisted into a reluctant smile. 'I loved my daughter,' he said, 'and the greatest tragedy is, I'm not sure I ever told her.'

'I tell my children I love them every day,' she offered, 'I don't always mean it,' she added with a smile. 'But I think they know, no matter how much they piss me off, no matter how mad they make me or how badly the screw up, we are a family and we can annoy the hell out of each other, but we always, *always*, have each other's back. And I'm sure Manon did too.'

He cleared his throat and turned suddenly, as if he was forcing himself not to cry. 'I'm not so sure about that,' he said with obvious sadness. 'Your children are very lucky to have you.'

Coco snorted. 'I'm not sure they'd agree with you, but I try. That's all any of us can do.' She reached over and touched his arm. He recoiled instantly. 'Try not to beat yourself up about any of this,' she said. 'I know it's tempting when you're in the eye of the storm, because you're only seeing the storm in front of you. Try to look through it and find things to latch on to. Memories you shared. Lying on a beach, having a picnic on a summer's day.'

He exhaled. 'I'm sure Manon did all of those things, but none of them would have been with me.' He shook his head. 'It's no exaggeration to say I spend most of my day either in a boardroom or on my private jet on the way to a boardroom. Manon was never part of the picture, now she will never be part of the picture.'

They lapsed into silence. Tomas Wall flashed Coco a helpless look.

'Captain Wall,' Pieter spoke finally after composing himself. 'Where are you in the investigation?'

'I... we...' Wall stammered.

Coco took over. 'We're still trying to figure out what happened to Manon.'

Pieter turned back. 'And have you?' He pointed at Wall. 'Because as far as I can tell, no one is really invested in discovering the truth, most likely because the truth, the *actual* truth is likely inconvenient to them.'

Coco shook her head. 'I can't speak for *École Privée Jeanne Remy*,' she said, 'but I can assure you, I have no desire to hide anything. It's not in my nature to keep quiet, even when I should,' she added with a smile. She did not look at Wall because she was not sure yet how honest or self-protective he was being.

Pieter clenched his fist. 'Directeurice Remy and Captain Wall here seem to want me to accept the boy who tried to kill himself, Elliot Bain, is totally responsible. Do you share their opinion, Captain Brunhild?'

Coco considered, still not looking in Wall's direction. She knew she should just agree with Wall and Remy, but until she knew otherwise, she could not. She took a deep breath, desperate for a cigarette to calm her fractured nerves, but she imagined Pieter

Houde in his five-thousand dollar cashmere suit would likely not approve. 'I agree there is powerful evidence to suggest Elliot Bain's involvement in…' she trailed off, 'something. However, until I satisfy myself completely, I can't offer you any assurances.'

He eyed her keenly, raising an eyebrow, interested. 'You don't buy it, do you?'

Coco shrugged. 'I don't know what I buy, just yet, Monsieur Houde.' She raised her hands. 'I'm not fobbing you off. I just want to make sure we're not missing anything. But, if the evidence points to it being a simple case of a love-struck teenager lashing out, then you're going to have to accept that, as hard as it might be.'

'And if it isn't so simple?' Pieter countered, glaring at Wall. 'If there is evidence showing there were others involved in what happened to my daughter?'

Coco finally looked at Wall. 'Then they will be held responsible. I'll see to it myself.'

Wall pushed himself to his feet. He turned to Pieter Houde. 'You wanted to see your daughter,' he said. 'Shall we?'

Pieter Houde stared at his daughter in her coffin. The early evening light seeping through the stained glass windows.

'I've never seen her so quiet,' he whispered. 'She was *never* quiet.' He laughed. 'We used to joke she never stopped making a noise from the second she was born. There was never silence.'

'Death is silent,' Coco said. 'My father used to say it's because it has to be. There's too much being said in death by everyone. We all look at death and it shocks us into trying to make sense of it, to piece together the moments which lead to it. But the most important part, the part we always forget is, it never makes any sense. All we can do is fight through it until we, hopefully, come out the other side.'

Pieter stared at Wall again. He was leaning against the

doorway, staring at his feet as if he wanted to be anywhere other than where he was. 'He won't tell me a thing, and I can't make him understand why I need to know.'

Coco nodded. 'Je comprends. The imagination plays tricks on us. We imagine scenarios far outweighing reality.'

'You've been here before,' Pieter said.

Coco looked around the room. 'Not here, but sure, I've been in many rooms like this over my life.'

'That's not what I meant.'

She stared at him. 'I know. And you're right.' She closed her eyes. The past is the past, she told herself. Her mind flashed a thousand images at once, it seemed. A summer, decades earlier. She would not go there, not again. She had barely made it out the last time.

'Just tell me, does it get any better?' Pieter asked.

She smiled at him. 'It becomes manageable,' she offered.

It was his turn to smile. 'Manageable sounds about as good as I could hope for. I have lived a wonderful life. I see the world daily. Business in Singapore? Fire up the jet, I say! And I have done it at the cost of my child.' He narrowed his eyes. 'So, I ask again. I need answers to my questions. The truth cannot be worse than what I imagine. Did she suffer? Was she brutalised?'

Coco took a deep breath, regretting the gin she had an hour earlier and also wishing she had had more. 'There is no evidence of rape,' she said, 'but as for the rest. Well,' she paused, 'I'm not an expert, but I would like to give the telephone number of my friend, the doctor who performed the autopsy. His name is Dr. Shlomo Bernstein, and he is one of the finest men I have known. I hold a low bar, but in his case it's true,' she raised her hand above her head, 'he's way up there. We call him Sonny, really, because although he sees the worst of us, he also sees the best of us. None of us want to end up in a morgue, but if we do, we have to be grateful for people like Sonny.'

'And what will this man tell me?' Pieter interrupted.

'The truth,' she replied. 'It won't be great, but it will be the truth and it will make you feel better. She didn't die peacefully,' Coco added, 'but it could have been worse.' She shook her head. 'And believe me, I realise what a completely stupid thing that is to say, but I also know what your imagination has told you happened to her. Just know, it was not that bad.'

Pieter clutched his chest. 'Tell that to my heart. It feels like it's going to burst out of my chest.'

Coco moved forward, realising his face was as white as the sheet which covered his daughter. 'Are you okay, Monsieur Houde?' she asked, her breath suddenly laboured, panic seizing her.

He moved back, pressing his hands against the wall. 'Désolé,' he said, 'I'm just a little light-headed. I haven't eaten properly for days, and I'm jet lagged. Yesterday I was in Australia, I suppose it's all… it's all…' he screamed, clutching his chest and falling to the ground.

'Call for an ambulance!' Coco screamed at Wall. He lifted his head, dumbfounded. 'Dammit, call a fucking ambulance, you idiot!'

SAMEDI
(SATURDAY)

10H00

Coco dropped onto a plastic chair in the conference room at the centre of the Commissariat de Police du 7e arrondissement. It groaned underneath her, wobbling sideways. She steadied herself on a nearby table and tutted loudly. 'Everyone's a critic,' she grumbled.

On the opposite side of the table, Dr. Bernstein laughed.

Coco turned to Cedric. 'Why has Commander Demissy called us in? Doesn't she know it's the weekend?'

He shrugged. 'She didn't say.' He stared at Coco, moving his head up and down. She was wearing her usual blue and green full-length woollen coat but it appeared to be getting dirtier by the day, blood stains mixing with food stains. 'Are you okay? You look a bit rough.'

'Another critic!' she cried, exasperated, before shrugging. 'As it happens, I have a gale force hangover. I had three separate...' she coughed, '*sexy* dreams last night. What does that mean, do you think?' she asked no one in particular.

Ebba, the forensic tech who had been sitting to Sonny's right, her head down, looked up, cold eyes fixing on Coco. 'It means you're a slut.'

'Ebba!' Sonny gasped. 'What did we say about improving your social skills, especially when dealing with your superiors?'

Coco tipped her head and laughed. 'Actually, she has a point. I wasn't my usual quiet, demure self in them.'

Behind her in the doorway, Commander Demissy cleared her throat. She entered the conference room, striding purposefully past Coco while shooting her a disparaging look.

Coco bit her lip, noticing Demissy was as usual dressed impeccably, her purple hijab neat and wrinkle-free. She glanced at her own coat and noted the blood stain appeared to be growing. She had tried cleaning it, but she had only succeeded in making it worse. She should buy a new coat, but had decided feeding her kids was probably more important.

Commander Demissy did not speak, instead stepping in front of the whiteboard and slowly and carefully placing a series of photographs across the middle. Manon Houde alive. Manon Houde in the freezer. Manon Houde on the autopsy table. Underneath, she placed several more photographs. Elliot Bain and his mother, before and after. She turned.

'Merci for coming in this morning,' she began, her voice deep and powerful. 'I know it's the weekend and you have,' she stole a look at Coco, 'families to enjoy, but considering events this week, I thought it prudent we put our heads together to try to close the case once and for all.'

'We may never close the case,' Coco interjected, 'because until Elliot Bain wakes up, IF Elliot Bain wakes up, there is little chance we will ever understand what truly happened to him or his mother.'

Demissy shook her head. 'Not closing the case is not an option, Captain Brunhild, especially if we want to keep our jobs.'

Coco's eyes widened in shock. 'That's a little extreme,' she sniffed. 'Sometimes we're just up against it and we have to accept we can't always win.'

'Failure is not an option,' the Commander retorted. 'Especially with Pieter Houde lying in intensive care after a massive heart attack. I spoke this morning with his doctor and at this stage it's touch and go as to whether he'll survive.'

'And I suppose that's my fault as well,' Coco muttered under her breath.

'Non, it isn't,' Demissy replied, 'but you led us into this mess.'

Coco opened her mouth to answer back, but noticed the

Sept Jours

anxious look on Sonny's face and thought better of it.

'And to make matters worse,' Demissy continued, 'he went to school with and remains good friends with the Prime Minister, who is, as you can imagine, suitably annoyed at the turn of events. And not to mention the fact we have had a case for almost a week and are no closer to making an arrest.' She faced Coco. 'Rightly or wrongly, Captain Brunhild, the Commissariat de Police du 7e arrondissement has a reputation, a reputation we are tasked with repairing, by people who have no faith in us doing so, all so they can say, *see, told you, women slash Muslims slash Jews slash foreigners can't be trusted in positions of power.*'

Coco, Sonny and Ebba exchanged a resigned look.

She shook her head. 'I shouldn't have to tell you, of all people, Captain Brunhild. We don't just have to work harder than anyone else. We have to be harder. You think I don't like you,' she paused, 'as it happens, I don't, but that's not the point…'

Coco appeared mock-offended. 'Moi? But I'm a diamond.'

Demissy tried to stop herself from smiling. 'My point is, we don't have the luxury of hiding behind statistics or claiming a crime is unsolvable. That's why we are here this morning, the five of us, to try to piece together what happened, because speaking it out loud in front of one another might just dislodge something we've overlooked. Don't you think?'

Coco gave a seemingly reluctant shrug of her shoulders.

'Bon,' Demissy said. She sat. 'Take us back to the beginning, Captain.'

Coco stood, crumbs from her breakfast croissant falling from her jumper. She cleared her throat. 'D'accord. Let's go back two weeks ago, when all of this began. It began sooner, of course, but we can't be certain of those facts. What we do know is, Manon Houde was intending to seize an opportunity when her class was going on a field trip for a week, to disappear from the school, presumably to meet a man. Except, we don't know that at all, not really.'

'What do you mean?' Demissy interjected.

'What I mean is, the only thing we know for certain is Manon Houde never left the school. The rest, the plans, the men, the planned escape, is something others have told us. Others, who have perhaps a vested interest in misleading us.'

Demissy shook her head. 'I understand what you're saying, but why leave the body to be found?'

'They didn't mean to,' Coco reasoned. 'They planned on disposing of the body, but for some reason never got around to it. Non, let's assume nothing, because I think that's where we're going wrong.'

'Then where do we start?' Cedric asked.

'We know Manon Houde, and most likely other students, all bribed their way out of the school,' Coco said. 'That's a fact confirmed by, amongst others, Captain Tomas Wall and the,' she paused, a sly smile appearing on her face, 'barman from *La Fontaine*. Both confirm they'd seen her in the bar, with at least one, probably more men. The suggestion is also they were older, but that's not something we can confirm. We also know she had a fake ID in the name Amélie, but we have no surname. So, there's not a lot we can do with that.'

'I took statements from the security guards, after Captain Brunhild spoke with them,' Cedric continued. 'One of them confirmed he took bribes, mostly from Elliot Bain, to allow students out of the school at night. I've passed the statements on to Captain Wall and his team, but he didn't really commit a crime, no doubt he's out of a job though.'

Coco tapped her chin. 'Which brings us to the day of her disappearance, or rather, the day after - Mardi morning when the group was ready to leave for their trip.'

'Isn't it strange they went anyway?' Sonny posed.

Coco shrugged. 'I don't see why,' she replied. 'The trip was booked and paid for, and it wasn't really their fault, and also because Elliot Bain confirmed his role in helping Manon escape.'

'Except he didn't,' Cedric said.

'The security guard confirmed someone snuck out of the school that night.'

'A man we know is a liar,' Commander Demissy interjected.

'Why would he lie about it?' Cedric asked.

She shrugged. 'There could be many reasons. Off the top of my head, I wouldn't rule out the possibility the security guard himself could have murdered Manon.'

'That still doesn't explain why Elliot took the blame,' Coco mused.

'Maybe he was working with the security guard. Some kind of kinky sex game, and the girl ended up dead,' Ebba suggested.

'I can't see it,' Coco said dissuasively, 'for one thing, all the security guard needed to say was he saw Manon leave, and that, along with the emails would likely be enough to put off anyone worrying too much about her for a while. And,' she continued, 'if Elliot was working with someone, someone who stayed in the school after he was expelled, then surely that person would have disposed of the body to cover themselves.' She shook her head in frustration. 'We're missing something, something obvious.'

Demissy tapped her fingers on the table. 'If we're considering Elliot Bain wasn't involved directly in the murder of Manon Houde, then what would make him get involved? Is this just about money? We know Elliot needed money and wasn't afraid to get his hands dirty.'

'I think you may be correct,' Coco nodded. 'It makes more sense to me to imagine a scenario where Elliot witnesses the murder of Manon Houde, and rather than calling for help, he sees an opportunity to make some money. Some real money, not the few euros he'd squirrelled away busting people out of the school.' She shook her head again. 'But that still doesn't explain why he would come back to Paris, kill his mother, and then try to kill himself.'

'Guilt is a powerful thing,' the Commander reasoned.

Coco flashed a doubtful look. 'Ecouté, let's leave the Paris connection to one side for the moment. I don't know why, but there's something about it and I think it's clouding the picture of what really happened in Saint-Germain-en-Laye.'

Commander Demissy tapped on the folders in front of her. 'I've gone through all the statements Lieutenant Degarmo took, and I see little there. Not from the students, the teaching staff, the catering staff, the cleaning staff. They all say nothing of merit, yet someone must be lying.'

An ominous, heavy silence descended on the room.

'We can't be sure who was or wasn't at the school at the time of Manon Houde's murder, because we know there was at least the possibility of bribing the security guard to turn off the CCTV cameras temporarily,' Coco said finally. 'But we know she never left the school. Therefore, she died somewhere in the school following her last lesson on Lundi and when she was discovered missing on Mardi morning. Once missing, Elliot Bain confesses to helping her escape, and he is immediately expelled and thrown out of the school. The police become involved later, after most of the students and the staff have also left the premises. Peut être, if the police had become involved earlier, we would have been better able to examine the premises and interview the suspect pool, but we don't have that luxury.'

'What about previous convictions?' Ebba asked.

'There's nothing there,' Cedric said. 'No one involved in the school has a criminal record.'

Coco bit her lip. 'Just in case, I asked my friend Etienne Martine in Montgenoux to do a follow-up search for me.'

'You shouldn't have done that, Captain,' Commander Demissy snapped. 'This has nothing to do with him.'

'I disagree,' Coco retorted. 'He works for the police, as far as I can tell he has access to far more search engines than we do. If someone is hiding something, Etienne is the man best placed to sniff it out.' She stared at the Commander. 'And if the Prime Minister is baying for our blood, shouldn't we do whatever we have to, to close the case?' She glanced at her watch. 'Etienne is due to call me soon. Let's hope he has news which might just break open the case, because if he doesn't, then,' she made the gesture of running a knife across her throat. Her face clouded. 'Oops, not really appropriate considering what happened to Elliot, but you catch my drift.' She paused again. 'Non, we don't have much, but we do have two things which I think are linked, I'm just not sure how.'

'And they are?' Demissy demanded.

'Manon's mysterious lover, or lovers, and the fact that Jacques Anders, the school gardener, is missing.'

Demissy shook her head. 'I read your report. There is a suggestion the gardener often takes fishing trips and doesn't keep a regular schedule at the school. He's a semi-retired loner. He could be anywhere and return when he sees fit.'

'Do you think he could be Manon's lover?' Sonny asked.

'I doubt it,' Coco replied, 'at least not the one she took to the bar. Captain Wall and the barman would most likely have mentioned if the young, beautiful teenager was shacking up with a sixty-eight-year-old toothless old fogey. But Jacques does interest me, primarily because of the Belladonna issue. Did he know it was being grown at the school? Was he growing it himself? Did he discover someone in the act? All of these issues, combined with his sudden absence, concerns me. I asked Captain Wall to put out a missing person report. He has, but nothing has come back so far. I checked with him this morning. He also confirmed no one has entered or left the school overnight.'

'Then we really are nowhere,' Demissy groaned.

'At least you married rich,' Coco mumbled.

Before the Commander could respond, the beeping of Coco's cell phone interrupted them. She glanced at the screen. *Hey, it's Etienne, call me when you can.* Coco turned to Demissy. 'I have to make a call. Are we done here?'

Demissy rose to her feet. 'For now. But I want us all to go over these statements again and again until we see what we're missing. And if we can't, get back to *École Privée Jeanne Remy* this afternoon. You and Cedric take more statements. Do whatever you have to do, but I want answers. Take Dr. Bernstein and Ebba, go over the school with a fine-tooth comb if you have to, mais, find me something, anything I can show the Prime Minister.'

Demissy moved towards the door, before stopping and turning back. 'I've been a Commander for less than a month. I intend to make it to my one-month anniversary, or so help me Dieu, I'll… I'll…' she trailed off, yanking the door open. 'Just find me the damn truth, for Dieu's sake.'

11H00

'Hey Etienne. It's Coco.' She had left the Commissariat and climbed up the narrow stairwell leading to the roof and was enjoying her third cigarette of the morning.

'How's it going?' he asked.

'Shit,' she retorted.

'Oh, I'm sorry,' he replied.

She snorted. 'Don't be. Shit is about as good as I can hope for. In fact, shit is a step up from my usual days.'

He laughed. 'Well, I don't think I'm going to make it any better.'

'You found nothing?' she asked, resigned.

'Not really,' he answered. 'There are no red flags as such on anyone involved in the school. All I found was a suggestion one teacher may, or may not, have had an inappropriate relationship with a female student while working in another school.'

'Ruben Badeaux?'

'How did you know?'

Coco sighed. 'Lucky guess. He was fired?'

'Non,' Etienne answered. 'He resigned. There seems to have been the suggestion the girl may have had relations with him as well as other teachers. Badeaux resigned before there was an investigation. The girl claimed a teacher had gotten her pregnant, but it turned out to have been her sixteen-year-old boyfriend. It seems they'd been extorting money from her older lovers, so it pretty much torpedoed any sort of investigation. She was expelled and that was the end of it, it seems.'

'Anything else?'

'I'm afraid not,' he continued. 'I've run the names through all of my usual databases and I don't see any alarm bells. Some of the parents of the students are pretty dodgy, but I don't see any suggestion of them being anywhere near the school.'

'And Manon Houde herself?' Coco asked. 'She'd disappeared before, and shacked up with some lowlife. Maybe he came back to reclaim her, or get rid of her for dumping him.'

Etienne sighed. 'He OD'd last year. Désolé, Captain.'

Coco blew a raspberry. 'Ah, well, it's pretty much what I expected.' She paused, taking a deep breath. 'And Captain Wall?'

'I accessed his police personnel file,' Etienne said, 'so, obviously this can go no further. A few years ago he seems to have gone through a rough patch. It seems they caught him drunk a few times when he was on duty. I checked the dates, and it appears to have been around the time his wife left him, which might explain why he went off the rails a little.'

Coco nodded. 'And that's it? He just never quite got to the bottom of a bottle for a while? I mean, he didn't shoot anyone by mistake, or anything?'

'It doesn't appear to be the case,' Etienne stated. 'And he was only made Captain last year. Therefore presumably whatever was troubling him before had passed.' He paused. 'I don't know what you were expecting, but he seems an okay, decent sort of flic as far as I can tell.'

Coco smiled. 'I'm glad. I think that's what I was hoping you'd say.' *He's got terrible taste in women,* she wanted to add, but did not. 'What about the gardener?'

'Rien,' Etienne added. 'No criminal record. He worked as a gardener for the local commune for almost forty years before he retired and took a part-time job at the school. Married once with no children. Pays his taxes etc. etc.'

Coco tutted. 'Not one person in the entire school has a damn record. Not even a parking ticket?'

'Not that I could find,' he added.

'Dieu, you are thorough!' she exclaimed. 'Merci, Etienne, for all your help.'

'Wait,' he interjected, 'I saved the best for last.'

'Then there is something?' Coco asked hopefully.

'Well, peut être,' he responded. 'I'm not sure how helpful it will be, but it's interesting all the same.'

Coco wound her finger. 'Come on, Etienne, spill.'

He laughed. 'It's about BIGFRITZ.'

'You found him?' she asked keenly.

'Non,' he answered quickly. 'And I'm not sure it will be possible. Mais, what I can tell you is where he sent the emails, or at least the IP address which helps pinpoint the location.'

'Etienne,' Coco wailed.

'You don't have to look very far,' he said. 'This isn't exactly kosher, so don't quote me on it without a Mandate. The emails sent to Manon from Fritz came from the same IP address.'

She scratched her head. 'What do you mean?'

'All I can say is, whoever Manon was writing to, it wasn't a lover in some other town or country even. It was someone in her school.'

'Why would she do that?'

'I can't say,' Etienne responded.

'I never bought those emails,' Coco said. 'Wait a minute. If someone wanted to make it appear she had just run off, they could do that, couldn't they? Set up a fake account and a fake correspondence?'

'Certainly could,' Etienne answered. 'The only other thing I can tell you is that Manon's email address is the one provided by the school and the only emails received were school related ones and from Fritz. The only sent emails were from Manon to Fritz. I don't know about you, but I find it hard to believe a seventeen-year-old doesn't use email.'

'Or at least not their school one,' Coco gasped. 'If Manon had a different email and never used her school one, then someone could have hacked it and be using it to set up a false alibi for her murder.'

'That's certainly possible,' Etienne confirmed. 'I could try to find Manon's other email address, but it would be next to impossible. Most of them are free. If I had her phone, or one of her devices, then I may be able to find something.'

'The police in Saint-Germain-en-Laye searched her room and her iPad, that's how they found those emails, but they mentioned nothing else,' she said.

'It could have been deleted,' Etienne interjected. 'If you get them to me, I could have a look at them for you.'

Coco considered. 'I may take you up on that, but for now I'll see what I can do at this end. Merci, merci, merci, Etienne.'

'That's okay. Désolé I couldn't find you a smoking gun, but if I can do anything else, just call, d'accord?'

'I will, but don't apologise. The email is interesting, and it might just be enough to smoke out whoever is behind this.' She laughed at herself. 'Listen to me, faux optimism. Well, when it's all you've got, it's all you've got!' She sighed. 'Love to everyone in Montgenoux.'

Coco disconnected the call, sucking on the cigarette. She glanced at her watch. 'Hmm, if we shake a tail feather, we might just get to *La Fontaine* in time for lunch.' She looked down at her clothes, lifting her blouse and sniffing it, her nose wrinkling. 'I'm sure I'll find something clean enough at the bottom of the laundry basket,' she told herself.

13H00

The barman's mouth opened to a wide smile. 'Back so soon,' he said cheerfully.

Cedric rolled his eyes. 'That's why you made me drive like a lunatic to get here.'

Sonny leaned in and whispered in Coco's ear. 'Which dream was he in?'

Coco turned her head. 'He was in all three,' she mouthed, before adding, 'and he was *fabulous*.'

Sonny snorted as the barman appeared next to them. 'Gin?' he asked Coco.

'Sure,' she answered. 'He's driving,' she said, pointing at Cedric.

The barman turned his head, eyes flicking irritably over Cedric. 'Your boyfriend?' he sniffed.

Coco laughed. 'Non, but he has seen my…'

Sonny slapped her hand. 'Coco, I beg of you! Don't finish that sentence.' He gestured towards a table. 'Let's take a seat.'

The barman nodded. 'I'll bring you your gin and take the rest of your order in a sec,' he said, running back in the direction of the bar.

Coco, Cedric, Sonny and Ebba moved around the table and took their seats.

'You can't be serious about him,' Ebba said. 'He's a kid.'

Coco shrugged. 'I never suggested I was,' she sniffed. 'I'm at the stage in my life, when I am only interested in looking, not touching, but as I'm not yet dead below the waist, I intend to look, and look a lot, comprende?'

Ebba glared at her. 'I understand nothing about you,' she said with a weary sigh.

'Why are we here?' Cedric whined. 'Commander Demissy said we had to go to the school.'

'And we will,' Coco replied. 'We're on our way, but we had to come here first,' she fluttered her eyes demurely, 'for research purposes purely, obviously.'

'Research purposes?'

She nodded, extending her hands. 'This very bar is where Manon Houde spent her time away from the school, and not just her, other students, teachers, cops.'

'Et?' Cedric asked. 'She didn't die here, so what does it matter?'

Coco moved her head slowly around the room. It was a bar, more or less the same as every bar in the country, or the world. 'She may not have died here, but she lived her. I was seventeen once,' she pointed at Ebba. 'Snigger and I'll make you wish your head wasn't so smooth and you had hair to cushion the blow,' she continued. 'As I was saying, I was seventeen once, and I lived in a place like this. It was my escape. My joy.' She smiled at the approaching barman. *'My education.'*

'I get that,' Sonny said, 'but I don't get how it's going to help us understand what happened to Manon.'

'Your gin,' the barman said, placing an extra large glass in front of Coco.

'Merci, barkeep,' Coco said demurely.

'My name is…'

Coco raised her hand. 'Don't tell me?'

His face crumpled in confusion. 'Pourquoi?'

'Don't ask,' Cedric muttered, 'I have a feeling you won't like the answer.'

Coco glared at him. She turned back to the barman. 'These are my colleagues. We're here because we are trying to understand what happened to Manon Houde.'

He frowned. 'You mean, Amélie?'

She nodded.

He shrugged. 'I don't know what to tell you. I wish I could tell you more. The truth is, I just didn't pay a lot of attention to her.'

'Too young?' Coco posed.

He smiled. 'And too stuck up. Girls like that look down at people like me. I see it all the time. We're just the "help," to them.'

'And there's nothing you can tell us about the men she was with?'

He shrugged. 'Old.'

'Old?'

'Yeah, like thirty, at least.'

Coco clutched her heart. 'Oy vey,' she mumbled, before adding, 'but not older? Like really, *really* old, forty or even older?'

The barman shuddered. 'Dieu, non. I suppose she had a type - white, old, smartly dressed.' He smiled. 'Like the cop.'

Coco audibly gasped. 'She was with a police officer?'

'Sure,' he replied, 'sometimes.'

Cedric glared at Coco. 'You knew about this, didn't you?'

Coco shrunk into herself, sipping her gin. 'Non, I didn't. I suppose you could say, I "suspected" but had no actual proof. Wall told me she came here, and I didn't think too much of it. But just to be sure, I had Etienne check. Wall is clean. There may have been a bit of an issue with alcohol at one point, but that's about it,' she concluded.

'That's it,' the barman interrupted, waving his finger. 'Captain Wall. I remember now, I saw her ID.'

'Her?' Coco interrupted, her voice shrill.

He nodded. 'Yeah, her,' he answered before adding, 'as I said, Manon had a type, white, old, smart…'

Coco and Cedric exchanged a confused look.

'It's just you made it sound as if it was a man,' Coco said.

'Sometimes it was,' the barman retorted, 'sometimes it wasn't.

It's the 21st century. That sort of thing is fluid these days, y'know?'

Coco shuddered. 'Non, I don't,' she mumbled.

Ebba leaned over to her. 'I bet that didn't happen in your dream.'

Coco sighed. 'Well, there were fluids involved.' She turned to the barman. 'Wait, you said Captain Wall was a woman, and you saw her ID. Why?'

'What do you mean?'

'Why did you need to see her ID?' Coco retorted. 'You pointed out, anyone over the age of thirty is old. So, why did you need to see her ID?'

The barman laughed. 'Thirty isn't old really. You'll see when you get there finally.'

Coco pushed herself back in her chair, flicking blue hair over her shoulder. 'True, sailor,' she exhaled.

Ebba retched. 'I swear to God, if you make me sick into my mouth one more time, I'm going to kill someone. And believe me, I know how to do it and leave not the slightest trace of evidence behind.'

Sonny smiled. 'Remember, play nice, Ebba.'

Coco turned her shoulder away from Ebba huffily. 'Her ID, sailor? Why did you see it?'

He leaned forward conspiratorially, like a spy in a terrible movie. 'She was on a stakeout.'

'A stakeout?' Cedric interjected. 'When and why?'

The barman stepped back. 'Can't you just ask her?'

Coco nodded. 'We will. But we want to hear your story first, because,' she smiled, 'because you tell it so well, sailor.'

'I swear to God,' Ebba repeated. 'Can someone get me a bucket of water?' she called to no one in particular.

The barman laughed.

'And what was this stakeout about? Did she say?' Coco asked.

He shrugged. 'It was a while ago; I don't really remember. But probably about someone dealing drugs, or selling stolen stuff. It's usually one or the other. We get all types in here.'

Coco turned her head as she considered. She leaned forward. 'Cedric, can you bring up the *École Privée Jeanne Remy* website? I seem to remember it has pictures of the staff.'

He nodded. 'Bien sûr.' He pulled out his cell phone, his fingers moving quickly around the screen. A few moments later, he passed it to her. She took it and nodded. 'Sailor. Do you see Captain Wall?'

He leaned forward. 'Yeah, that's her.'

Coco stared at the cell phone. She took a deep breath and showed it to Cedric.

'Putain,' he muttered. 'We should get to the school.'

Coco nodded. She stood. 'Everybody is hungry. You should have some lunch, and then we'll go to the school.' She stepped away from the table.

'Where are you going?' Cedric asked.

'To speak to the actual Captain Wall,' she responded. 'I want to make sure he didn't have any knowledge of the other Captain Wall.'

'And if he did?' Sonny asked.

She took another deep breath. 'Then he'll be in a cell with Mordecai, if I have any say in it, but if he didn't, then he might just be able to fill in a few of the blanks.' She smiled at them. 'Enjoy lunch. I'll be back in less than an hour, one way or another. I'll either have another cop handcuffed to me, or we'll have a better idea of what we're dealing with at that damn school.'

14H00

'Why did you want to meet me here?' Coco asked.

Tomas Wall did not respond. He took a deep breath, sucking fresh air deep into his lungs. 'When I was growing up, my Grand Mére had a painting on her bedroom wall. It wasn't real, just a print, but I used to think it was beautiful. It was called *The Terrace at Saint-Germain, Spring*, and painted by a man called Alfred Sisley,' he said. 'She used to tell me, this is your home, you should be proud. I don't know what happened to it after she died, but I used to come down here - the north bank of the River Seine, and look towards Paris. I wasn't proud of where I lived then. I dreamed of escaping, going to Paris, making my fortune, falling in love, the usual nonsense.'

Coco leaned over the railing, turning her head towards the distant Paris. 'We all have the same sort of memories,' she said, 'dreaming of escaping the places in which we were born, desperate to be free of the shackles.'

'You weren't born in Paris?'

She shook her head. 'Non. I was born in Saint Nazaire, and I couldn't wait to get away from it.'

Wall smiled. 'And you did.'

Coco laughed. 'Not exactly the way I intended. I left when I was nineteen, pregnant, and alone. I went to Paris to disappear, and I did.'

'And you made it.'

'It was hard,' she responded, 'and I made so many mistakes. By the time I was twenty-one, I had two screaming babies and not a man in sight. I was lucky, my grandfather had left me a tidy sum of money, so it meant I could afford to live for a while, to pay someone to look after the kids while I trained to be a cop.'

'A strange choice of career, non?'

She shrugged. 'I never had the sense to do anything else, and it was all I had ever wanted to do. So I did, but I had to work hard for it, twice as hard as anyone else, but I wanted it so badly I wasn't going to take no for an answer.'

'I can imagine,' Wall said. 'You had more courage than I ever had. I dreamt of leaving but never did.'

Coco pushed her windswept hair away from her face. 'But you made a go of it. I think about Saint Nazaire often, and how my life would have been different if I'd stayed.'

'With the father of your baby?' he asked. 'Désolé, it's none of my business.'

'Man, we were hot and heavy,' she said. 'In the way love is at that age - all-consuming and everything.' She smiled sadly. 'But he was going places, and if I'd stayed, well, we would have ended up hating each other. He would have given up his dreams and settled for some dead-end job. Non, there was no point in us both ruining our lives.' She watched the river as it moved quickly past them. 'Do you come here often?'

Wall nodded. 'Usually when I need to get away, or think. It reminds me of the painting and simpler times.'

She turned to him. 'D'accord, we've done the skirting around the issues, now it's time to level with me.'

He exhaled. 'I don't know where to begin, but I want you to know before we start, that I'm not crooked, or corrupt, not like your ex, I promise you.'

Coco raised her hands. 'Don't make promises like that. I'll decide for myself, that's the only way it's going to work for me.'

'I guess by now, you've had my background checked,' he began. Coco nodded. He continued. 'Then you'll know I had an alcohol problem for a while. Still do I suppose, but I know my limits, and I know when to stop. But that wasn't always the case.'

'They promoted you last year,' Coco said, 'which tells me

whatever happened is behind you.'

Wall snorted. 'I just replaced one set of problems with another.'

'What do you mean?'

He took another deep breath as if he was having to force the air into his lungs. 'When my wife left me, I thought I'd never get over it.' He looked at Coco. 'I know how pathetic that makes me sound, but it's the truth. She left me for another man and she never looked back. She didn't even want our son. She said it was all my idea in the first place, that she'd never wanted the nice, neat life, but she'd gone along with it because she had no other choice. As soon as she had another choice, she took it,' Wall added. 'And for a while, I didn't finish drinking.'

'But then you did,' Coco interrupted. 'What happened?'

He swallowed. 'There was an accident. I hit a wall with my car. It was the wake-up call I needed to get my life in order, but it was not without a price.'

'Somebody saw you and knew who you were and blackmailed you,' Coco stated. Wall turned his head to her, his face crumbling. She recognised it instantly because it was the same expression she had witnessed on Mordecai Stanic's face - it was relief. Relief at not having to pretend any longer. 'And I'm guessing the person you almost hit was Directeurice Jeanne Remy.'

'How do you know?'

She shrugged. 'It makes sense. I get the impression Jeanne Remy likes to have favours she can call in. And did she? Call in favours, that is?'

Wall turned away from her. 'Not in the way, you imagine.'

Coco shook her head irritably. 'You don't know what I'm thinking. Answer my question.'

'It was just little things,' he said finally. 'I swear to you. I'm not corrupt.'

'That's not for me to judge, nor for you to swear to,' Coco

hissed with more venom than she intended. 'What did you do for her?'

'You've seen her,' Wall replied. 'That damn school is her life. It's all she has, and she's fiercely protective of it. But as you yourself said, kids are kids no matter how smart they are and sometimes they get in trouble.'

Coco nodded. 'Bien sûr, they do.' She considered. 'Remy knew some of the students were sneaking out of the school, didn't she?'

'Oui,' he replied. 'That's the problem with some kids who come from parents with bottomless pockets. They don't give a shit about consequences. All Remy is interested in is her reputation and she'll do anything to protect it. So, occasionally she calls on me to get a student out of trouble.' He raised his hand. 'I know what you're thinking, but we're just talking about stupid, childish things, stuff we wouldn't generally waste our time with, anyway.'

'Such as?'

'It all started when a couple of kids went on a drunken crawl through the centre of town, damaged a few planters, nothing substantial, just the usual nonsense,' he said. 'So, when Remy called me up and "reminded" me of my own drunken indiscretion and how I'd gotten away with it and was back to being a fine upstanding person because… because…'

'Because of her, and her silence,' Coco finished.

Wall sighed. 'The worst part is, she had a point. I had my career still because of her, and was it really such a big deal to let the kids go without charging them, possibly ruining the distinguished careers they had ahead of them.' He stared at her imploringly. 'You have to see that. We probably wouldn't even have charged them, anyway.'

'That's so not the point,' Coco interrupted.

He lowered his head, the muscles in his wide neck flexing. 'I know,' he mouthed.

'And what else?'

'The same sort of thing,' he answered. 'Fights in a bar, a couple of DUIs. I made the charges go away and drove them back to her. I swear I wouldn't have covered up any serious crime. You have to believe me,' he pleaded. 'Please say you believe me.'

Coco lit a cigarette, waving it angrily towards him. 'You're making me break my rule. I've already smoked my daily allowance today.'

He smiled sadly. 'I'll buy you a pack of cigarettes, Charlotte.'

'I don't accept bribes,' she retorted quickly.

His face flashed with horror. 'That's not what I meant, honestly it isn't.'

She laughed. 'Relax, I'm messing with you.' She sucked on the cigarette. 'This is a mess, Tomas.'

'I know,' he replied. 'I'm going to lose my job, aren't I?' he asked desperately. 'Oh, Dieu. I have a son. I know he's seventeen, but he's a boy. He's not fully cooked yet, he's not even partly cooked yet. And his damn mother is useless. We don't even know where she is. Oh, Dieu, Dieu, Dieu!'

She reached over and touched his arm. 'Calm down, Tomas. This doesn't have to be so serious.'

'It doesn't?' he asked with clear desperation.

'If you're telling me the truth,' she began, 'then you're right. I'd have probably read the kids the riot act and kicked their sorry butts back to the school. It's not as if you accepted payment for it… is it?'

'Of course, not,' he retorted. 'She called me and asked me to help, that's it.'

She nodded. 'I get it, and I'm sure others would to.'

'Then you're not going to report me?'

Coco did not answer immediately.

'Captain Brunhild?' he pressed.

'If you're telling me the truth,' she answered finally, 'then it's none of my business if you use your discretion in the relationships you cultivate with your local community. Mais,' she paused, 'if you're not, I'll make sure you're sorry.'

'I am telling you the truth.'

She nodded. 'What about Manon Houde?'

He shook his head. 'I had nothing to do with that, I swear,' he said.

'Mais, you knew her before, didn't you?'

'It was one time, I swear,' he cried.

Coco shook her head. 'Oh, Tomas, she was seventeen!'

'I know! I know!' He shouted. 'And that's why I didn't take it any further.'

'You didn't sleep with her?'

'Of course not,' he retorted. He took a deep breath. 'Look, I saw her one night in the bar. I'd had a pretty shitty day, and I just wanted to get loaded and laid, in whatever order it came. Manon was there, on her own, and she came on to me. She came on to me, and I was flattered.'

'How did you find out she was seventeen then?' Coco interrupted. 'Because we know she had fake ID.'

Wall buried his head. 'Her teacher told me.'

'Her teacher?'

He nodded. 'Rueben Badeaux. He cornered me in the toilets. He said he wondered how my Commander would like me sleeping with a seventeen-year-old student. I was mortified.'

'And what about him?' Coco asked.

Wall frowned. 'What do you mean?'

'Badeaux. How did he seem? Angry?'

He shook his head. 'Non, I wouldn't say angry, more…' he trailed off, his face crinkling as he tried to recall.

'Jealous?' Coco suggested.

Wall locked eyes with her. 'Jealous,' he confirmed.

Coco exhaled. 'That girl certainly had a lot of people at her feet,' she said. 'What happened after your bathroom chat with Badeaux?'

'I made my excuses and left,' he said.

There was something about his face which bothered, Coco. 'What aren't you telling me?'

'I want to call you Coco,' he said, staring at her in a way she was sure she had not been looked at in a very long time, 'so badly.'

She shook her head. 'We're not there yet,' she snapped with more force than she intended. 'What aren't you telling me?' she repeated.

'Rien,' he answered with evident desperation. He clenched his fists. 'When I went back to the table, I explained to her who I was, and that I knew she was a student. She said it didn't matter to her, so it shouldn't matter to me.'

Coco's mouth twisted into a sad smile. 'She was certainly a character, that girl.'

Wall nodded. 'You could say that. She didn't want to take no for an answer. But I made sure she did. I may have been a drunk then, but I wasn't a sleaze bag, Charlotte.'

'I believe you,' she said after a moment, 'I don't know why, I certainly shouldn't, but I do.'

'I can't tell you how much that means to me,' Wall said with a contended sigh.

'Don't get excited,' she blurted. 'You said she didn't want to take no for an answer? What do you mean?'

He shrugged. 'She was angry. She threatened me, I told her she had nothing to threaten me about. We'd met once in front of dozens of witnesses, and I'd done nothing but shared a drink with a woman with a fake ID. She got angrier and angrier. *Nobody dumps me,* she said. And I told her, I wasn't dumping her because I'd never been with her and if she really wanted to cause trouble for me, then she'd better be prepared for it to come out she was sleeping with her teacher.' He smiled. 'That stopped her in her tracks.'

'And then she disappeared,' Coco said.

Wall repeated. 'And then she disappeared.'

'How did you find out about it?'

'Jeanne Remy called me to report her missing,' Wall said. 'She told me I didn't really need to bother to search for her as it was clear she'd ran off with a boy.' He paused. 'I can't say I was surprised. I went to the school, looked at her emails. It pretty much confirmed what I imagined, anyway. She'd gone off with some man.' He stared at Coco. 'I feel pretty rotten about that, right now,' he said.

Coco reached over and touched his arm. 'Don't. I think her candle was already snuffed well before then.' She turned away, watching a seagull darting across the water. It seemed so serene and focused and carefree. All the things she imagined she never would be. 'I can't imagine there was anything you could have done to change what happened to Manon. Tell me, when you spoke with Jeanne Remy, how was she?'

'What do you mean?'

Coco considered. 'I mean, how did she seem? Worried? Anxious? Guilty?'

'She was definitely worried,' he replied. 'You've seen Pieter Houde. He's not the sort of man to cross, especially for someone like Directeurice Remy.'

Coco nodded. 'Did you tell her about your... interaction with Manon?'

Wall did not answer.

'Tomas,' Coco she said, 'if you're not completely honest with me, I'm going to stop calling you Tomas, and call you Captain Wall. And neither of us want that, because it'll make it all official and very annoying.'

Wall stared at her, looking as sad a man as she thought she had ever seen. 'The directeurice was concerned, obviously, but she made it clear that I omitted my connection, or Manon's behaviour, or the fact she had been seen regularly out of the school.'

'Didn't that strike you as odd?'

'Pourquoi?'

'Because it was odd,' Coco retorted.

Wall shook his head. 'I didn't see it that way. Remy made me understand the kind of girl Manon was. And I can't say I disagreed, but more importantly, I really believed there was no real reason for concern. The facts were reasonably clear. Manon had a secret boyfriend, probably several, and she wanted to get away. The emails proved it. That was the girl I knew briefly. And then when Elliot Bain confirmed he had helped her escape, there really was nothing else to do.'

Coco nodded. 'And in hindsight?'

'I know you might have trouble believing me,' he replied, 'but I'm still not sure what I could have done differently.'

Coco did not say it, but she was inclined to agree with him. 'Back to Manon,' she said. 'You told me you saw her in the bar. Was that true?'

'Bien sûr, it was true,' he answered desperately. 'And this was later, much later.'

'And you maintain, you don't know who she was with? Was it her teacher, Ruben Badeaux, peut être?'

He sighed. 'I wish I could answer that, but I can't be certain. I've told you all I can about that.'

Coco nodded. 'Then let's move on,' she snapped.

'Move on?'

She nodded again. 'If you want me to help you, then I have to believe you. And the fact is, I don't believe men at all, but I'm going to give you a chance to look at my face and not lie.' She lowered her head. 'I'll give you a chance to start the process in which I might actually begin again trusting the species of men. Look at me and don't lie.'

Wall lifted his head towards her, his eyes staring at her. 'Ask

Sept Jours

your questions,' he whispered.

'Have you had sex with Directeurice Jeanne Remy?'

Wall's eyes widened in horror. 'Non, definitely not.'

She stared at him. 'But you have with Manon's teacher, Margot Tasse, haven't you?'

He nodded. 'There's no crime in that. Sometimes we hook up. She's lonely, I'm lonely. We have nothing in common, but we have fun sometimes, that's all. It's nothing serious, and it doesn't happen very often.'

'What about Caron Voland, Manon's other teacher?'

She noticed his reaction instantly. The flinch, the twitch of the eye. He said nothing.

'Tomas,' she pressed. 'What about Caron Voland?'

'It was a long time ago. I was drunk, very, very drunk,' he whispered. 'And it was only once,'

Coco lifted the lapel of her coat. The breeze from the river suddenly made her feel chilly. 'She was with you, wasn't she?'

'Charlotte, s'il te plaît,' he begged.

'You said you would be honest with me, Tomas, and that is the only way I'm going to help you. What about Caron Voland?'

'I didn't even know she was a teacher,' he said finally, 'or maybe I did, I can't say for sure. We met in the bar, had a few drinks, a lot of drinks in fact, and we decided to…' he shook his head, 'Dieu, this is so embarrassing.'

'Head to the car for a bit of back-seat bouncing?' Coco finished his thought for him.

He did not look at her, but slowly nodded instead.

'And then?' Coco continued. 'You drove her home?'

'That was the plan, and then we had the accident… I had the accident.'

Coco's eyes flashed. 'She was driving, wasn't she?'

He sighed. 'I was too drunk, and I have to tell you, I'm not really clear about any of it. I might have been driving for all I know, mais…'

'And that's how Directeurice Remy became involved,' Coco posed. 'Caron Voland rang her boss and told her she needed her help, and Remy being Remy, all she thought about was protecting her precious school.'

Wall nodded slowly.

'This is a mess, Wall,' she added.

'Je sais,' he replied. 'I've been a fool, but as I said, it was my wake-up call. I got reasonably sober after it. Sober enough not to let it affect me anymore, anyway. I've been better since, that's all I can say.'

Coco nodded. 'Then, let's move on. Tell me about Elliot,' she said. 'I only spoke to him briefly, and to be honest, you're the only person I trust enough to give me a true opinion of him.'

'You trust me?'

She smiled. 'Don't push it, Wall. Piss me off, and I still might turn on you, because the jury's out on you. Back to Elliot Bain. Was he lying to you, do you think? I mean, we know he was lying, but what was your impression of him?'

Wall considered his response. 'I think he was just a kid out of his depth. He asked about his mother a lot.'

Coco pulled back her head in surprise. 'You didn't mention that before,' she said.

He shrugged. 'Why would I? There wasn't really any reason for it. I just thought it was normal. He was worried because he didn't want his mother to know he might be in trouble with the police.'

Coco shook her head. 'And yet he was quite happy to admit to something he most likely had nothing to do with, which was likely to get him expelled.'

'Or make his escape,' Wall retorted. 'We keep coming back to the same thing. He wanted to get out of the school because of what he had done to Manon.'

Coco closed her eyes, immediately seeing Elliot Bain's cherub face, his smooth olive skin and rosebud lips. She could not explain to herself why she was seeing innocence on his face. But she was, and she could not shake it. She sighed. 'The only thing we know for certain about Elliot Bain is that he wanted money.'

'Because he didn't have any.'

She nodded. 'I know that, and believe me, as someone who knows all about having not a cent to her name, I understand the attraction. But why did he need money? And why did he need to get out of the school, and,' she paused, 'what would he do to get a lot of money?'

'Are you suggesting someone paid him to kill Manon Houde?' Wall asked. 'I just can't see it.'

'Nor me,' Coco replied. 'But a kid who's desperate for money, might just help someone who has some and needs his help, no questions asked.'

'Manon's murderer.'

'Oui.' She lit another cigarette. 'I'll take you up on your offer to buy me some cigarettes saying as it's your fault I'm smoking so much.'

'Gladly,' Wall replied. 'Will you ever forgive me?'

'There's nothing to forgive.'

'Forgive me enough to think of me differently?' Wall asked directly.

'Don't push it,' Coco retorted. 'You're only good to me in my fantasies at the moment, and that's how it'll stay.' She paused. 'For now, anyway.'

Wall threw back his head and laughed, his entire body reverberating. 'Dieu, that felt good. I'm not sure I've laughed, *really* laughed in a very long time.' He stared at Coco. 'You said, for now?'

She pointed at him. 'I said don't push it.' She turned her head. 'For a while, at least.' She looked at her watch. It was getting late. She needed to get home, but she also needed the case to be closed. *Désolé, Helga*, she thought. *I'll make it up to you when it's all over.* 'There's one other thing,' she said to Wall.

'Oui?'

'Fake IDs. Where did they come from?'

'I don't know, for sure,' he answered. 'But I believe it also had something to do with Elliot.'

Coco nodded. 'And what do you base that on?'

'Rien,' he replied. 'Gut. I told you, I used to round up students and send them back to the school. It was mostly drunk kids in bars, or horny boys with prostitutes, but there was one time, only one time, I saw Elliot in town. He was with a man known to the police here, a man who has his hands in many pies, such as fencing stolen goods and…'

'Providing fake IDs,' Coco interjected.

Wall nodded. 'Oui. He spent a few years in prison for providing immigrants with pretty convincing passports. But again, I can't say anything for sure about what Elliot Bain was up to.'

'What did he say when you caught him with that man?'

'He said he was buying drugs,' Wall replied. 'And it seemed reasonable and probable. I dropped him at the red door and didn't really give it a lot of thought.'

'D'accord. It's time to go back to the school.'

'Do we have to?' Wall asked.

Coco nodded. 'Time to find justice.' She touched his arm again. 'Je suis désolé, Tomas,' she whispered. 'I have no intention or interest in dropping you in it, or getting you in trouble, but I need to find justice for Manon Houde, and whatever his faults, also for Elliot Bain. I'll try to keep you out of it, but you have to know people react badly sometimes when they're backed into corners.'

Wall gulped. 'If I have to pay for justice to be served, then I'm okay with that.'

Coco smiled. 'That's an excellent answer, Tomas. That's a

very good answer. Let's go to the school and finish this, and if you play your cards right, I might finally let you call me, Coco.'

15H00

As she stood in front of the panoramic window which dominated Directeurice Jeanne Remy's office, Coco wished she had dressed differently. Not that she necessarily had a lot of better choices in her wardrobe. The "slacks" she wore had taken on an unnaturally puce colour, which she considered odd, as she was fairly sure they had been beige to begin with. Her trusty blue and green checked woollen jacket still contained the remnants of Elliot Bain's blood, as well as a smorgasbord of various types of food. Now, with the expectant gaze of Remy and the three teachers, Caron Voland, Margot Tasse and Ruben Badeaux, she felt uncomfortable, which was odd for her, considering she had spent most of her life trying to find a way to ignore enforced opinions about her. She considered removing her coat, but realised she was probably wearing no bra under an ill-fitting Julien Doré t-shirt. *Oh well*, she mused, *at least I have my looks and sparking wit.* It was not a lot, but it was all she had. And all she needed. She turned her attention to the people gathered in the room and she realised one thing which mattered the most - *I am not the problem in this room.*

The door to the office swung open and Cedric led the three students, who were in Manon Houde's class, into the room. Ada Fortin, Fabian Auch and Enzo Garnier flopped huffily into chairs near their teachers. Coco could see instantly the bravado they had shown previously had deserted them. *Bon,* she thought. *I might make it home in time to put my kids to bed, finally.* She looked at the expectant faces and realised whatever happened next; she had a feeling it would not be so easy.

She cleared her throat. 'Merci for you all agreeing to meet with us this afternoon…'

'What is this about?' Directeurice Remy interjected. 'I'm a

busy woman and I…'

'And you're a liar,' Coco snapped. She smiled upon noticing Remy's shocked expression. 'And now that I have your attention, I would ask you to only speak when I ask you a question.'

Remy spun her head toward Tomas Wall. He was slumped in a corner seat next to Sonny and Ebba and appeared to be pressing his body into the smallest shape he could manage.

'Don't look to Captain Wall for help,' Coco hissed. 'This is my investigation now, and as far as I can tell, you have nothing on me to use. The fact I've already hit rock bottom has proved to be oddly freeing for me. I'm blackmail proof. There is nothing left anyone can do to me that hasn't been done.' She paused to allow the information she had just imparted to sink in. It took just a moment for the flash of recognition to cloud the Directeurice's face. She lowered her head, folding her hands in her lap.

'Bon,' Coco continued. 'Let's begin. I came into this investigation five days ago because of something awful that happened in Paris in my apartment building. A turn of events which had nothing to do with me, but if it hadn't it may have resulted in the murder of a young girl going unquestioned. Manon Houde died over a week ago and from that moment on, I believe we've been played and that there has been one lie after another, one clever misdirection after another, each time assuming the police will either look the other way, or,' she stole a look at Wall, 'are too stupid to notice the glaring discrepancies.'

'What do you mean?' Sonny asked.

'I slept on the car journey back here today, and it helped, because it forced me to focus on what happened here, not what happened in Paris. And once you take Elliot Bain's attempted suicide out of the equation,' she replied, 'I believe it becomes much easier to clearly understand the discrepancies.'

'How?' Ebba countered.

Caron Voland shook her head. 'As hard as it is for me to

believe, because I was Elliot's teacher, and I was very fond of him, I'm afraid we have to accept facts. Elliot is responsible.'

Coco faced the mousey, nervous teacher. She was dressed differently than the last time they had met. Coco considered she would even go so far as to suppose Caron Voland had dressed up. She was dressed in a simple olive pant suit, but it was silk and expensive and made the teacher appear much less dowdy. 'I agree. We do have to face facts, and you're undoubtedly correct. Elliot does bare responsibility for what happened to Manon Houde.'

Directeurice Remy clapped her hands. 'Finally! We agree at last.'

Coco shook her head. 'I think we agree on very little, Directeurice Remy, and by the end of this discussion, we will agree on even less.'

Enzo Garnier sniggered, running a hand through his dyed green hair. 'Good one,' he laughed.

'You were talking about misdirection,' Sonny said, as if he was attempting to keep Coco on track.

'Ah, oui,' she responded, flashing him a grateful smile. 'If we were to believe the chain of events as presented to us, then it was all quite simple. Manon Houde had a secret lover, and she bribed her way out of school to be with him. She chose the time of her disappearance to coincide with a planned trip with her teacher, Monsieur Ruben Badeaux and the four other students in her class - Elliot Bain, Ada Fortin, Fabian Auch and Enzo Garnier. Except there was one gaping plot hole.'

'Her disappearance was noticed right away and therefore the alarm had to be raised,' Cedric added.

'Exactement, Lieutenant Degarmo!' Coco cried.

'Then what went wrong?' Sonny asked.

'There was no escape planned,' Coco answered. 'That can be the only explanation.'

'But I've seen the emails between her and her secret lover,'

Directeurice Remy interrupted, 'as have you. Manon Houde's intentions were blatantly clear and obvious. Not only on this occasion had she followed such a path, but she had done so on at least one other occasion.'

'Oui, I have seen the emails,' Coco conceded. 'And you are probably correct. Manon Houde *appears* to have been a young woman completely in control of her life, and most likely the people around her. And oui, she had a lover. She probably had several,' she added, looking at no one in particular. 'I can't speak to the validity of those emails, other than I can inform you we have confirmed the location from which the emails from Manon's lover came from.'

'Then you know where she was going,' Ada Fortin said.

'I don't believe she was going anywhere,' Coco answered. 'At least, not for a rendezvous with her secret lover.'

'What are you talking about, Captain Brunhild?' Directeurice Remy snapped.

Coco moved in front of the window. She wanted to be standing front and centre when she spoke next. She knew she had one chance and one chance only to gauge for a reaction. 'The emails between Manon and her supposed lover originated from the same place.' She paused. 'This school.'

Jeanne Remy frowned. 'What are you talking about?'

Coco smiled. 'I'm talking about bullshit, that's what I'm talking about.'

Remy dropped her head. 'Captain, s'il vous plait, we have children here.'

Coco snorted. 'There are no children here,' she retorted. 'And the fact you see my language as something which should be reprimanded rather than the cruel and terrible things which have happened in this school, tells me all I need to know about you.'

'You know nothing about me, or my school,' Remy shot back.

Coco shook her head at the Directeurice. 'On the contrary, I know all I need to know. The rest I'm sure we'll learn in the court cases which follow.' She smiled at Remy. 'As quickly as you thought you knew me, I knew you. We both may be wrong, or we both may be completely accurate. Either way, I feel completely comfortable in saying I don't believe a word of what you say.'

The three students laughed. Coco turned to them. 'The same goes for you,' she shot.

Remy tapped her watch. 'You're going to have to get to a point at some point, Captain Brunhild.'

Coco laughed. 'You're right.' She waved her hands in the air. 'Let's take away all the smoke and mirrors, and the confusion and look again at what we have. Manon Houde had to have known she would be missed, therefore, the planned escape and its cover become moot. We know she was murdered sometime on Lundi evening, between her last class and her no show at the rendezvous for the trip. We know a search was conducted, and that sometime during Mardi morning, Elliot Bain confessed to his part in her escape. He was quickly expelled and left the school. The police became involved, mais…' she stole a look at Wall, 'because of the overriding circumstances of the disappearance and the lack of any actual evidence of anything untoward, there was really little point in investigating further. Under those sorts of circumstances, I would have probably done the same.'

She moved across the room. 'We have to assume Manon Houde never left the school. It's the only assumption which makes sense. We also know she was poisoned using Belladonna, or as it's sometimes known, deadly nightshade. Now, there's something about that which has troubled me. Poisoning is,' she paused, 'an unusual choice for a murder weapon. They used to say it was a woman's preferred method. I'm not sure I agree with that necessarily, especially in the 21st Century. It means little, a man may choose to use it just as a diversion, so as always, I pay little attention to psychological profiles.'

'It is my understanding the cause of death is still undetermined,' Directeurice Remy interrupted, 'in any definitive way.'

Coco glared at Wall, angry that it appeared he had shared so much information with Remy. She shook her head angrily. 'She died in one of two ways,' Coco conceded, 'but she didn't crawl into the freezer herself. The issue of criminal charges will come later, that's for the Juge and the Procurer to figure out. But there will be charges, *many* charges, I'm sure.' She turned her head slowly to the expectant faces. 'We now know Manon Houde, and most likely many other students have been sneaking out of the school for a long time.' She pointed at the Directeurice. 'Before you begin your protests, you should know a short time ago, I spoke with Captain Wall and he told me everything. *Everything*,' she emphasised the last word, blowing through the small gap in her front teeth.

'I doubt that, very much,' the Directeurice snipped.

Coco shrugged. 'That isn't my business, not at this moment.' She stared at Wall. 'Captain Wall is ready to deal with whatever he has to deal with. He is a good man, and he deserves better. But he knows he will pay a price, and being the good man he is, it's a price he will pay in exchange for justice.'

Tomas Wall smiled at her and nodded as if passing on his agreement.

Coco continued. 'We have a separate witness who has confirmed Manon was a regular at the bar, *La Fontaine*. He will also make a statement concerning the identification of some of Manon Houde's lovers.' She paused, shaking away a memory from her dream when she had been taking a statement from the barman, sans his clothes. She centred herself again, staring at the Directeurice. 'I'm not sure how this would have ended had Elliot Bain not dragged the Paris police into it, but I suspect it would have been very different.'

Margot Tasse turned her head towards Tomas Wall. 'You seem to be suggesting the local police incapable of solving a crime.' She licked red lips. 'Whereas, I believe the Saint-Germain-en-Laye police to be extremely capable.'

Coco fought the urge to say, *I bet you do.* Instead, she turned away.

'Let's think about this logically,' Coco said. 'Why was Manon's body not removed after her death? Why was she thrown into a freezer and left? Because presumably everyone involved must have known, she would have been discovered, eventually.' She exhaled. 'I think in the end, it wasn't rocket science, and it all came down to one thing.' She shrugged. 'There was no need to hurry.' She continued. 'The school was empty and the Saint-Germain-en-Laye police weren't treating it with any kind of seriousness.' She paused. 'Non, I believe it boiled down to a simple logistical problem. How to remove a body from the school when access is so limited? The dumbwaiter may have moved Manon Houde into the kitchen, but the only way to get it out of the school would be down the only staircase in and out of the school, and of course, that is practically impossible. There are cameras, security guards, students.'

'Then what was the damn plan?' Ebba gasped, before pushing herself back in her chair, obviously embarrassed by seeming so enthralled in Coco's speech.

'I can think of only one,' Coco answered with a smile. 'And it's relatively simple. This all began with a young man.' She took a breath, throwing from her memory the slicing open of his throat a foot away from her. Her voice broke when she spoke again. 'A brilliant, highly intelligent young man. I haven't checked his prior school records, but I imagine Elliot Bain was very different before he came here. As far as I can tell, the only real thing he learned here was the difference between the haves and the have-nots.'

'That's not fair,' Jeanne Remy interrupted.

'Peut être,' Coco responded. 'But it seems Elliot Bain saw an opportunity to make some money, and that's what he did. For whatever reason. For his own reasons. I have a suspicion, but nothing to base it on at this point.' She stepped away, staring out of the window. 'I can't be sure of how or why, or when it all changed for him, but I think I have a pretty good idea.' She spun around. 'At first, I believe he acted as a middleman. The poor scholarship kid, grateful for any scraps thrown at his feet. He wanted money, or he needed money, whatever,' she said, 'I imagine the rich kids saw him as a patsy. I hope it bothered him to begin with, and in the end, he realised it was his chance to redress the balance somehow. To make sense of the cards the universe had dealt him.'

'What is your point, Captain?' Remy snapped.

Coco took a deep breath. 'I believe Elliot became a middleman between the rich students and the security guard. The kids didn't want to risk getting caught sneaking out, but they didn't mind throwing a few notes at the poor student and the underpaid security guards. That way, their own hands were clean should the plan fail.'

'I hate to state the obvious,' the directeurice interrupted, 'mais there is a logical reason why Elliot needed to make a lot of money. He was on drugs.' She shrugged. 'I'm sad to say, it happens, particularly to children from disadvantaged backgrounds.'

Coco's nostrils flared, and she pulled back her head sharply, narrowing eyes in Remy's direction. She opened her mouth, ready to unleash a verbal torrent on the directeurice, but she stopped herself. Not because she agreed with Remy, but because she did not want to prove her point for her. The apartment building she shared with the Bain's was the pits, Coco would be the first to agree, but it did not mean the people who lived inside were monsters or criminals. *The people who lived inside were not monsters or criminals.* The words struck Coco and in an instant she remembered something. Something which had been bothering her and which she could not articulate. She filed the thought away. She had to concentrate on the issue at hand, the rest would have to wait.

'You may have a point, Directeurice,' Coco said finally. 'However, when Elliot was admitted to the hospital, they ran a toxicology screen. Not only was he clean at the time of the incident, there was no evidence of any long-term drug activity.'

Remy pursed her lips and turned her head.

Coco continued. 'That's not to say he wasn't involved in providing drugs. We know he became involved with a criminal in Saint-Germain-en-Laye and found another way to make money.' She turned to the three students. 'Par example, I know he provided fake IDs. But I have to wonder what else he may have brought into the school?'

The students did not respond.

'Elliot may not wake up from his coma,' Coco said finally. 'So, getting in trouble with the police is the least of his worries right now. And I'm not asking you to drop anyone in it, but did Elliot bring drugs into the school?'

Ada Fortin sighed. 'Just a bit of weed, nothing hard.'

'And booze, sometimes,' Fabian Auch added.

Directeurice Remy turned, glaring at the teachers. 'Did you three know about this?'

Ruben Badeaux thew a sly glance at Caron Voland and Margot Tasse. He shrugged. 'I saw nothing directly,' he answered.

Margot sighed. 'I heard rumours, but I saw nothing to worry about.'

'Nor me,' Caron added.

'You saw nothing to worry about?' Remy shouted. 'These are children in our charge.' She shook her head. 'Mon Dieu. The scandal with be the end of us.'

Coco nodded. 'I think it will, in one way or another.'

'Directeurice Remy,' Caron Voland interjected. 'We talked about it between and we decided the students were going to do what they wanted, no matter what we did. In the end, if they wanted to smoke a little marijuana, then why not do it here, in the gardens, in a relatively safe, secluded environment, rather than sneaking out into town and becoming involved in who knows what.'

'You should have told me,' Remy snapped.

'You're right,' Caron conceded.

'But if we had, you would have put a stop to it and that would only make the situation worse,' Ruben interrupted. 'And we had a handle on it. We were watching, not obviously, but we were making sure nothing got out of hand.'

Remy shook her head. 'You don't understand the ramifications of what you've done.' She took a sip of water. 'The only good thing is, at least they expelled the drug pusher from the school.'

Ada Fortin shook her head, throwing her braids over her shoulder. 'Elliot was a good guy,' she said.

Enzo laughed. 'You would say that, because you had the hots for him.'

'So did you,' she snapped, 'at least I have the guts to admit it.'

Coco closed her eyes momentarily. She saw Elliot instantly - olive skin, rosebud lips, with a face anyone could love. It dismayed her she had been so wrong about him. It did not matter about the circumstances; she had looked in his eyes and did not see the young man she learned about. A drug dealer? A criminal? There was something wrong. She had to believe it, or had she come so far in losing her ability to spot evil when it was standing in front of her. The thought terrified her. She had never imagined her lover, her boss, the father of her two youngest children could be the man he was. If it was the same with Elliot Bain, what did it mean about her future as a police officer? Was she as wrong about Elliot as she had been about Mordecai Stanic?

'Captain Brunhild?' Cedric called out. 'Captain Brunhild, are you okay?'

Her eyes snapped open. She was back in the room.

'He always needed money,' Fabian said. 'It was tedious.'

Coco frowned. 'For what? The evidence suggests it wasn't for drugs.'

He shook his head. 'I never saw him taking drugs. In fact, he was quite anti-drugs, as far as I could tell.'

'And booze,' Enzo added. 'He didn't like to drink.'

Coco looked at Sonny. 'If a kid needs a lot of money, what does that suggest to you if it isn't for drugs or booze?'

He shrugged. 'Gambling?' he suggested.

'Or hookers,' Coco added with a smile.

Directeurice Remy made the sign of the cross on her chest. 'Mon Dieu, tell me he wasn't smuggling prostitutes into the school.'

Despite her mood, Coco smiled. She almost wished he had been. Why did Elliot need money? The thought bothered her because the only thing she could think of was he wanted to look after his mother, his widowed mother. The widowed mother it appeared he had beaten to death. It made no sense. And yet something else occurred to her.

'A chain of events,' she said aloud. Everyone looked at her, confused. 'A chain of events,' she repeated.

'What are you talking about?' Directeurice Remy asked, her voice laced with clear irritation.

'A chain of events,' Coco repeated for a third time, pacing in front of the large window. She looked down at the long, winding staircase, imagining the first time Elliot Bain had made his way towards the school. Was he filled with excitement? Filled with wonder and pride at having the chance to make his parents proud. To afford his mother a comfortable life after losing her husband in such a tragic way. No matter what Elliot had gotten himself mixed up with, Coco hoped she would have time to talk to him about it.

'Captain Brunhild,' Cedric called out again, his eyes wide with evident concern. 'You drifted again.'

She nodded. 'Désolé, it won't happen again.' She turned back to face everyone in the room. 'Because I know who murdered Manon Houde, and I think I know how they intended on getting away with it. It was her lover, at least one of them, wasn't it, Captain Wall? You murdered Manon Houde.'

15H15

Tomas Wall's eyes widened in horror. 'Captain Brunhild,' he cried, 'we talked about this. I *never* had a relationship of any kind with Manon Houde.'

'I did not have a sexual relationship with that woman,' Coco replied, in a mock American accent. 'Relax, Wall,' she said, waving her hands. 'I'm talking to the fake Wall, or should that be the *faux* Wall?'

'Captain,' Cedric waved his finger like a moving clock.

'Blah, blah,' she retorted. She moved towards the teachers. 'Whatever Elliot Bain was, he was very enterprising. He didn't just provide fake IDs for the students. He provided them for the adults too. Didn't he Mademoiselle Voland?'

Caron Voland gasped. Although she was a slight, demure woman, Coco could tell by the way she turned her head, she was not afraid to stand up for herself when she needed to.

'You seem to have all the answers,' Voland said.

'I wish,' Coco retorted. 'But I think I'm getting there. So, Mademoiselle Voland. I get it. You're a teacher, life has passed you by, and then someone like Manon Houde comes into your life, and suddenly you see, what? Possibilities? Remembering the girl you had a crush on when you went to camp as a kid? Maybe you were too afraid to explore that part of your sexuality, or maybe you had once and Manon awakened something you'd been suppressing for years. Either way. It's the truth, n'est pas?'

Voland said nothing. The only sound was the grinding of her teeth as she clenched her jaw.

Coco continued. 'How did it begin? Was it all a lie? Was she just using you because you were her teacher - old and boring, but useful?' Coco bit her tongue. She did not want to be so mean, but she believed it was the only way in which Voland would bite, and Coco needed her to bite, if there was ever to be a chance to truly understand what had happened at the school.

Voland remained silent. She lowered her head. The only sound in the room was the antique clock on the wall. Slowly, Voland lifted her head. 'It was not a lie.'

Coco nodded. 'I guessed as much. For you, at least. I'm not as sure about Manon.'

'She loved me,' Caron Voland hissed. 'You can't lie about that sort of love. Not really, not so convincingly and for so long.'

Coco's lips twisted. 'I agree, and you're probably right. All I meant to say was, I believe Manon, like a lot of kids, hell not even kids anymore, can compartmentalise their lives, their loves. And some people just manage to love more than one person at a time. I believe you when you say Manon loved you, but you have to know she also loved other people.' She turned to Voland's right, where the biology teacher, Ruben Badeaux was sitting, his lips pulled into a tight grimace. 'Isn't that correct, Monsieur?'

He, like Caron Voland, remained silent, his head remaining rigid in the opposite direction.

Coco sighed. 'And here we are, back to the wall of silence, the combined need for self-preservation. I have to tell you, it's boring, and it's nasty. Like dirty nasty. Because you all are supposed to be the adults, the ones charged with caring for and guiding these young adults into becoming something special.' She took a breath. 'Hey listen, I get self-preservation. I could have done with it myself in the last few years, but I chose to do the right thing and to be accountable. And that's what you are all going to do, or so help me, I'll drag you out of here kicking and screaming if I have to.' She frowned at Voland. 'I get you had a thing with Manon. I don't know whether it meant more to you than to her. We'll probably never know the answer to that now. I imagine it devastated you when you discovered she was seeing other people, especially your colleague Ruben Badeaux.'

'I didn't know,' Caron shook her head forcefully.

Coco shook her head. 'Oh, I think you did.' She frowned. 'What I don't get, is what did the fake ID have to do with it? Why did you pretend to be Captain Wall? Because I know you did, there's no point in denying it. The barman at *La Fontaine* has already confirmed it and identified it was you. Mais pourquoi? What was the point?'

Caron Voland sighed. 'It was her idea. Manon's. She said she wanted to run away with me but that her father would never let her, that he would always look for her.'

Coco nodded. 'And that's why you needed a fake ID, but why use Captain Wall?' she asked again.

Voland shrugged. 'Manon said it was a good idea. A police ID. If anyone stopped us, then I could say I was taking her somewhere for questioning,' she stopped, looking at Wall. 'She said she knew Wall - that he was a drunk and if we got caught, we could use it to make sure he didn't arrest us or turn us in.' She covered her mouth. 'I know how stupid it all sounds, but it was intoxicating. It was a fantasy. We were running away together. We were escaping.' She stared wide-eyed at Coco. 'Somebody like you would not understand what it's like to just "exist," to not be noticed, to not be picked, or cared for, or cared about.'

'Somebody like me?' Coco asked in surprise.

Caron Voland looked around the room. 'I see how people look at you. They don't look through you, or around you. They look at you and the way they look at you tells me they like what they see.'

Coco pointed at her stained coat. 'Well, I am a bit of a fashion icon,' she said.

Caron smiled with clear sadness. 'They like you. Nobody has ever liked me. Not even my own parents liked me. But Manon, liked me.' She shrugged. 'I'm not completely naïve. I know it was different for her. Maybe a psychiatrist would say I reminded her of her dead mother, or some such nonsense, but it didn't matter in the end. We must measure the moments which give us pleasure in our own way, because they are so fleeting.'

Cedric stood and moved next to Coco. 'This is all very charming, I'm sure, and a lovely story, mais what the hell went wrong? What happened the day she died?' he asked.

Voland took a breath. 'I saw her the night before. I snuck out, following her into town. I knew she was up to something and then I saw her. Laughing the way she laughed with me, touching his hair the way she touched mine, her tongue darting in and out of his ear as she whispered, no doubt telling him what she was going to do to him later.'

'We're talking about your colleague Ruben Badeaux?' Coco asked.

'Oui,' she replied, not looking in Badeaux's direction. 'In the end, it didn't matter. You were right, Captain Brunhild. As she told me later, I wasn't the only person in her life, and nor was Ruben. There were likely several others too.'

'What happened?' Cedric pressed.

'Seeing her with Ruben that night, it all seemed to come crashing down around me. I was so confused. Did she love me? Did she love him? I felt like such a fool. I was a fool, a lonely old spinster who had the audacity to believe someone like Manon could love me. Me, a woman with nothing to be proud of, no money, no figure to make head's turn. I ran back to the school. I didn't want to see her. I didn't want her to see the hurt and pain on my face, because it would have been like adding insult to injury.' She gasped for breath. 'But mostly because I didn't want to see her face be cruel to me. I wanted her to have always been my perfect flower.'

My perfect flower. The words struck Coco. 'What happened next?' she asked.

'I barely slept that night,' Caron continued. 'I tossed and

turned. I was so angry and embarrassed and humiliated. I spent the following morning walking around in a daze like a zombie. I couldn't bear to look at Manon, but of course I had to. I had to carry on. I had to be normal. I was so grateful for the trip being the next day, because I knew she'd be gone and I could just find a way to deal with my pain in her absence.'

Coco and Cedric exchanged a look. 'Then she was always planning on going away with her fellow students?' Coco asked.

'Oui, bien sûr,' Caron answered.

Coco frowned. 'Mais, it makes little sense.' She slapped her head. 'Or it makes perfect sense.'

'In what way, Captain?' Sonny asked.

'Because none of this ever made sense,' Coco reasoned. She looked to Caron. 'You said you had made plans to run off with Manon. You weren't planning on going last week then?'

She shook her head. 'Non, not yet. It was all up in the air. Manon had little money after her father cut her off, and I had even less. It was a dream, but little more than that at this stage.'

Cedric moved next to Coco. 'What are you thinking, Captain?' he asked.

She smiled at him. 'That it's all beginning to make sense.'

15H30

Coco moved towards Caron Voland. 'If your plan was just to get through the day until Manon left on her trip with her fellow students, then what went wrong. What went so tragically wrong?'

Caron turned away. 'After class, Manon said she had to talk to me. I tried to tell her I was busy, but she said it couldn't wait. She couldn't go away with an atmosphere between us.'

'Then she'd seen you at the bar?'

Caron nodded. 'I thought I'd left fast enough, but she saw me. She knew I'd seen her with Ruben.'

Coco gulped. 'And she wanted to make it right?'

'Oui,' Caron replied. 'She told me to meet her in the gardens. We used to go there you see,' she added lowering her voice, '*for privacy*.'

'And what happened?'

'She tried to... to... convince me of her love for me,' Caron said, her cheeks flushing. 'I don't know what came over me, but I think I saw her for the first time, and more importantly, I saw the foolish woman I had become.'

'And that's when you decided to poison her?' Coco asked.

Voland nodded. 'It was just there. I saw it growing so beautifully over her shoulder. I'd been growing the Belladonna for an experiment. I swear that was the only reason. I was intending to show my students how easy it was to grow, and what they could do with it.'

'You knew that sort of thing isn't allowed,' Remy said.

Caron nodded. 'Je sais. This all began because I'd just been talking with Jacques, the gardener, one day. He'd been growing plants in one form or another for most of his life, and somehow the conversation came around to Belladonna. He told me how beautiful it was, and how easy it was to grow. He'd done it himself. I didn't really see the harm in it.' She spun her head around the room. 'You have to see, there was nothing premeditated about it. We found a nice secluded spot, and I imagined it would be a great educational experience.'

Coco scratched her head. 'And how did that translate into murdering Manon?' she asked.

'I told her to meet me later,' Caron replied. 'We often used to meet in the woodshed. It was warm and cosy and private. It was a place for lovers and a place very few people knew about. It's hidden behind the oak trees, you see. Very few people even know it's there. She came, and we ate. It was easy to disguise the Belladonna in a salad. She didn't even know she was eating it. In the end, I wanted her death to be beautiful,' she whispered, 'to see the blush of passion on her cheeks from the Belladonna. I wanted us both to die, but in the end, I didn't have the courage. That's always been my problem. I never had the courage to do anything.'

'What happened next?' Cedric asked.

'She changed,' Caron answered. 'It was almost as if she was drunk. Like she'd been injected with a truth serum or something. She was cruel, horribly cruel. She told me she'd only agreed to come to the school to satisfy her father because she didn't want to go to some finishing school in Switzerland. She wasn't interested in science, or anything really, just in having fun, to have money. To have men, or women, it didn't really matter to her in the end. She told me she only slept with me to make sure she got good grades, enough to finally convince her father she'd sorted herself out, so he would give her back her credit cards.' She shuddered. 'She turned her back on me, laughing as she left the shed. I followed her outside. I couldn't believe that's all I was to her. A way to get good grades. I swear, before I knew what was happening my hand was on her, I just tried to stop her, that's all.'

'And she fell and hit her head,' Sonny added.

Voland nodded. 'It all happened so quickly. She was stumbling all over the place, and she fell and hit her head on the stones. It was raining by then. I stood and watched her blood disappearing into the earth.'

'You didn't try to help her?' Cedric asked.

Caron did not answer, but after a moment shook her head. 'There was no point. She was gone.'

Coco took a deep breath, and then another. 'I believe you. And I thank you for being honest. It might just help you with what comes next for you, but we're not there yet.' She faced the room. 'There's a lot more to this story, and for Manon's sake, if you cared about her at all, I hope you'll continue to be as honest.' She stared at Directeurice Remy. 'No matter how difficult it may be for you, or how much pressure they have placed upon you.'

'How did she get back to the school?' she asked after a minute had passed.

'I knew about Elliot,' Voland replied. 'And what he would do for money. I went and looked for him and told him what had happened. I promised it was an accident but that no-one would believe me. He said he understood and that he would help me, but he needed money, and a lot of it.'

Coco frowned. 'That's what he said? That he needed a lot of money?'

She nodded. 'Oui.'

Coco looked at Cedric. 'This keeps coming back to money. Pourquoi?'

'If it helps,' Voland said. 'When I asked him why he needed money, he said it was for his mother, to get her away. Those were his words. To get her away.'

'And how much money are we talking about, exactly?' Coco asked.

Voland did not answer. Coco nodded. 'Oh, for fuck's sake,' she cried. 'That's why none of this makes sense.'

'What do you mean, Captain?' Cedric asked.

'Money. Always about fucking money.' She sank into a chair, suddenly feeling exhausted. She pointed at Tomas Wall. 'Directeurice Remy, Captain Wall here told me about your deal, your desire to protect your school. It should have been harmless - protecting a few kids when they went on a drunken bender, caused a bit of trouble around the town. Easy to solve. But what do you do when you've got a problem that isn't so easy to solve?'

'I promise you, Charlotte, I didn't help them cover up a murder,' Tomas Wall called out.

She nodded. 'For what it's worth, I believe you. But by helping them, you helped create this whole horrible mess, and that's something you're going to have to deal with.' She turned away from him. 'Elliot Bain wanted money and perhaps he saw a way of making a lot of it.' She pointed to Voland. 'I haven't checked your financial records yet, but I have a feeling your pockets aren't so deep.' She faced the Directeurice. 'But I imagine yours are. And I also imagine Elliot knew that too.' She shook her head. 'Oh, I've been so stupid.'

'Then so have we all,' Sonny said.

'You murdered Manon Houde, Mademoiselle Voland,' Coco continued. 'Primarily because of your jealousy of a relationship she was having with your colleague Monsieur Badeaux and you called the two people you could think of to help you get out of it.'

'Two?' Cedric asked. 'You mean Elliot and Captain Wall?'

She shook her head. 'Non, Elliot and the deep pockets, Directeurice Remy.'

'I was asleep,' Remy snapped. 'Everyone knows I take sleeping pills for insomnia.'

'Oh, stop it, Jeanne!' Caron Voland hissed. 'You hadn't even taken your pills yet, and you didn't that night.' She looked at Coco. 'After... after it happened, and Elliot told me how much money I needed to find, I went to the Directeurice and told her the whole story - about the affairs, the drugs… I had to make sure she helped me and the only way to do was that to appeal to the only thing which mattered to her.'

'The reputation of the school,' Coco concluded.

Voland nodded. 'It's all the old witch cares about.'

'Caron!' Remy scolded.

'She's right,' Coco snapped. 'Once she told you what happened, it was you who came up with the grand plan.'

Sonny scratched his head. 'She did? What plan? I don't understand?'

Coco flashed him a sad smile. 'In the end, it was very simple. But simple plans have a tendency to go wrong easily.' She turned to the Directeurice. 'Once Caron Voland told you about Elliot Bain's involvement in getting people drugs, alcohol, fake IDs, I imagine you came to a very quick conclusion. He could be bought. What was it? Did he even put up a fight when you called him into this office. Was it easy? Did he agree without a second thought to spending the rest of his life paying for something which had nothing to do with him?'

Tomas Wall finally lifted his head. 'I really don't understand, Charlotte.'

She took a breath. 'Once you take a step back, it's easy, really. None of this made sense because it went wrong. Elliot Bain needed money badly and in this room he, Directeurice Remy and Caron Voland figured a way to save the school and get rid of the problem of Manon Houde's death. He would take the blame.'

'That makes no sense, whatsoever,' Cedric interrupted.

'I agree,' Coco responded. 'And I don't know why exactly he was so desperate for money for his mother. That answer lies in Paris and we'll deal with it tomorrow. But in this room, in this space, these two old women took advantage of him - for his need for money to help his mother. A deal was made, wasn't it, Directeurice? You knew there was no way to move Manon's body easily, so you did the next best thing. You hid it and had Elliot admit to helping her escape, which resulted in his expulsion. What I'm still not sure about is, you must have all known it would have come out, eventually. The body would have been discovered. What was the plan?'

Caron Voland sighed. 'It was Elliot's idea to expel him from the school. It was the only way he would agree to the plan. He said, *get me out, send me some money and once I have it, and once my mother is safe, I'll confess to the police I killed Manon and where I had left her body.*' Her lips twisted. 'It seemed the perfect plan,' she said.

'Except it wasn't,' Coco added. 'Mais, pourquoi?' She looked at Remy. 'You sent the money?'

She nodded reluctantly. 'Oui, to a bank account under a different name, bien sûr.'

Coco considered her response. 'Then what went wrong? Why didn't he follow through on the plan?'

'He was a troubled child,' Voland said. 'He killed his mother, obviously.'

'Non!' Ada Fortin cried. 'Elliot loved his mother. Everything he did was for her. Nothing else makes sense. He loved her. I loved him. He was amazing.'

Enzo Garnier reached across and touched her hand. 'He was amazing, and I loved him too.'

Coco smiled at the two young students. 'He's not dead yet, kids. And when he wakes up, let him choose which one of you two he thinks is amazing, because as far as I can tell you all are just kids who mess up and who deserve chances.' She paused, turning back to the Directeurice. 'D'accord. Elliot changed the plan by deciding to kill himself. What did you do?'

Remy took a breath. 'There was nothing we could do. We knew it was only a matter of time before it all came out. I had hoped for longer, but I supposed it wouldn't matter,' she stole a look at Captain Wall. 'There was never any reason for this to be

Sept Jours

about anything other than Elliot Bain.'

'Except he had different plans,' Coco replied. *'Different plans.'* She frowned, turning to Caron Voland. 'Wait a minute, you said Elliot told you he would confess once he was sure his mother was safe. Is that what he said? Were those his exact words?'

Voland shrugged. 'I believe so. Is it important?'

Coco pursed her lips but did not answer.

'Safe is an odd choice of words,' Ebba said. 'Even if he was arrested for murder, it's not like she would need a new identity or something. The money was in a different name. There was no reason for him to worry about her being safe.'

Coco nodded at the forensic tech. 'I agree.' She smiled. 'And that tells us everything about him. She wasn't safe, and he wanted to make sure no matter what happened to him, she would be.'

'But, she's dead,' Ebba replied. 'Which in my book, suggests she wasn't very fucking safe at all.'

Coco's eyes widened. She stared at Ebba, a memory suddenly appearing before her. She looked to the floor and remembered something. A letter at her feet. 'Ebba, when we get back to Paris, I'm going to need your help. I have an idea.'

Ebba shrugged nonchalantly, looking almost pleased. 'Yeah, whatever.'

Coco took a deep breath. 'D'accord. We are done here for now. Cedric is going to take statements from you all, while we figure out what the hell we're going to do with you.' Coco moved towards the door, stopping in front of Caron Voland. 'What happened to Jacques the gardener? Are we going to find him buried in the garden somewhere?'

Voland looked offended. 'Non, of course not! He knew about the Belladonna. We figured it would be a good idea to get him out of town for a while. He's on a fishing trip in Germany.'

Coco glared at Directeurice Remy. 'I'm sure your father would be very proud of how you throw his money around to protect yourself and this damn school.' Without looking back, she called over her shoulder. 'I'm going home to kiss my babies. You can go to hell.'

DIMANCHE (SUNDAY)

10H00

Ebba Blom's fingers moved so quickly across the keyboard, Coco was having trouble seeing what she was typing. She stepped away, stretching her body and yawning loudly. She had slept fitfully, and for the first time in a week, there had been no dreams about errant and very different and desperate men. Just darkness. They had returned in silence from Saint-Germain-en-Laye and after putting her two youngest children to bed and sharing a pizza with the two eldest, Coco had retired to her bedroom and spent the next few hours filing her reports on the computer. She knew she needed to get it all out when it was still fresh in her mind. Whatever happened next was out of her hands, but she wanted to make sure there would be consequences for all those involved, even if that included Captain Tomas Wall, although she was not sure he deserved the kind of punishment he likely had coming for him. He had been a fool, and he had made mistakes, but she believed him to be a good man. The thought bothered her, however, because she realised it would likely be a long time before she trusted her instincts again.

'I'm not finding anything,' Ebba interrupted. 'Are you sure about the name?'

Coco sighed, suddenly feeling very dejected. She had been so sure of herself, and confident, but now... She shook her head. 'I'm not sure of anything. And besides, I'm probably imagining the whole thing.'

Ebba nodded. 'Close your eyes,' she suggested, 'and concentrate. Go back to the moment and try to visualise it.'

Coco guffawed. 'The last time someone said that to me I ended up butt naked and tied to a...'

'Captain Brunhild.'

Coco grimaced. 'She's behind me, isn't she?' she whispered to Ebba.

'Oui, I am,' Commander Demissy said, the click of her heels indicating she was walking towards Coco's desk. 'And she is curious as to what on earth you are doing in your office on a Dimanche morning when it's difficult enough to get you here on an actual working day.'

Coco spun on her heels. 'Oh, you know me, busy busy busy. And when I have stuff to do, I'm not one to sit on my fat… to sit on my laurels. What about you? You don't have some fancy recital to attend?'

'Non,' Demissy replied. 'I have brunch with the Procurer. He has a meeting this afternoon with the Prime Minister, who as you can imagine is very keen to learn where we are with the Manon Houde case.'

'I filed my reports last night,' Coco stated.

The Commander nodded. 'And despite the atrociously bad French grammar and appalling spelling mistakes, they were…' she paused as if the words were too difficult to speak.

Coco smiled. 'Go on, Commander. You can do it.'

'The reports were very good. Concise and informative,' Demissy added. 'You and your team did a very good job.'

Coco shrugged. 'I'm not so sure about that. It still feels like a job half done.'

Demissy shook her head. 'The Procurer and the Prime Minister will be more than happy. I'll see to it. It wasn't even our investigation, and we solved it when the local police couldn't, or peut être, wouldn't.' She stared at Coco. 'I read your footnote regarding Captain Wall with interest,' she said. 'And it's quite a limb you went out on. Considering your… considering your circumstances, are you sure you wish to make your opinion public record?'

Coco nodded slowly. 'Oui, I am. I'd be a hypocrite otherwise.

And as we all know, I have many faults, but hypocrisy is not one of them.' She sighed. 'The bottom line is, Tomas made an appalling mistake, a mistake he deserves hauling over the coals for, but nothing more. If my opinion means anything to anyone, which I'm not sure it does, then I have to state it.'

'Bon,' the Commander said. She moved her head, studying Coco in a way which appeared to Coco as if she was actually impressed with her. The expression disappeared as quickly as it appeared. The Commander waved her hand. 'Well, go home. You deserve the rest of the day off. I'll see you bright and early tomorrow.'

'Non, I still have work to do,' Coco replied.

The Commander's eyes widened in surprise. 'Is this about Elliot Bain?'

'Oui.'

She tutted. 'Captain Brunhild, as much as I appreciate your apparent newfound dedication, I'm afraid unless Elliot Bain wakes up and cooperates, we may never know exactly what went on in his apartment.'

Coco shook her head irritably. 'That's because I'm missing something, I just know it. Elliot was willing to take the blame for a murder he had nothing to do with, just so he could get enough money to make sure his mother was safe. Well, she wasn't safe. He was too late, and for whatever reason it was more than he could bare. I don't believe he tried to kill himself because he was worried by me, or what had happened at the school. It was because he'd failed in his plan.'

'And you're basing that on what, exactly?' Demissy asked.

Coco looked slyly at Ebba.

'Captain?' Demissy pushed.

Coco took a breath. 'All the talk about false IDs at *École Privée Jeanne Remy,* reminded me of something I had thought nothing of at the time,' she shook her head, unwashed blue hair falling over her shoulders, 'I'm still not sure I do.' She stared at Demissy. 'I hate saying this to you of all people, but I base this on one thing - gut instinct. There was something strange, something off. That's the only thing I'm completely sure of. And I *really* hate the thought I'm missing something and if I don't figure out what it is, it's going to bother me for the rest of my life.'

'Is this about Nita Bain's supposed "ethnic" boyfriend?' Demissy asked.

Coco shook her head. 'Not really. The old dear who lives next door could have just made a mistake. It could have just been the television. It might explain why Elliot Bain wanted to make sure his mother got away.'

'Except there was no evidence of anyone being in the apartment, other than Nita Bain, her son, and the old lady from next door,' Ebba interjected.

Coco shrugged. 'He could have cleaned up after himself.'

The Commander sighed. 'If Elliot Bain knew who he was, why didn't he just say it to you, rather than being so nondescript?'

'I can't answer that,' Coco said reluctantly. 'Mais, I know I'm missing something, and it's right there in front of me. Something so simple, I didn't even give it a second thought when I should have. If only I could remember… if only…'

Demissy offered her a smile which appeared sincere. 'In our jobs, we have to accept that sometimes, just sometimes we can't find all the answers. Being a police officer is often not glamorous, and the people we deal with aren't movie stars…'

'Fuck Jesus in a Rodeo!' Coco screamed, causing Demissy and Ebba to jump. 'It wasn't *Blanchard*, Ebba,' she gasped. 'I remember now. I saw the name and thought to myself, ha, I wonder if she got to snog Leonardo DiCaprio!'

'What on earth are you talking about, Captain?' Demissy cried irritably.

Coco shook her head, blue hair covering her face. She shook

it away. 'Mon Dieu, it's all coming back to me. I saw the name, and it amused me, because I thought it was the same as the chick in the "Titanic" movie, but I made a mistake. It wasn't Blanchard, was it? It was Blanchett, but with one T. Try that Ebba. Try Blanchet with one T.'

Ebba nodded, her fingers moving quickly, eyes narrowing as she stared at the information on the computer screen.

'Are you going to explain to me what is going on?' Commander Demissy demanded. She sunk into a chair. 'And do I even want to know?'

'I hope it will all become clear soon,' Coco said biting her lip, staring anxiously as Ebba continued typing, before adding, 'ish…'

After several minutes had passed, though it seemed longer to Coco. Ebba pushed herself away from the screen. 'Holy shit,' she mumbled, before raising her head apologetically. 'Sorry, Commander Demissy.'

'What the hell is it?' Coco interpreted, running around the desk. She flicked on a pair of broken glasses and stared at the screen. 'Holy shit,' she repeated.

Demissy tutted. 'S'il vous plaît,' she cried, 'can we at least pretend to be professionals?' she asked. She moved towards Coco and Ebba, muttering irritably after stepping on several greasy, empty fast-food cartons. 'What am I looking at?' she asked, staring at the screen.

Coco clapped her hands, grabbing Ebba's bald head and kissing the top of it. She pulled back. 'Well, that was weird, like kissing a really weird baby.' She pointed to the screen. 'You might want to hold off on your brunch, Commander.'

'Why on earth would I want to do that?' she demanded.

'Because if you do,' Coco answered, pulling out her cell phone and clumsily stabbing her fingers against it. 'You might just have a neat little bow to tie up the entire case. Ah,' she said, speaking into the phone. 'Allô? Who is this? *Chantel?* Is Cedric there? Cedric. He's blond. Built like a brick…' she lowered her head demurely, 'well built,' she added politely. She sighed. 'Listen, honey, turn him over, slap his face, ask him if his name is Cedric Degarmo. And if it is, tell him to put on his boxer shorts and come and pick up his boss, *pronto*.' She threw the cell phone onto her desk, unable to hide the smile on her face.

11H00

Coco stood at the entrance to her apartment block. Rue de Penfeld. She turned to Cedric. 'Do you know why I chose this apartment block to move into after I was…' she took a breath before continuing, and then shrugging as she realised she had no reason to be ashamed, 'after they evicted me from my last place?'

Cedric shrugged, wafting his hand as if he could not care less.

'Because me and the kids were sitting on the old sofa, watching an old episode of "Murder, She Wrote" and Jessica Fletcher moved to this fancy, schmalzy apartment in New York. *Penfield House,*' she added in a grand English-affected accent. 'Growing up, my kids loved "Murder, She Wrote," at a time when they still loved me, because they imagined I was Jessica Fletcher.' She stopped, snuffling and wiping her nose with her sleeve. 'So, when I had minus nothing in my bank account and a choice of nowhere to go, I saw this place, Rue de Penfeld. *It's almost the same,* I thought. *It's a sign. We can be like Jessica Fletcher here, living our best lives, running in and out of our apartment block doing important shit, being important. Being together.*' She glanced at the tramp sleeping in the doorway.

Cedric nodded. 'And how did that work out for you?'

'Reality is a bitch,' Coco replied. 'But you know, catch the older kids in the right mood and we still all sit down together and watch the show, and now and then I see it in their faces. This isn't such an awful life. We all live it, and at the very least, we have each other. I have nothing to give my kids apart from that.'

'It's enough,' Cedric said.

'Try telling that to Elliot Bain,' Coco added. She pushed open the door.

Cedric followed her. 'We don't know what happened to him.'

Coco strode with determination towards the spiral staircase, moving up it with a determination she never had before. 'I intend to find out exactly what happened to Elliot,' she said, stabbing her finger upwards. 'But the answer lies up there, c'mon.'

Coco kicked her foot against the door. It did not budge. She kicked it again. She glanced over her shoulder. Cedric yawned and looked away. She kicked it a third time with enough force to cause her to wince, pushing her hand to her side.

A soft voice called out from behind the door. 'Who is it? Who's out there?'

Coco stepped back as the door to the adjacent apartment opened and Madame Cross peered into the hallway.

'Ah, Madame Cross,' Coco said cheerfully. 'We're waiting for our forensic team, but as usual, they're nowhere to be seen. Don't worry, we'll just wait here quietly and won't disturb you.'

'Forensic team?' Madame Cross asked, her interest evidently piqued.

Coco nodded. 'Oui, but I can't really talk about it,' she said, lowering her voice as if confiding to a friend, 'confidential police business and all,' she added with a wink. She smiled sweetly at the elderly lady. 'Don't worry, we'll be quiet, and we'll be out of the way before you know it.'

Madame Cross threw open her door. 'Nonsense, you can't wait in the hallway. I wouldn't be a good citizen if I left you to stand out there. Until your colleagues arrive, you can wait in my apartment.'

Coco smiled. 'You're too kind,' she said, before calling over her shoulder, 'come along, Cedric.'

'Can I get you anything?' Madame Cross asked. 'Café? Thé? I

think I may have a little sherry, though it's rather early, n'est pas?'

'We're fine,' Coco responded, thinking a sherry might actually not be such a bad idea at that moment. She moved around the room. It was, as she imagined, the same as any elderly person's apartment anywhere in the world. The smell was the same. Dust and resignation. She moved towards the fireplace. It was crowded with photographs. 'Your husband?' Coco asked, pointing at a dusty black-and-white photograph of two young adults, dressed in wedding finery.

Madame Cross nodded. 'Oui.'

'And this?' Coco asked, moving further along, pointing at another photograph. The same woman, another man, also in their best wedding finery. 'And this?' She pointed at a third framed photograph. The same woman. A different man. Different finery.

'How is Elliot?' Madame Cross inquired.

'Oh, he's fine,' Coco shrugged nonchalantly. 'His doctors expect him to make a complete recovery.'

Madame Cross turned away. 'Oh, that's good news,' she said. 'Such good news,' she added with a saccharine sweetness.

'Such good news,' Coco repeated, holding the old woman's gaze. She had seen the attitude before, on her daughter's face, on her own face. It was not new. It was defiance. It was control. It was anger.

Madame Cross tutted, throwing her head back and cackling. 'Oh, for goodness' sake. I'm too old to beat around the bush.' She pointed at the straining buttons on Coco's coat. 'You want to ask me questions, you fat, ugly trout? You do it with a fucking Avocat by my side. I know the score. Now arrest if you must, but I assure you, I won't roll over. Not just because I'm old, but because I hate the fucking police!' Madame Cross grabbed a knitted jumper from the sofa. She stuck her two fingers up towards Coco. 'Vive la fucking France, you old dyke!'

12H00

Commander Demissy stared through the one-way mirror into the interview room and shook her head. Madame Cross was smoking a cigarette through a long, thin ivory holder, blowing it slowly and deliberately into the face of the young Avocat who had been unfortunate enough to have been on call that morning. Demissy turned slowly towards Coco and Cedric.

'What the hell is going on?' she asked.

'You're looking at Madeline Stram, formerly Madeline Jermais, and most recently Madeline Blanchet,' Coco responded.

'Your statement said her name was Cross,' Demissy said.

Coco nodded. 'It did. I suspect it was her birth name. And of course, I believed it when she told me it was her name, because that's what she said it was,' she added. 'And, obviously, we didn't see the need to check otherwise. I mean, why would we?' She shook her head. 'I won't make that mistake again,' she hissed.

Demissy looked at Cedric. 'Do you understand? Because I sure the hell don't.'

He shrugged. 'She reminds me of my Grand Mère,' was all he said.

'And that's exactly how she got away with it for so long,' Coco interrupted. She smiled at their confused faces. 'I'm not suggesting I'm smarter than either of you,' she said, leaving a long pause before continuing, 'mais, I had a little bit of extra information. You see, on the day we found Nita Bain's body, this old femme couldn't resist sticking her nose in. Just another old busybody, we thought, telling me about Nita's,' she paused, moving her fingers into an air quote, '"ethnic" boyfriend, but non, I think she wanted to make sure she was around because she knew what she had done. She wanted to get into the apartment, to see what had happened. So, she offered to give us the spare key she kept, and that was, for us most fortuitous.'

'I'd love to know how,' Demissy interjected.

'Because in her anxiety, she panicked, and she dropped her letters on the ground,' Coco said, moving her body into a mock bow, 'and me being me, the kind soul I am, I picked them up.'

'Ah,' Demissy retorted. 'That's when you saw the different name.'

'I'm very confused,' Cedric added.

'I thought nothing of it,' Coco continued. 'I mean, why would I? For all I knew, she could have had a kid living with her. The truth is, I didn't really give it a second thought at the time, but after everything that happened in Saint-Germain-en-Laye and the whole, fake ID business, it was there, niggling away at me. Why did Madame Cross have a letter in a different name?'

'Why did she?' Cedric asked.

'We'll figure that out later. It could be anything. A probation letter, par example,' Coco retorted. 'All I know is the letter was addressed to Madame Madeline Blanchet. This morning Ebba searched for me in the police database. Madeline Blanchet served twenty-five years in prison for beating her husband to death with her walking stick. The case itself wasn't so remarkable. He was an old man, he "just" died. The autopsy showed massive trauma, but it was assumed he'd just fallen. The difference in this case was his Merry Widow. Madeline Blanchet had been down this particular road before, at least twice we know of.'

'Messieurs Stram and Jermais,' Cedric concluded.

She nodded. 'Both died in very similar circumstances, leaving behind rather large insurance policies in the name of their dear wife.'

Demissy frowned. 'How did she get caught?'

'According to what I've read,' Coco replied, 'some overzealous insurance adjuster. He connected the dots and contacted the police. The court papers seem to show she didn't even bother to deny it.'

'What does this have to do with Nita Bain?' Commander Demissy asked.

Coco looked towards the window into the interview room. 'We'll find out soon enough when I interview her, but I imagine it had a lot to do with Madeline Cross being old and most likely broke after all that time in jail.' She took a deep breath. 'Or maybe she's just a sadist who gets off on inflicting pain on others.'

'She looks so… so innocent,' Cedric offered.

Demissy stared at him. 'There's no such thing, Lieutenant. The sooner you learn that, the better you'll do in life.' She glanced at her watch. 'My brunch is in half an hour, Captain Brunhild. Can you finish this up by then?'

'What's in it for me?' Coco asked. 'A pay rise?'

Demissy walked away. 'Well, you'll get paid this month, at least,' she called over her shoulder.

12H30

Madeline Cross stared at Coco. 'I'm glad you're dealing with my case, Captain,' she said. 'It seems fitting since we're both women whose misfortune lies directly at the feet of men.'

'It does?' Coco retorted in surprise.

'Do you imagine I kill men for the fun of it?' Cross posed.

Coco did not answer.

The old woman laughed. 'Well, I suppose I did occasionally, but really it was more about survival. Survival of the fittest, you might say. Men imagine they are the superior sex, which is where they make their biggest and stupidest mistake.'

The young Avocat cleared his throat. 'Madame Cross, I'm not sure this is very helpful…'

Madeline patted his arm. 'Cher, merci for your input, but really, you're only here to make sure the dyke doesn't beat me? So, do us all a favour, sit there and talk only when you enter puberty.'

'Why does everyone think I'm a lesbian?' Coco muttered to herself. 'I've never done the bouncing dance,' she paused, before adding, 'lately.'

'Ask your questions, Captain,' Madeline Cross slapped her hands onto the table. She tipped her head towards the mirrored window. 'Do we have watchers? Am I being filmed? "Streamed" Isn't that what they say these days on the television box.' Her eyes widened. 'What does that even mean. How is a person streamed, sans water?'

Coco sighed. She slammed her fists onto the table. 'Enough with your bullshit, old lady. I don't know you, but I know enough to understand the one thing you are not, is naïve. I'm not as old as you, so hopefully I have a lot more time. But if you want to be in your top dog prison cell in time for supper, let's cut the crap and cut to the chase. Be brutal and be honest with me. Why did you murder Nita Bain?'

Madeline stared at her. 'I know I'm going to jail again, but can't this be fun?'

Coco shook her head. 'I'm the very definition of fun. Seriously, open a dictionary and look up Coco Brunhild, and it literally says, *fun*.' She shook her head again. 'Mais, non, none of this can be fun. Elliot Bain is fighting for his life and if he does wake up, I want to be able to explain to him why his mother died.'

'He was a brat,' Madeline spat.

'He's a teenager,' Coco retorted. 'Bien sûr, he was a brat. They all are. I admit my,' she coughed, 'interaction with the kid was *limited*, and testing, mais, I have learned something about him this last week. Something I probably wouldn't have bothered to look for, if he'd been around. But because he couldn't speak for himself, me being the Jewish mother I am, I decided to try to speak for him. He messed up, he was most probably messed up, but I believe his actions were informed by the need to protect his mother.'

Madeline pressed her lips and blew a raspberry.

Coco tutted. 'Oh, quit with the attitude. I spend my days doing the same thing because I know it annoys people, but also because I know it stops them looking too closely at me.' She leaned forward, peering into Madeline's face. 'But I am peering at you. And I see you. Hell, I could be you, if I was a sociopath, that is, but I do get you. You hate people because they've always mistreated you, for whatever reason, I really don't care, but quit hiding behind your crazy old lady mask. It means nothing, and the truth is, you're just nasty, and I suspect you've always been nasty.' She stood up and pushed her chair backwards. 'And I will not pander to you, because that's all you want. You want attention. And I get it. I'm a woman who is desperate for attention, so long as no one actually looks at me.' She slapped her fist again. 'N.I.T.A B.A.I.N. What happened to her? Spill it, you old bitch.'

'She was weak,' Madeline cackled as if she was proud of herself. 'And eager to please.'

'Eager to please?' Coco repeated with bite. 'Eager to please?' she repeated.

Madeline shrugged. 'You know the type.' She ran her hand through thinning white hair. 'She sees an old dame, frail and fragile.' She laughed. 'I'm old. I'm a dame, hell, I'm even frail, but fragile?' She chuckled. 'I'm not fragile.' She tapped the side of her head. 'There's nothing fragile about this.'

Coco nodded. 'Then what was it? Why did Nita have to be your next victim? Was it because you figured you're so old now? You're all dried up, and you figured you'd never be able to bag yourself a rich old homme again? A man you could secretly beat to death with your walking stick once he'd changed his life insurance policy in your favour?'

The old woman shrugged again. 'Well, I wouldn't quite put it that way, but you do have a point.'

Coco pulled back her hand, realising she had never wanted to hit someone as much as she wanted to hit the nice looking old woman. It troubled her, and it made her realise something important. People are most often horrible. She hated the fact she had to pander to Madeline, but she knew she had to. 'What did she do that was so annoying?' Coco asked.

'She underestimated me,' Madeline said. 'She came in, she shopped for me, she lifted me up when I asked. Do you know what it's like to be boring?' She pointed at Coco. 'Non, of course you don't, blue hair, clothes you can't be bothered to clean. You're beautiful and you don't even care. People like you, but you don't care. You need none of the things normal people do, and that's why you do this job. You need clarity. You need to understand why Nita Bain had to die, and why Elliot Bain chose to kill himself.' She smiled. 'It'll drive you crazy when I don't tell you, won't it?' She laughed again. 'And I won't tell you, for that exact reason.'

Coco nodded, moving closer to Madeline. She touched her woollen overcoat and then with a swift movement; she grabbed her, yanking her into a standing position and throwing her with some force against the wall.

'You think I give a flying fuck you're one hundred and ninety-two years old?' Coco hissed. She jerked her hand back towards the Avocat who had jumped to his feet, his eyes wide with fear and confusion. 'Sit down, Justin Bieber,' Coco shouted. She turned back to Madeline, lowering her back into her seat. 'Now talk, you decrepit old bitch, before I rip out your tongue.'

Madeline positioned herself back in the chair. 'The last time I was arrested, the cop said I reminded him of his Grand Mère.' She paused. 'I vomited in my mouth when he said that, because I'd seen the outline of his groin in his pants and I'd figured I'd offer him a little light relief, y'know what I mean?'

Coco shrugged. 'I do, but I wish I didn't. Carry on, ancient one,' she said.

'Despite everything, getting old is no fun,' Madeline said. 'And then you get someone like Nita Bain,' her mouth twisted into a sarcastic grimace. 'All pretty and perky, and keen and helpful.' She shuddered. 'It made me sick to the bottom of my fucking stomach. When they moved in, barely a day later, I'd hardly had a chance to check them out. But there she was, all cheery, standing on my doorway with a warm croissant.'

She laughed. 'Just lovely,' she added, before shaking her body, 'and just fucking boring. Like everything else in my life since I got old.' She stopped. 'Peut être, I was blaming the wrong person. I mean, it wasn't really her fault.' She stared at Coco. 'Sweetness grates on me. Nita Bain grated on me. It only took ten minutes. I stumbled against the wall. I'd gotten up quickly and was light-headed. She caught me and lifted me like I was a lightweight back to my chair. *An old lady,*' she said the words as if they were poison in her mouth. 'I didn't mean to,' she added earnestly. 'I mean, it wasn't as if she was one of those impotent men I'd shackled my horse to.' She placed her hands in front of her. 'I poked my first husband in his ribs because he annoyed me. He apologised. I poked him again and do you know what happened?'

Coco nodded. 'He apologised.'

Madeline laughed. 'He apologised for upsetting me, can you believe that?' She exhaled. 'So, I made sure he apologised a lot from then on in.' She pointed to the young Avocat next to her. 'This foetus will make a big deal about it in my trial, if he knows what's good for him,' she added with a wink in his direction. 'Mais, my father used to like to,' she exhaled, smiling, before adding, 'touch me.'

'I don't know if that's true,' Coco interrupted. 'And if it is, that's awful and very sad.' Her eyes narrowed. 'I may not be the kind of flic you're used to, old woman, but I am the kind of flic who will always say to people like you. I COULDN'T GIVE A FLYING FUCK. Get therapy, get help, but don't kill other people and think it's okay. I wouldn't,' she said. 'I want to kill people most days, but I don't.' She sighed. 'Alors, let's stop assuming I have only half a brain and tell me what it is you're really about. Why did you kill Nita Bain?'

'She annoyed me,' Madeline responded. 'When I fell, she picked me up forcefully. *Don't handle me like I'm a sack of potatoes*, I shouted at her. I slapped her face and instead of being upset with me, she actually apologised, like the limp-dicked men I married.' She laughed. 'All of my husbands were weak, and their weakness was what they imagined I should have too. The demure wife. The homemaker.' She blew a raspberry. 'They were all fucking bores. ALL men are fucking bores.' She smiled at Coco. 'I haven't had sex for twenty-five years and I miss it. But it annoys me I need a man to do it for me.'

Coco snorted. 'Are you crazy? Of course, you don't.' She shook her head. 'Dieu. Anyway, this is all irrelevant.' She stared at

Madeline. 'If you weren't such an asshole, I might have actually liked you. You have spirit, you're a murdering bitch, but you have spirit. Mais, what you did to Nita Bain and her son is unforgivable.' She turned her head. 'Why was it necessary?'

Madeline smiled. 'She let me. I poked her, and she didn't mind. Well, bien sûr she minded, but she let me do it. She wanted to help me. *I'm in pain,* I'd cry, and she'd eat it up. *My husband died*, I'd cry, and she'd say, *so did mine, and I'm angry too*. She'd try to tell me to stop lashing out, but I did, time after time, and I'd say sorry, and she'd say she understood, if it wasn't for her son, she'd do the same, blah blah blah. It was all pathetic, and it was all boring. She bored me. Ramming my walking stick into her chest was the most fun I've had since my last husband.' She stopped and guffawed.

Coco pulled her head back. 'I think the worst part about all of this is, you were just bored. You had no husband to abuse. You were out of prison - you had no family, no friends, nothing. And for someone who has no moral compass, it must have irked your rotten, soulless core when suddenly there comes along this incredibly sweet neighbour. Someone who wanted to help you, to care for you. And I imagine, all you saw in her was someone making you feel old and useless.' Coco closed her eyes. She had never met Nita Bain alive, but she imagined the woman she had been. 'Nita Bain was a woman who'd lost so much and realised how lonely life could be. She thought you were lonely, didn't she? And that's what made her accept your brutality. She understood your anger. Hell, she was widowed so young. She probably lived the same pain, and I imagine that is why she let you abuse her. She had no friends. She had no family and with Elliot at school you were all she had.' She stared at Madeline. 'She wanted to help you. She wanted to make you feel better.'

'Because she was a stupid fool,' Madeline laughed.

'What about the boyfriend?' Coco asked. 'I imagine it was a lie when you suggested Nita Bain had a secret boyfriend.'

Madeline laughed. 'She was a pig. She was lucky to have found one man to fuck her. If he hadn't died, he'd have probably moved on, anyway. Men do that, especially to dried-up old prunes.'

'What happened when Elliot came back?' Coco asked.

'I heard the arguments,' she answered. 'Nita was angry with him. There were problems at the school. He said he was going to make it all right.' She breathed. 'He went out that morning. He had business to take care of, he said. I went into her apartment and Nita told me she was leaving and that she didn't blame me and wasn't upset with me.' Madeline snorted. 'She didn't blame me? As if I had done anything to be blamed for! *You'll be fine without us*, she said. Anyway, she said, Elliot was taking her away. They were going to start a new life far, far away from Paris. She said she forgave me.' She threw back her head and cackled. 'Forgave me! I gave her the hardest dig with my walking stick, just to show her how little I thought of her forgiveness. She hobbled off like a dog who'd just been kicked up the arsehole!' She cackled again, forcing her body into convulsive coughing.

Coco took a breath, which felt as if it was the deepest one she had ever taken. 'And I'm guessing that terrified you. You were suddenly facing losing your biggest champion, your punching bag.'

Madeline smiled. She lifted her walking stick and stabbed it in Coco's direction.

T.H.E O.N.L.Y W.A.Y Y.O.U.R.E L.E.A.V.I.N.G. M.E. I.S. I.N. A. B.O.D.Y. B.A.G.'

She spelled out the words with a repetitive stab of the stick.

Coco leaned forward. 'And that's what you did, didn't you?'

Madeline shrugged. 'Peut être. Or, peut être, it was that brat of a son of hers.' She laughed. 'The court case should be a lot of fun. I have fuck all to look forward to these days. It'll be a pleasant change playing the dotty old lady in a trial. At least I'll be well looked after, they wouldn't dare not!'

Coco moved towards the door. 'I can't say I know Elliot

Bain, but I can say I believe he was prepared to sacrifice everything to get his mother away from that apartment. From you. I imagine he knew his mother was in trouble, but she wouldn't tell him why, or from who. And poor Elliot probably never imagined it would be the nice old lady from across the hallway. All he knew was he had to get his mother away. But he was too late. And because of you, the monster you are, at seventeen years old, Elliot Bain believed his only choice was to end his own life. I hate you for that, you despicable old bitch.'

Madeline cackled. 'He should have been better prepared. Too little, too late. Typical man.'

Coco opened the door.

'We're not done here, Captain,' she called out. 'We have lots more to discuss, and I enjoy chatting with you.'

'We are most certainly done here,' Coco snapped. She smiled. 'And I'm going to do the only thing I believe you can't stand.' She stepped into the hallway. She turned back. 'I'm going to ignore you. Au revoir, Madame whatever-the-hell-you're-calling yourself. I hope you're remaining days are long and eventful, and that someone finally makes YOU their bitch.' She slammed the door behind her.

19H00

'You wouldn't believe the day I've had,' Coco said. She dropped her oversized antique Chanel bag on the floor, rummaging in it and pulling out a large cardboard box. She opened it, spreading the contents on the small square table. Her movements were slow and deliberate, and she moved the pieces into place.

'You're a kid,' she said. 'You've probably never heard of Monopoly, but believe me, if you come from a big family who all hate each other, this little game is HUGELY important. I can't emphasise it enough. It is HUGELY important. One Christmas, our whole holiday was saved because my uncle, who hated my aunt by the way, managed to win. If he hadn't, he would have gotten ridiculously drunk, picked fights, which would have ended in several people stomping off. It would have been brutal, a lot of fun, but brutal all the same.'

Coco moved some metal objects onto the table. 'I'm the dog,' she said, 'and before you say it, not because I'm a dog, just because it's the cutest piece. So, let's get started, but I guarantee you, before you know what's happened, I'll have hotels on Avenue des Champs-Élysées and Rue de la Paix and you'll be screwed.' She stopped, hearing someone clearing their throat behind them. She glanced over her shoulder. Commander Demissy was gesticulating for Coco to come out of the room.

Coco sighed. 'Don't move a muscle,' she said. 'I'll be back in a minute. The wicked old witch of the west is here.' She stood up and left the room, closing the door behind her. 'Yeah?' she snapped.

'Don't be disrespectful, Captain,' Demissy said.

'It's still the weekend,' Coco retorted. 'And as far as I know, I'm not on the payroll right now.'

Demissy pointed through the small round window in the door. 'He's still in a coma. He may never come out of the coma. Without a next of kin, decisions may have to be made for him…'

Coco raised her hand. 'Not as long as I'm here. Just because the kid has no one to watch out for him, doesn't mean the kid has no one to watch out for him, even if it's just me.'

Demissy smiled. 'That's not such a bad thing,' she said, 'but it isn't your responsibility. You have your own job to do. A job you are…'

Coco smiled. 'Go on, Commander. You can do it again.'

'You did reasonably well, Captain,' Demissy said.

Coco cackled. 'Those exact words will be on my tombstone. *Here lies Coco. She did reasonably well.*'

'I didn't mean it as an insult.'

Coco shrugged. 'I know. And it's okay with me. Reasonably well, is better than most people manage in their lives.'

Demissy shook her head. 'You're very strange.' She paused. 'But, somehow we've almost made it through our first month together.'

Coco nodded. 'True enough. You might hate me, Commander, but you'll never be bored with me.'

'I'll settle for praying you just don't get us both sacked, or worse,' she responded. She looked to the hallway. 'I should go.'

Coco smiled. 'What's the hurry? I'm just about to thrash the kid at Monopoly, why don't you join us…' she trailed off, 'unless you're scared the weird flic with blue hair might actually beat you?'

Demissy snorted. 'I'm scared of nothing, Captain Brunhild.'

Coco pushed open the door. 'You're scared of liking me, and you're terrified I'm going to beat you at Monopoly. Prove us both wrong,' she said. 'I'm the dog.'

Printed in Poland
by Amazon Fulfillment
Poland Sp. z o.o., Wrocław
15 October 2021

32159a30-a24c-45e5-8379-944929093b64R03